ACCLAIM FOR MARK COGGINS' RUNOFF

"[D]eliciously quirky ... panache to spare."
—*Kirkus*

"What could be better than a fun fiction about the real dangers of electronic voting? Coggins shows us that elections can be hacked and the cover-up can be murder."
—Ellen Theisen and John Gideon, Co-Directors, VotersUnite.Org

"Classic noir, brought bang up to date. August Riordan is a hero with a heart. You're with him every inch of the way as he stalks the mean streets of San Francisco's Chinatown, confronting crooked pols, anarchist squatters, psychopathic software engineers, and cleaver-wielding gangsters, with betrayal lurking around every corner. A wild ride."
—Peter Tasker, author of *Samurai Boogie* and *Buddha Kiss*

"Great PI novels are as hard to come by as honest elections, but Mark Coggins' *Runoff* comes through in spades—Sam Spades, that is."
—Craig Johnson, author of *Kindness Goes Unpunished* and *Death without Company*

ACCLAIM FOR MARK COGGINS' RUNOFF

"*Runoff* by Mark Coggins is a smart, funny, spooky ... often touching, always entertaining romp through ... San Francisco's highways, byways, and alleys of corruption. (Hammett eat your hat and laugh.) It's great fun and a must read."
   —James Crumley, Dashiell Hammett award-winning author
      of *The Last Good Kiss* and *The Right Madness*

"Street savvy and wit make August Riordan an appealing gumshoe in the San Francisco tradition. *Runoff* has my vote."
   —Twist Phelan, author of *False Fortune* and *Spurred Ambition*

"*Runoff* is at once a biting, witty, very timely commentary on our flawed electoral system, and a fast-paced page turner you won't be able to put down. Mark Coggins has written the must-read PI novel of the year. "
   —Jason Starr, author of *The Follower*

"Firmly entrenched in the classic private eye mold of Hammett and Chandler, Coggins exposes the dark underbelly of American politics ..."
   —*Publishers Weekly*

RUNOFF

#4 in the August Riordan Series

RUNOFF

Mark Coggins

BLEAK HOUSE BOOKS

MADISON | WISCONSIN

Published by Bleak House Books,
an imprint of Big Earth Publishing
923 Williamson St.
Madison, WI 53703

This is a work of fiction. Names, characters, places, and incidents either are the product of the author's imagination or are used fictitiously, and any resemblance to actual persons, living or dead, business establishments, events, or locales is entirely coincidental.

ISBN 13 (cloth): 978-1-932557-53-4

Printed in the United States of America.

11 10 09 08 07   1 2 3 4 5

Library of Congress Cataloging-in-Publication Data has been applied for.

Set in Adobe Garamond Pro

Cover and book design by Von Bliss Design, based on a concept by Peter Streicher
www.vonbliss.com

For John D. Coggins Jr.

"It's not the voting that's democracy; it's the counting."
—Tom Stoppard, *Jumpers* (1972) act 1

"People never lie so much as after a hunt, during a war or before an election."
—Otto von Bismarck

"Win or lose, we go shopping after the election."
—Imelda Marcos

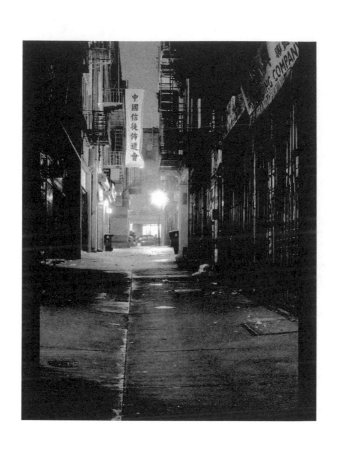

THE MIDNIGHT RIDE OF JOHN DEERE

I SHOULDN'T HAVE BEEN SURPRISED WHEN THE BACKHOE materialized out of the Chinatown fog, ran onto the sidewalk and took out a column supporting the pagoda roof of the Bank of Canton.

But I was.

Parked under a sagging fire escape on Wentworth Street—once known as "Salty Fish Alley" for its vats of fish and shrimp curing in salt—I was reading a back issue of *Down Beat* by penlight in the front seat of my Galaxie 500. It was close to two AM and I had been there since midnight trying to get a lead on the thief who had been knocking off San Francisco ATMs over the last month. He'd been targeting free-standing machines in front of banks, and while it was obvious that heavy equipment entered the equation somewhere, no one had actually seen how it was being done.

My motivation was a $10,000 reward the Bay Area Bankers Association had offered for information leading to the arrest and conviction of the suspect. Given that I had made a total of twenty-five dollars from my private investigation business since the beginning of the crime spree—and that only because I'd answered the phone in my office when someone had called with a survey on fiber supplements—I figured there were worse ways to spend my time than trying to earn the reward. What I didn't figure was getting lucky on the first night.

I dropped the magazine and fumbled open the door. I ran to the mouth of the alley and then across Washington Street to the front of the bank. The fog, the slickened pavement and the lights on the backhoe stabbing through the swirling vapor-like search beams gave the scene an eerie, landing-rover-on-a-distant-planet sort of appearance.

Big was a small word for the guy in the driver's seat. Neck bolts aside, he looked like someone the villagers should be chasing with torches and pitch forks, but was dressed like it was just another day on the construction site, right down to his work boots and hard hat. He had bulldozed the ornamental column out of the way and was busy lowering the bucket of the front loader to the place where the ATM joined its concrete pedestal.

I had decided to pull the stakeout duty on a whim after playing some jazz bass at a nearby club, and it suddenly occurred to me that I hadn't brought a gun or any other means of persuasion, apart from my irresistible personality. But that didn't stop me from putting my beak into it. I came up to about five feet of him, shined the puny penlight up in his face and shouted, "What do you think you're doing?"

Engine noise and focus on the task at hand kept him from hearing me or noticing the penlight. He drove the blade of the bucket into the ATM and gunned the motor to put the horsepower to work. I waved my hands and shouted again to no effect, and then finally hit on the idea of chucking the penlight at him. It bounced off his hard hat and flopped into the loader bucket. That got his attention. He snapped his gaze in my direction and I got my first clear look at his face. It was big and red, with a lopsided goatee of coarse red whiskers encircling his mouth like bad topiary. He wore glasses with cheap black rims that were patched at the bridge with adhesive tape.

He yanked his foot off the gas and twisted around in the seat to see me better. "What are you doing?" I repeated when the sound of the backhoe's exhaust had subsided.

He frowned. "What's it look like I'm doing?" His voice was deep and rumbly, like barrels going down a ramp. "Demolishing the building. A better question would be what are you doing? Please stay back so you're not injured."

His matter-of-fact response made me doubt myself for the slightest moment. I felt my jaw sag open as I pondered what to say. My glance strayed to the dashboard of the backhoe. There was no ignition key in the switch, and below the dash was a tangle of wires, several of which had been stripped. I gestured at the obvious hot-wire job. "Leave the keys in your other frock?"

He looked at the dash involuntarily and then brought his eyes up to meet mine. A grin spread slowly across his face. "You might have something there," he said, "but don't get frisky about it."

He did something fancy with a hydraulic lever and tromped on the gas. The backhoe growled in response, and the loader bucket surged against the ATM with a wrenching, scraping sound.

If you ever try to stop a guy in a backhoe with your bare hands, you'll soon find it's a little like trying to stop a tank with the same implements. I couldn't think of anything else to do but rush the driver's cage and try to pull him off the seat. I managed to get my foot on the stepwell and my hand on the roll cage bar when he reared back and planted a work boot square in the middle of my chest. I went sailing out into the street, where I landed in a pothole full of cold, muddy water and conked my head on a conveniently placed manhole cover.

I spent most of the next few moments groaning, rubbing my head and trying to squirm out of the water, but I discerned a brittle crunching noise over the sound of the backhoe's diesel, followed by a loud clang. Then I heard the backhoe moving away, the pitch of the motor falling and rising as the guy with the red goatee worked the transmission through the close-ratio gears.

I staggered to my feet in time to see him turn the corner down Wentworth Street. The source of the clanging noise was readily apparent: the Bank of Canton's flossy automatic teller machine now rode in the backhoe's loader bucket. I stumbled after him, pulling my cell phone out of my jacket pocket as I ran. By the time I got to the mouth of the alley, the backhoe was already at the end of the block, where Wentworth dead-ended into Jackson. He turned left and disappeared from view.

I tried to punch in 911 on the phone while running, but the backlight on the display kept going off before I could locate the next digit. I finally gave it up as a bad job and pulled up by the door of a brush painting studio, which was at least partially lit by a dim yellow bulb in the Chinese lantern over the entrance. A giant panda gave me a bored look through the window while I called the 911 operator and told her about the theft. She did her best to be sympathetic and helpful, but I couldn't make her understand that I wasn't talking about an ATM mugging. "I realize you're upset," she said finally. "We'll get a patrol car to the scene as soon as possible. Just be sure to stay by the teller machine until they arrive."

"I'm trying my damndest," I snarled into the phone. "But it keeps moving on me."

I flipped the cell phone shut and broke into a sprint, crunching over a broken liquor bottle as I rounded the corner at Jackson. The guy with the goatee was nowhere in sight. I keep pounding pavement up Jackson, crossed the intersection with Grant—swiveling my head to check it as I went—and then turned back to see a huddled bundle lying square in my path. I couldn't stop, but I managed to put enough oomph in my next stride to leap over the obstacle. I landed heavily on the other side, clutching a rainspout to stop myself from reeling back.

"Watch it, boyfriend," croaked a voice behind me. "Gene Kelly you're not."

A homeless woman with a complexion like dried apple core levered herself out of a half-zipped sleeping bag to stare at me. I'd seen mummies that looked healthier.

"Sorry. Did you see a backhoe go by here a minute ago?"

She slumped back onto the ground. "Try Ross Alley. I think he turned up there."

I nodded my thanks and hurried up Jackson again to the next intersection with Ross. Some African cultures believe that evil travels in a straight line, but mischief—if that was the right way to refer to the guy with the goatee—could evidently negotiate some circuitous routes. Originally home to gambling houses and brothels in the wild Barbary Coast days, Ross Alley is a very narrow throughway that has retained enough of its character to be featured in movies like *Indiana Jones and the Temple of Doom*. As I entered, I could see several places where the backhoe had scraped the walls getting by—and I could also see the machine itself at the end of the block.

Goatee was at the controls, raising the loader up to the level of a dump truck parked perpendicular to the alley. As I crept closer, I saw that there was another man sitting behind the wheel of the truck. There wasn't any doubt where the ATM was going if I didn't succeed in stopping them, but my problem was compounded: I still had no gun, and there were now *two* guys with heavy equipment to deal with.

I cast about the alley for something to use as a weapon. The choices were limited: flattened cardboard boxes outside the door of a fortune cookie factory; a rickety-looking bicycle chained to a gas meter; and five or six little cairns of bricks or cobblestones piled up in front of other businesses. The bricks were the obvious choice. I wondered why they were there until I remembered the recent renovation of Chinatown's Commercial Street. Commercial had been one of the last streets in San Francisco to retain its brick paving, but when it came time to replace sewer lines below the street, city officials decided they were too weak to stay and replaced them with concrete. Many Chinese residents had salvaged the old bricks and placed them in and around their businesses because they were believed to promote good *feng shui.*

I made a silent apology to the owner of a one-chair barbershop as I scooped up a dozen fist-sized stones in front of his establishment and piled them into a makeshift carryall fashioned out of my jacket. I crept down the remaining stretch of alley and slipped out behind the backhoe and around the dump truck to stand about ten yards from the driver's partially open window. He had turned in his seat to watch as Goatee raised the loader bucket to the level of the dump bed, and had no idea I was there. Until I threw the first brick.

The first one came in low, pounding the door with an incredible thud. The driver jumped like he had sat on an electric juicer and twisted back to look out the window. I wouldn't be human if I didn't admit to getting the slightest bit of satisfaction from the crazed expression on his face. Not that I took time to savor it. I had the second brick airborne before he caught sight of me, and fortunately for him, it bounced off the truck's side mirror. The third one was right on target, flying through the open part of the window and landing somewhere inside.

He'd ducked in time to avoid the missile, and stayed down as the fourth one I threw put a spiderweb crack in the window's safety glass and clattered down the side of the truck to the ground. I had a fifth in hand when he popped up, put the truck in gear and barrelled down Washington Street into the deepening fog, leaving Goatee with the backhoe's loader bucket high in the air and no place to put the ATM.

I doubt if Goatee had even been aware of the bombardment up until that point—I made damn sure he was now. I heaved the brick in my hand toward him, trying to thread my way under the loader and between the roll cage posts to nail him in the driver's seat. My throw sailed high, hitting the bottom of the loader. The brick exploded into shrapnel-like fragments. One must have nicked him because I heard him curse loudly, then yell even louder, "You fucker!"

While I reached for another brick, he punched the gas and pulled the backhoe around to head in the opposite direction down Washington. My next heave missed entirely, shattering on the pavement behind the back wheels. I trotted after him with my jacket-load of bricks, but he was going too fast for me to keep up and throw at the same time. When he reached the intersection with Grant, he hung a sharp right. With the front loader raised high like pincers and the back shovel and boom curled up like a tail, the backhoe in profile resembled an attacking scorpion. It also appeared unstable. The back wheels came off the ground during the turn, overbalanced by the weight of the ATM. It lunged out of view behind a building and then I heard a hammering crash, a shrieking, skidding noise and the sound of glass breaking.

I dropped the bricks and hustled the remaining fifty yards or so up to Grant. On the left side of the street, the backhoe had jumped the sidewalk and toppled into the plate glass window of a fancy art gallery. An alarm was ringing in the back of the building, bits of glass were scattered over the sidewalk like wedding rice and the ATM had rolled out of the loader bucket and come to rest beside a gigantic stone Buddha in the center of the store. I ran up to the backhoe to see if Goatee had been injured, but there wasn't a trace of him in the driver's cage. I found his hard hat in the middle of the road, picked it up and then did a slow 360-degree revolution like Dumbo at the Ice Capades. Nada. He had given me the slip.

I was looking up to see if he had somehow flown away when I heard the wail of an approaching siren. The patrol car was on me in less than a minute, skidding to a stop on a diagonal across from the art gallery. I had already locked my hands together on top of my head, but the cops came out of the car with guns drawn, barking at me to lie down on the road. The one on the passenger side was a husky, corn-fed kid with a buzz cut who I didn't recognize. The driver was a fellow Irishman who I knew slightly from a bar on Clement called the Plough and Stars. I'd played a gig there one night and he'd come up to introduce himself after the show. "McQuaid," I shouted as I dropped to my knees. "It's me—Riordan. I'm the one who called this in."

He rose from his crouch behind the driver's door. He was a small man with a slender torso and the body armor he wore made it seem like he was puffing out his chest. "I wondered if it was *that* Riordan." He turned to his partner. "It's okay, Jerry, I know him."

I stood and met them as they holstered their guns and walked to the front of the gallery. They looked over at the ATM and then they looked down at the wreckage.

McQuaid turned to me. "Freelancing for the reward?"

"Yep."

"Where's the perp?"

"Hell if I know."

I glanced over to Jerry, who was staring down at the backhoe, completely entranced. "John Deere," he said almost dreamily. "Now that's a tractor. My grandfather swore by John Deeres on the farm. Said they used to call them Pumping Johnnies when he was growing up because of the funny pumping sound their engines made."

I gave the kid what was probably a goggle-eyed look. "This one sounded pretty normal to me—not that I was paying much attention."

McQuaid smiled at his partner and explained, "Jerry's from Oklahoma. But what you might want to pay attention to is the owner of this building."

"Oh yeah?"

"Yeah. The bank may be very happy you saved their ATM, but I don't think Leonora Lee will be pleased to find it in her front parlor, so to speak."

"You don't mean—"

Jerry laughed. "Oh yes he does. I'm from Oklahoma and even I know who Leonora Lee is." He ran his hand lovingly over the shovel of the overturned backhoe.

"The Dragon Lady of Chinatown."

ENTER THE DRAGON

THE RING TONE OF MY CELL PHONE sounded annoyingly like the beep the backhoe made when backing up. I managed to retrieve the phone from my nightstand and lay it next to my ear without prying open my eyes.

"Hello, Gretchen," I growled into the handset.

"Good morning, August," said a playful voice. "How'd you know it was me?"

"The jury is still out on this cell phone business. I haven't given the number to anyone else."

"Well, let me be the first to welcome you to the twentieth century. But in case you hadn't noticed, this is the twenty-first."

Gretchen Sabatini was my secretary, confidant, gal Friday—and one time fiancée. She was also on a mission to cure me of my Luddite ways. As a private investigator, not having a cell phone had become more and more of a bother, and on a recent case had almost cost the life of a very good friend. Gretchen hadn't even waited for me to come to the obvious conclusion. She had simply signed me up for the service one day and left the phone on my desk. "Thanks for the update on the time," I said. "But could you get a little more specific than the century?"

"It's 11:20."

"And you're waking me up after four hours of sleep because …"

A fiendish giggle spilled out of the phone. "Because you're having tea with Leonora Lee at the Lee Family Association building at one PM."

"Tell her I'll take a rain check. I'm rotating my tires."

"No can do. Her secretary was quite insistent. It might be a coincidence, but there's a great picture of the Lee building on the front page of the *Chronicle* Web site this morning. The article suggests that a certain San Francisco PI had a hand in recent remodeling activities."

I blinked open my eyes and rolled over to look at the ceiling. A dilapidated spiderweb clinging to the light fixture hovered and danced on the ambient breeze. I said, "Doesn't anyone read the paper on paper anymore?"

"Online is better for *breaking* stories."

"Thank you for that."

"Well, I'll let you get gussied up for your meeting. Ms. Lee's secretary emphasized that she expects the dress of visitors to be appropriate for a formal business occasion and that she is a stickler on punctuality. And her lair—I mean her office, of course—is in the penthouse."

I thanked Gretchen in a less-than-sincere fashion and hung up to look in my closet for my confirmation suit.

I lived on the top floor of a four-story building on the corner of Post and Hyde. Although it was late November and Northern California had already gotten more than enough precipitation for the ski resorts in Tahoe to open early, it was an unusually clear (and cold) day and I decided to walk the dozen or so blocks to Chinatown.

I also decided the short pants that went with my confirmation suit weren't appropriate, so I'd settled on a charcoal three-button number that Gretchen had picked out for me when we were still seeing each other, and a wool and cashmere blend topcoat she bought for me to go with it. As long as we stayed above the ankles I was looking pretty good, but my socks had holes and my shoes were the same scuffed wingtips I always wore. I figured there was a limit to the sartorial splendor I was willing to expend for a meeting where I was going to get yelled at.

I went down Post, past the newly redesigned Union Square with its vast, multicolored granite promenade that made people look like pieces on a chess board, hung a left on Grant and came up to the green-tiled gate that led into Chinatown. The streets around the square had been fairly thick with Christmas shoppers, but they were pikers compared to the dedicated ranks of souvenir-hunting tourists moving up and down Grant after I got through the gate.

Wall-to-wall stores on both sides of the street were set up to cater to them. You could bag your limit cheaply in the shops that specialized in back scratchers, paper parasols, skull caps with fake queues and purses that looked like Chinese take-out boxes, but the bigger game was to be found in the places that sold antiques, artwork, jade and coral jewelry and silk cheongsam dresses with slit skirts and mandarin collars. I elbowed my way along the sidewalk—and sometimes the gutter when I couldn't get by—up to the intersection with California where the old Saint Mary's Church stood. An inscription in large gold letters on the clock tower read: "Son, observe the time, and fly from evil." Apparently intended for those who frequented the nineteenth century brothels across the street, it drove home the point that I was already five minutes late for my appointment with the Dragon Lady.

I half walked, half jogged the rest of the way up the street to the Lee Family Association building. The backhoe was gone, broken glass from the window had been swept from the sidewalk and plywood sheeting had been nailed in the window frame to cover the damage. A street musician sitting on a stool in a courtyard at the side of the building played a two-stringed Chinese violin, nodding and smiling at me as I double-checked the directory for Leonora Lee's office. She was in the penthouse as Gretchen had said, but there were eleven other floors of Lee family enterprises on the way. These included the damaged gallery, offices for a Chinese language newspaper, a real estate development firm and just below the penthouse, a *Gourmet Magazine*-reviewed restaurant called the Jade Phoenix.

I dropped a buck in the jar of the violin player and walked further back in the courtyard to a pair of elevators. After a little bit of trial and error it became apparent that the closest one didn't go to the penthouse and I needed to pick up a red phone on the wall next to the other to be let up. The phone rang for a long moment and then I heard a woman say something like, "Nee HaOW."

I figured that for hello, but that didn't buy me much. "Sorry," I said, "I don't speak Chinese."

"No problem," said the same woman. "Is this Mr. Riordan?"

"Yes. Is this Ms. Lee?"

She laughed pleasantly. "It is, but not the one you think. I'll open the elevator for you. Press the button marked P."

I started to say thank you, but she had already hung up. I replaced the phone, waited for the elevator doors to clang open and then took a quick ride to the top. The room I stepped into was walled in glass on two sides, affording spectacular views of North Beach, Telegraph Hill, the Financial District and the Bay—but the view inside was even better.

A paralyzingly beautiful Chinese woman waited for me by the elevator. She wore a red linen dress with black and white beading around the collar and a short matching jacket with the same beads around the cuffs and outer edge. I expected it came from Paris or Milan, and I knew it didn't come cheap. Her hair fell to her shoulders and curled back in a soft flip that made me think of the 1960s, but looked swell anyway. Her face was angular with high cheekbones and was exquisite as all get-out, her figure lithe and shapely. A scent of something light and floral emanated from her like a warm glow. She curled her lips into the tiniest of smiles and I thought I'd been given the high sign for the rapture.

"Mr. Riordan?" she asked.

"That's the old me," I said. "I think I've been transported to a higher plane."

Her eyebrows went up a fraction of an inch. "Really? Are you sure you just didn't get off on the wrong floor?" She must have seen something in my face, because she continued almost immediately, "Kidding. May I take your coat? It's cold outside, isn't it?"

I peeled off the topcoat and passed it to her. "Sorry," I said. "I guess I'm already in enough trouble without adding to it. And, yes, it's cold. Which way to the execution?"

She graced me another of her tiny smiles. "It's nothing so bad as that. Leonora is in her office. Come with me."

We went across an antique Chinese rug with a pagoda scene against a cobalt blue background and up to an office door that was flanked by matching three-foot-high vases glazed in the same cobalt color. My escort knocked softly on the door and then pushed it open without waiting for a response. The room inside was dominated by a carved rosewood desk as big as Napoleon's tomb. Behind the desk sat a tiny woman in a tailored suit with jade jewelry at her ears, wrist and neck. Her dark hair was pulled back in a cruel-looking bun that didn't get within shouting distance of flattering. It was hard to guess her age: she might have been a severe-looking forty or well-preserved sixty.

She rose as we entered and put her hand across the desk for me to shake. I had to come right to the edge and lean far across to grasp it. "Mr. Riordan, I presume." She twitched her mouth open to display her front teeth in an expression that looked more like a baring of fangs than a smile, then said, "You're late."

"Yes, I—"

"Never mind. Please have a seat."

The door pulled closed behind me and I glanced over my shoulder like an idiot in the weak hope that I hadn't been left alone with her—but of course I had. I sat down in a carved rosewood chair next to a matching table with a Chinese tea service laid out. "Listen, Ms. Lee," I began. "About your window …" My voice trailed off as I realized the Dragon Lady was still standing behind the desk peering down at me.

She looked me over carefully, and then after a moment sighed and returned to her high-backed chair. "You know how I judge a man?"

"By his deeds?"

"By his shoes."

"That was going to be my next guess."

"A man who doesn't pay attention to his shoes doesn't pay attention to other details. He is lazy, and lazy men do not become prosperous."

I looked down at my scuffed shoes and self-consciously positioned my feet under the chair. "Look, Ms. Lee—"

"Mrs. Lee, please."

"Look, Mrs. Lee, I'm sorry about your window and all, but being a community-minded person, I would hope that you appreciate the greater good I was trying to accomplish by catching the ATM thief. I'm betting your insurance will cover the expense, and if it doesn't, I suppose we could discuss damages, but I don't see the need for this dressing down. And—for your information—lazy men do not run around after backhoes at two in the morning. Misguided ones, perhaps—but not lazy."

She looked at me with eyes that were tinged with something, but damned if I could make it out—amusement, perhaps. "You misunderstand me, Mr. Riordan," was all she said. She gestured at the table beside me. "Would you pour the tea?"

I fumbled the delicate porcelain teapot around and managed to get the tea into the matching cups without breaking anything.

I picked up the cup closest to her with the intention of passing it over, then hesitated, wondering if I was supposed to doctor it with something first. She was miles ahead of me.

"Chinese tea never contains sugar, milk or lemon."

"Rightie-o." I stood and placed the cup on the desk in front of her. I hoped getting to the point was somewhere on the agenda, because character assassination and butler duties were getting to be a drag. I dropped back into my chair and picked up my tea to sample it. It was good.

She sipped at hers, leaving a purply red mark from her lipstick on the rim of the cup. "I say you misunderstand me because I am not concerned about the window. If I chose to be concerned, it would be about the $8,000 ceramic bowl that was also destroyed."

I felt heat rise to my cheeks. I hadn't considered that anything else in the store had been in harm's way.

"I didn't ask you here to discuss damages; I asked you here to thank you. I *am* a community-minded person, and I am also a minority owner of the Bank of Canton and several other San Francisco financial institutions. I contributed to the reward fund, so I'm gratified that it motivated you to prevent the theft of our ATM." She raised her cup in a little toast. "So thank you."

To say I hadn't seen this one coming was putting it mildly. "Er, you're welcome," I managed. "But I didn't actually catch the thief."

"No, not yet. We will be very pleased to pay the reward to you when you do."

"Okay." I shifted in my chair. I had the feeling there must be another size six pump ready to drop. "Was there anything else?"

She hugged the cup to her chest with both hands as if to draw warmth. "Yes, there was. You followed the recent city elections of course."

Although I hadn't voted, it was hard to live in the city and not be aware of them. The mayoral contest had been the big ticket item, with three major candidates vying to take over for the outgoing incumbent, Charlie Hill. The favorite was Hill's hand-picked successor, Hunter Lowdon. Young and handsome, Lowdon was a political moderate: he was popular with business—particularly the tourist industry—because of his tough stand on the homeless problem, but he still retained Hill's affinity with labor, including the big unions in city government like the transit workers.

To the right of Lowdon was Alan Chow. He was a conservative businessman involved in retail. He had the support of the "downtown" business interests, including banking and real estate, and was popular in the predominately Chinese neighborhoods of the city, like Chinatown, Sunset, Richmond and Vistacon Valley. These had gone for Hill in previous elections, but were looking this time to put a candidate of their own in office. Leonora Lee was a big backer of Chow.

Finally, there was Mike Padilla. Padilla was a firebrand lawyer from the Green party who was interested in controlling development and improving the lot of the citizenry in San Francisco's poorer neighborhoods, like the Mission and Hunter's Point. His base was built in those neighborhoods, but he had other supporters throughout the more liberal districts like the Haight and the Castro.

The handicapping before the election had Lowdon winning by a wide margin, Chow garnering a respectable tally—but less than what would be required to force a runoff—followed by Padilla with a single-digit percentage of the vote. The handicapping, it turned out, was pretty much wrong. Lowdon and Padilla split the vote forty-five percent to forty percent, and Chow ended up in the single-digit zone. A runoff election was scheduled in early December for Lowdon and Padilla to duke it out.

I nodded at the woman across the desk. "Sure," I said. "I followed the elections. Your candidate lost."

The Dragon Lady frowned. "Don't be impertinent. Yes, Mr. Chow lost, and to be honest, I did not really expect him to defeat Lowdon, but I was at least hoping he would force a runoff and perhaps encourage Lowdon to include more of our thinking in his platform. Now I will be happy if we simply manage to defeat Padilla."

"I don't really have a dog in this fight, but it seems pretty obvious that you and the rest of Chow's supporters are going to go as a block to Lowdon. Even those few percentage points should be enough to push him over the top."

"Not if the election is rigged."

I laughed. "Mrs. Lee, I've felt like Alice down the rabbit hole ever since I walked in here. What could possibly make you think the election will be rigged and what—if you don't mind my asking—does it have to do with me?"

"I'm afraid the runoff will be rigged because I'm convinced the November election was. I want you to figure out who did it, how it was done and prevent it from happening in December."

I blinked at her. "Do you want fries with that too?"

"Please. It's not as fantastic as it sounds. As you probably know, the city installed touch-screen voting systems for this election. My computer experts tell me there are a hundred ways to tamper with these machines, and very little in the way of audit controls to detect the tampering. I also have election experts who've done statistical analysis of historical voting patterns in the city—as well as racially motivated voting behavior—and what happened in the November election is completely inconsistent with past elections. A small example is that Padilla actually captured thirty-four percent of the vote in Chinatown. Impossible."

I wasn't sure what to make of her comments about touch-screen voting, but I agreed with her assessment of Padilla's chances in this neighborhood. "Okay," I said cautiously. "But that still doesn't explain what you expect to accomplish by hiring me. Why not use your experts? Or better yet, have Chow protest the election and trigger a formal investigation. Isn't that the way election irregularities are supposed to be handled?"

"Chow is a weak-willed idiot."

"And I bet his shoes are scuffed too."

She slammed her teacup down on the desk, sloshing tea over the side. "Mr. Riordan, I may have been wrong when I implied you were lazy, but I'm developing some good ideas for new labels to apply. Please do me the courtesy of hearing me out without further injections of sarcasm. As I was about to say, Chow refuses to protest the election. He's afraid of being labeled a conspiracy theorist and hurting his chances in future campaigns."

"May I ask why you selected me, then? I mean, apart from the fact that we ran into each other."

"I've done my research. I've talked to some of your former clients and contacts I have in law enforcement. I know you've successfully handled some high-profile cases involving technology. I'm offering you $1,000 a day until the election—which is less than a week from now—plus a bonus of $20,000 if you discover the person or persons behind the fraud."

My bank balance was so low it would fit under a lizard, so a thousand bucks a day was going to be hard to pass up. But despite my putative success with "technology" cases, I hardly felt qualified. "I appreciate the offer," I said. "But I know nothing about touch-screen technology. In fact, when it gets right down to it, I'm pretty much a technophobe. I wouldn't know where to begin with something like this."

"You begin with the appointment I set up for you this afternoon with Professor Ballou at Stanford University. He's a computer scientist and an expert on touch-screen voting fraud. He can provide all the expertise you need. In the end, this isn't really about technology.

It's about investigative skills and the ability to get in someone's face until he or she gives you the information you want. Based on this interview, you seem like you'd do that well."

I thought about it for a moment. Assuming there was actually anything to be found, I still had zero conviction that I'd be able to uncover it, but I couldn't see walking away from the easy money. I also knew that I could lean on my friend and sometime assistant Chris Duckworth to help me with the technology aspects. "All right. I'm game."

The Dragon Lady brought a hand up to the jade pendant around her neck. The stone was the size of a hockey puck. She rubbed the surface of the jade and produced another fang-baring smile. "Excellent. My daughter has a check for your retainer and the details on the appointment with Professor Ballou."

"Your daughter?"

The Dragon Lady actually laughed this time. "Yes. Are you surprised? Her name is Lisa. She was Miss Chinatown last year." When I was slow to respond, she came around the desk to escort me to the door. I rushed to return the teacup to the table and stood to walk with her.

"Good luck," she said, and put her hand out to shake goodbye. "I'd like regular reports. You can phone them in to Lisa and I'll follow up if there's anything critical."

"Roger that," I said before she hustled me out the door and back into the reception area. Lisa was sitting at a smaller rosewood desk off to one side. Music came from a stereo on the desk and I recognized the tune as "Things Ain't What They Used to Be" from the Ellington songbook.

She looked up as I approached. "Did you take the job?"

"She made me an offer I couldn't refuse."

"Congratulations, then. I'm sure you'll do well."

I came to a stop at the corner of the desk and stared down at her. It was hard to get over what a stunner she was. "You and your mother are much more confident on that point than I am." I nodded at the stereo. "You a jazz fan?"

Her face brightened. "Yes I am, as a matter of fact. Just the old stuff, though. My dad was a band leader and he got me hooked. He used to play in the restaurant downstairs."

"Really? What instrument does he play?"

"He played drums. He called himself the Chinese Buddy Rich." She smiled at the memory and looked over my shoulder to the view of the Bay, not really seeing it. "He passed away some time ago."

"I'm sorry to hear that." An awkward moment went by. I caught her eye again and blurted, "I'm playing bass in a jazz quartet tomorrow night at Shanghai 1930. You should come and see me."

She gave me a broad smile that nearly floated me out the Golden Gate. "First with the higher plane stuff," she said, "and now with the invitations. You're a fast mover, Mr. Riordan."

"August."

"All right, August, I'll think about it. In the meantime, you need to get a move on if you're going to make your appointment with Professor Ballou." She opened a drawer to extract a business envelope. "This has a retainer check, directions to Dr. Ballou's office and contact information for us."

"Including your phone number?"

"Including my *office* phone number." She stood and snatched my coat from where it lay on a chair next to her desk. She passed the coat and the envelope over. "Now I think you should go before you work yourself up to a marriage proposal."

I bowed in what I hoped was a chivalrous fashion. "If marriage be premature, perhaps a token of your esteem that I be reminded of you on my quest. A kiss, for instance?"

She brought a hand to her mouth to suppress a laugh and looked around her desk. Her eyes settled on a pad of Post-it notes. She peeled one off and stuck it to my lapel. "There, good knight. You shall bear my royal colors."

I looked down at the droopy, yellow square and shook my head. "I wonder if this is how Saint George got started." I made my retreat to the elevator, stepped inside and turned to look at her.

"You've got your cultures confused," she called out as the doors were closing. "Saint George *slayed* the dragon. You're on her payroll."

YOU *CAN* FIGHT CITY HALL

MINGLING AGAIN WITH THE HORDES OF TOURISTS on Grant Street—and getting poked repeatedly in the ribs for my trouble by a rotund woman carrying a paper parasol—I had a sense of coming back to the real world. It now seemed more than a little fantastic that I had been hired to investigate election fraud in one of the largest cities on the West Coast. I peered in the envelope Lisa had given me and looked at the retainer check. Drawn for $5,000 on the Bank of Canton with the neatly written memo, "mayoral election investigation," it at least had the patina of legitimacy.

I made it as far as Old St. Mary's before lingering doubts about the case arrested all forward progress. I felt like I needed some kind of confirmation that there was any basis to believe there had been election irregularities. I sat down on one of the stone benches outside the granite-trimmed doorway of the cathedral and pulled out my cell phone. With the aid of the overpriced directory service and a few calls into the city hall switchboard, I learned a number of things. The first was that asking the switchboard operators for information was like asking for a DNA sample. The second was that—surprisingly enough—city elections were run and monitored by the Department of Elections with oversight by something called the Elections Commission. Finally, I learned the director of the department was a guy named Jerry Bowman. I asked to be transferred to his office and Mr. Bowman himself picked up on the second ring, which suggested I'd been given his private line. I figured the switchboard operator must like him even less than she liked me.

"Department of Elections, Jerry Bowman," he said in a toneless voice as boring as high school Latin.

I couldn't think of any subtle way to ask him if he thought the last election he ran was rigged, so I decided to play it straight. "Mr. Bowman, I'm a private investigator named August Riordan. I've been hired by Leonora Lee to look into concerns she has about the mayoral election results. I wondered if you would answer a few questions for me."

I didn't hear anything for a long moment and then there was the sound of a heavy breath being drawn. "I've already spoken to Mrs. Lee about her concerns. There's no reason to think there were significant problems with the election. If she feels otherwise, her best recourse would have been to encourage Chow to protest the results. Now the deadline has passed."

The cold from the stone bench was seeping through my topcoat. I shifted my buttocks around so I could limit the frostbite to one cheek. "I understand, but Mrs. Lee has a particular concern about the touch-screen voting systems that were put in place for this election. Maybe if you could see your way clear to explain the voting fraud safeguards, I could pass the information on and Mrs. Lee and I both would be out of your hair."

"Interesting suggestion Mr. Riordan," he said in his toneless voice, "but I don't think that's the best use of my time. I can get you out of my hair with the press of a button. Like this."

I folded up the phone and watched as a six- or seven-year-old boy broke ranks from the stream of tourists and attacked invisible enemies near my bench with the plastic samurai sword his mother had bought him. There was a lot of gesturing and hacking, but very little in the way of real results. I was feeling a little like that about my activities the last twenty-four hours.

I opened the phone again to call Gretchen to reschedule my appointment with Dr. Ballou for tomorrow. It seemed a better use of my time would be making the director of elections work harder to get me out of his hair.

San Francisco's city hall is larger—and more opulent—than many state capital buildings. Part of the opulence comes from $400 million that was lavished on it for repair and retrofit in the wake of the 1989 Loma Prieta earthquake, including about a half million worth of 24-carat gold leaf that was applied to the massive copper dome. I parked on the Polk Street side in a spot that was clearly reserved for a city official—permit holder number seventy-two, to be exact—and went up the same steps that Marilyn Monroe and Joe DiMaggio had trod on the way to their short-lived 1954 wedding.

Inside were artifacts from another famous—if not nearly so happy—event in the building's history: metal detectors. Dan White, the assassin of Mayor George Moscone and Supervisor Harvey Milk, had gone out of his way to avoid these by climbing in a basement window on the north side of the building with his .38-caliber revolver loaded with dum-dum bullets. I had left all my hardware in the car, including the knife I usually kept sheathed on my ankle, so the only things I had to drop into the basket before stepping through the detector were my keys and the heavy, half-dollar-sized medal of Saint Apollonia I carried in my pocket.

I retrieved my stuff from the guard and wandered into the rotunda. Marble was the operative word here. The walls, the floor and the grand staircase leading to the surrounding balconies were lousy with it. And when they couldn't use marble, they'd limped by with granite, polished oak or cast iron trimmed in more gold leaf. I sojourned across the cavernous space, through a marble archway and up to a building directory in a vestibule by the elevators. The Department of Elections, it seemed, was housed in the basement, room forty-eight.

The basement had every bit as much stonework as the rotunda, but with the lower ceilings and the lack of natural lighting, it came off more like a men's room at a train station than an architectural masterwork. The Bicycle Advisory Committee and Animal Care and Control were the only other departments down here, so it wasn't hard to guess where Elections fell in the political pecking order.

Room forty-eight was actually a suite of offices with double doors that opened on a reception area. Behind an oak counter near the entrance stood a towering, Ichabod Crane-like figure with eyebrows long and bristly enough to attract pollinating bees. As I approached, he squared a stack of absentee ballot request forms and pushed them to one side on the counter. His eyebrows shot up his forehead in a welcoming—if weedy—expression and he said, "How may I help you?"

"I'd like to speak to Jerry Bowman."

"Do you have an appointment?"

"No, I don't."

He patted the forms again, not making them any squarer. "The director doesn't usually see people without an appointment."

"I think he'll want to see me."

He looked me over appraisingly and I realized that the Dragon Lady might have been onto something with her insistence on formal business attire. "I suppose I could check with him. Would you tell me your name and the topic you'd like to discuss?"

"Greg McQuaid," I said, borrowing the name of my pal the cop. The topic was going to be harder to manufacture. I glanced behind the counter to a poster on the wall that talked about voter outreach and community participation. "I'm here to talk to him about outreach to the Irish community."

The guy behind the counter didn't quite smirk. "Really?"

"Yes, really. Irish-American voters have the lowest turnout of any ethnic group in the city, yet as a block, they donate the largest amount to political campaigns. I want to discuss outreach programs to encourage voter participation." I paused in significant way. "I think he'll understand."

Ichabod made an elaborate shrug—moving his eyebrows in tandem with his shoulders—and went down a hallway that opened off the reception area. I turned away from the counter and watched as a pimply guy eating a Clark Bar opened and closed drawers in the tall filing cabinets that ringed the waiting area. He didn't seem to be a department employee, but I couldn't figure out what the heck he was doing. He felt my eyes on him and looked over. "FPPC forms," he said, and stuffed the last of the Clark Bar into his mouth.

"FPPC?"

He nodded as he chewed. "Fair Political Practices Commission. They require forms for campaign disclosures and contributions to be open for public inspection." He licked chocolate off a finger and then extended it to point at me in an accusatory way. "Irish don't give dick."

I snorted and turned back to the counter. In a moment, Ichabod returned with an odd look on his face. "Mr. Bowman is in conference. I suggest you call to make an appointment for another time. I'm sure he'll be happy to see you then."

"How about if I just wait?"

"I don't know how long he'll be."

I glanced at my watch. It was already three thirty and I realized I hadn't had anything to eat all day. I'd seen a sign pointing to a cafeteria, so I decided to beat a tactical retreat there, refuel on the tater tot casserole—or whatever other delicacy they had coagulating in the steam trays—and come back to wait out Mr. Bowman. I nodded to Ichabod and went out the office doors.

The cafeteria was down a corridor that paralleled the one Ichabod had taken to see Bowman. At about the twenty-yard point was an unmarked door that was slightly ajar. If the floor plan included a private entrance to the director's office, this is the place it would be. I checked to see if anyone was watching, and then tugged at the knob. The latch slid off the strike plate and the door came open further. Inside I could see a slice of the carpet and a corner of a dark mahogany desk. I figured this had to be it. I tapped on the doorframe. "Excuse me, Mr. Bowman?" I said. My voice sounded tentative to my ears, like a grade-schooler asking permission to go to the bathroom.

Tentative or not, Bowman didn't answer. I pulled the door open wider and stuck my head into the room. Ichabod had told me that Jerry Bowman was in conference. The only thing the big man behind the desk was in conference with was a letter opener—right through the neck.

His head hung lifeless off the back of the chair, his mouth gaped open and his eyes bulged in a fixed stare at the ceiling. The handle of the letter opener—a miniature medieval sword with a silver crossguard and jeweled pommel—gleamed cruelly at the side of his neck. Blood had flowed from the wound to cover his dress shirt like a ghastly bib. The skin on his bald head looked mottled and gray and I didn't have any doubts that he was dead.

I came up to check anyway, but couldn't bring myself to probe his neck for the carotid artery. I lifted a meaty wrist and didn't find any sign of a pulse, but he was still warm to the touch and there didn't seem to be any indication of rigor. All that made sense since I'd talked to him less than an hour before. I dropped his hand back to his ample gut and a plastic cap of some sort tumbled from his palm to land on his chair near his crotch. I didn't like where it landed, but I didn't like any of this. I pushed his chair back a little to get maneuvering room and used a key from my ring to daintily spear it. I held it up to the light.

It was small and nearly square in shape, a little larger than a piece of Chiclets gum. It was made from a translucent purple plastic and had a clip on it to attach to a shirt pocket. I supposed it could have been a cap for a felt tip pen—perhaps the kind used for highlighting. I set it down on the desk blotter and squatted to look on the floor for my hypothetical pen. I found paper clips, a penny and receipt from a hardware store. I stood up. The desk was clear of writing implements and I didn't want to muddle the scene any further by opening drawers.

The fact of the matter was I was stalling, and I knew it. Although the cap had been in Bowman's hand, it may not have had any more significance than the hardware receipt. I simply didn't want to face the music with the cops. I briefly considered walking, but Ichabod and the guards at the front of the building would be able to identify me and my selection of Greg McQuaid as my alias had been particularly unfortunate. I shoved Bowman back under the desk and rubbed the places I'd touched his chair with my handkerchief. No use giving the cops any more than necessary to get excited about.

I looked down at Bowman a final time. Dark blood welled in his mouth like crude oil in a drill hole. I shivered and turned away.

The lock button was down on the knob of the interior door, so I exited the way I'd come, dragged myself up the corridor and into the Elections Office. The guy with the Clark Bar was gone, but Ichabod was hunched over the counter looking bored, his chin resting in his palms. He frowned when he saw me. "I told you I didn't know how long Mr. Bowman would be."

"Try an eternity."

BLACK PENNY

IN MY LAST ENCOUNTER WITH LIEUTENANT "SMILING Jack" Kittredge in an interrogation room at the Hall of Justice, he'd arranged for me to sit under a leaking sewer pipe and then personally flushed the toilet in a stall in the men's room above. This time when a uniformed officer directed to me to a chair, I first made sure there were no overhead pipes and then moved to a different seat after the officer left for good measure.

Kittredge came through the door a moment later, flashing his trademark choppers. "I just won twenty bucks." He held up a crumpled Jackson.

I stared at him for a long moment. "I'll bite. What for?"

He laughed and pointed at the video camera on the ceiling. "We were watching on the monitor. I bet you'd switch seats after Johnny dropped you off."

"Do the words Abu Ghraib hold any particular association for you, Kittredge?"

He sat down across from me, taking care to perch on the very edge of the grimy-looking chair. He always had at least a thousand bucks worth of designer suit on—today's was an olive green worsted with a faint maroon line running through the fabric—and he was fastidious as hell about his appearance. He winked at me. "Sure. Isn't that the new falafel place they opened on Market?"

"That's right. And I hear they need a guy to grind the garbanzo beans into paste. You should apply—something tells me you'd be very good at it."

"Lighten up, Riordan. If I ever gave you the third degree for real, you'd know it. This is just a little friendly hazing." He paused to shoot his cuffs. The movement caused a cloud of musky cologne to waft across the table. "So tell me, how is it that you keep stumbling across dead bodies? If a person didn't know better, he'd think there was a cause and effect relationship."

Kittredge and I had met on an earlier case when I discovered the body of a young Japanese woman. There was no good answer to his question, so I let it hang there with his cologne.

"Start flapping your gums already—or who do you think we're going to blame this on?"

"The Bossa Nova?"

He thrust his shovel chin out. "Just tell me what the hell you were doing in Bowman's office."

"I wanted to ask him about election irregularities."

"In this last election?"

"That's right."

"You told the guy at the counter you were Greg McQuaid and you wanted to talk about Irish voter turnout."

I cleared my throat. "That was just a gag to get in to see Bowman."

"Did you know there's a cop named Greg McQuaid?"

"Yeah, I know him slightly."

"What made you pick his name?"

"It's Irish."

Kittredge rolled his eyes. "We cops generally frown upon having our names used as aliases in criminal activities—that's something you might want to note down for future reference."

"There was nothing criminal going on. I had already given my name to Bowman when I talked to him on the phone and I knew he wouldn't want to talk to me again."

"The conversation went well, did it?"

"He told me there were no problems with the election and hung up."

"And that was a little less than an hour before you found him."

"That's right."

Kittredge flared his nostrils and sniffed. The view from where I sat was like two bores from the Caldecott tunnel. "You were a little vague with the responding officer about *why* you were looking into problems with the election."

I held up my hands. "You know what I do for a living. Somebody hired me."

"Somebody hired me," Kittredge repeated in a mocking tone. "Maybe you should have that stitched on a pillow. You can set it right next to the one that says, 'I was only following orders.'" He leaned onto the table. "Well, don't give me any crap about client confidentiality. I want the name of the person and I want it now."

I had to fight to keep from smiling. He wasn't going to be any too happy to have it, especially given the recent turmoil in the SFPD. An only-in-San-Francisco scandal involving the deputy chief's son and an off-duty brawl over a bag of fajitas and its ensuing cover-up—dubbed "Fajitagate" by the press—had swept the chief, the deputy chief and about half the command force out of the department. The new chief was a squeaky clean veteran with thirty years of service, mostly in administrative roles. She was also female and Chinese, and not surprisingly, was vigorously supported by Leonora Lee and the rest of the Chinese community. I knew that Kittredge had been connected to the old administration and was not nearly so tight with the new chief.

"Leonora Lee," I said slowly. "Last name spelled L-e-e. Called by some the 'Dragon Lady of Chinatown.'"

Kittredge slumped back into the chair. "You're not serious."

I produced the signed check and laid it out on the table with a flourish. "Pay particular attention to the amount."

He glared down at it. "I'm going to confirm this. Your story better damn well pan out."

"It will."

"Then when did she hire you?"

"Just today. See the date on this *$5,000* check?"

He looked down again and shook his head in disgust. "Let's get back to Bowman. Did you see anyone leave his office before you went in?"

"No, the hallway was empty."

"And you decided to go in because …"

"Because the door was open and I wanted to talk to the guy. It's as simple as that. I didn't have any idea he'd be dead. I wasn't even sure it was his office."

"Did Lee tell you to go talk to him?"

"What? You think she had him bumped and then sent me over there to discover the body?"

He jerked his chin at me. "Just answer the question."

"No, Lee didn't send me there. I went off my own bat."

Kittredge stared at me for a second and then rubbed his face with both hands. The news about Lee seemed to have knocked him off his perch. "What reasons did Lee give you to believe there were election problems?"

"Not a lot, to be honest. She just seemed convinced that the results didn't match historic voting patterns. That's the main reason I went to see Bowman. I wanted to understand if there was really anything to it."

He nodded, and I could see that he didn't relish the thought of Bowman's death being mixed up with election fraud. It would be much better for the department—and the city as a whole—if it turned out to be the result of a lover's quarrel or something equally mundane. "And apart from the letter opener sticking out of Bowman's neck, you didn't see anything unusual or noteworthy in the office?"

"No, not really. I told the officer on the scene about the cap that fell from his hand when I tried to take his pulse. I didn't see a matching pen, but I didn't open the desk either."

"You damn well better not have. The last thing we need is you polluting a crime scene." He reached into his jacket to take out a card. "Here," he said, and shoved it across the table. "We're done. Call me if you think of anything you accidentally left out." He emphasized the word accidentally with little quote marks in the air.

"Aren't you going to give me the usual warning about steering clear of the investigation? Or maybe my connections are a little too solid this time?"

He stood up. "Not solid enough to let you jump up and down on my neck, Riordan."

I picked up the card and my check and stood with him. "Was the letter opener Bowman's?"

"Yeah. He had a little plastic base for it in the shape of a stone in a drawer. It was labeled 'Excalibur' like the King Arthur story, get it?"

"Yeah, I get it. So whoever killed him didn't plan it."

"Or they knew about the letter opener already, or they realized they couldn't get a weapon into the building and planned to get creative once they arrived." He paused. "Now get lost. You're like the last dirty black penny at the bottom of the jar. I don't want you around here anymore."

I stepped past him. "But you know the old saying, don't you Kittredge?" I said when I had my hand on the door. "The bad penny always comes back."

PAJAMA CHAT

L UCKY CHARMS USED TO BE ONE OF my favorite breakfast ce-
reals, but General Mills ruined it for me when they began
messing with the recipe, adding purple horseshoes, red balloons,
tri-color rainbows, etc. to the original marshmallow lineup of pink
hearts, yellow moons, orange stars and green clovers. Imagine how
pleased and surprised I was, then, when I found boxes of "factory
seconds" containing only frosted oats and orange stars at the local
Smart & Final. I snapped up two cases of them and have been en-
joying a breakfast experience that hearkens back to a simpler time
ever since.

Preparing a big bowl the morning after my interview with
Kittredge, I found the milk had gone bad so I had to float the cereal
on orange juice that itself was a week past its expiration date. The
juice tasted okay, but it did clash a bit with the orange stars, which
were a paler yellow-orange color. I was halfway through the bowl
and nearly all the way through the *Chronicle* article on Bowman's
death—"SF Election Director Murdered; First Attack in City Hall
since Moscone Shot"—when my cell phone rang. I traipsed across
the room to snag it from the coffee table and then returned to sit at
the folding card table where I ate my meals. I saw the calling number
had been blocked, but flipped open the phone to answer anyway.

"This is Riordan."

"Mr. Riordan, this is Leonora Lee. I got your number from your secretary."

Given Bowman's death, I wasn't surprised the Dragon Lady was calling, but something about talking to the woman—even over the phone with her at least a couple of miles away—made me sit up straighter. "Ah, no problem. What—what can I do for you?"

"It's nearly ten. I was expecting to find you at your office or out working on the investigation. Your secretary says she doesn't know where you are. I hope not at home lounging around in your pajamas."

I looked down at the green and white check pattern of my JCPenney pajamas and fingered the low-thread-count cotton. "No," I said. "No, of course not."

"Professor Ballou tells me you rescheduled your appointment with him. May I ask why?"

"It's pretty simple. I wanted to get the perspective of the guy who actually runs elections for the city before I talked to anyone else, so I moved the appointment."

"I see. I had a conversation with a Detective Kittredge this morning. He seems, by the way, to start his work day much earlier than you. He suggested that the reason you went to see Bowman was because you doubted my assertion there was fraud in the last election."

"Not exactly—"

She rode right over me. "And having tried to see Director Bowman and found him dead, do you now take the idea of election fraud more seriously? And was this newfound certainty worth broadcasting my business to the police?"

I picked up the cereal spoon and swirled the remaining Lucky Charms in the bowl into an angry orange whirl. "Look, Mrs. Lee, the reason your interest in the election is known to the police is *because* Jerry Bowman is dead. The cops aren't stupid. They would have had to investigate the possibility of a political motivation for the murder, and the fact that you had discussed your doubts with Bowman would certainly have come up—through his staff or from his appointment calendar."

Her voice took on a new shrillness. "Are you insinuating in any way, shape or form that I had a motivation for harming Bowman?"

"Simmer down," I said, and dropped the spoon into the bowl. The momentum of the orange juice caused the handle to sweep around the rim like a second hand. "I'm not insinuating anything. I'm just saying that your interest would have become known in the normal course of the investigation, even without my involvement. Besides, I believe you have a pretty important friend in the department who will make sure your business stays private."

The line was silent for a moment and then she said, "Perhaps," in a cooler tone.

It was clearly time to seize the initiative before she wound herself up again. I said, "You implied it earlier, but just to get it out on the table—do you believe the murder is politically motivated?"

"Of course. The stakes are very high and you would do well to take that to heart. If Bowman was killed for what he may have learned about the fraud—or to stop him from revealing his own part in it—it's entirely possible someone investigating will be putting themselves at risk."

"You're making this sound like a very dark and sinister conspiracy. Who's behind it? Padilla?"

The Dragon Lady didn't quite snort. "Not him personally. He's just an overgrown boy who got a law degree from Stanford and decided to dabble in politics. But like any candidate, he's supported by people with particular agendas. Special interests, as they say. Some of the people in his camp have some very strongly held beliefs and are prepared to do whatever it takes to advance them."

"This is the Green Party we're talking about. You think they're going to kill to advance the cause of recycling?"

"You're being naive, Mr. Riordan. The left has a history of violence at least as checkered as the right. Remember the Symbionese Liberation Army?"

"I don't remember what they stood for, except that they demanded food for the poor as ransom for Patty Hearst. What do you think these special interests in the Green Party want?"

The Dragon Lady laughed. "You live in San Francisco and you can't guess? What's the most precious resource in the area?"

"Real estate. Housing."

She laughed again. "Yes, housing. That's the first time in this conversation I've heard anything to give me hope I haven't wasted my $5,000 retainer. I suggest you keep housing—or the lack of it—in mind as you continue your investigation. Now I'm going to let you go so you can get back to work. Please don't miss your appointment with Professor Ballou again."

I pushed the cereal bowl away. The Lucky Charms had assumed an unappetizing, bloated appearance. "I'll be there with bells on."

"Good. One last thing. I see you are in the paper two days in a row."

"My name wasn't mentioned in the Bowman article."

"No, it wasn't," she said. "Look on page A24."

She clicked off and I folded the phone and set it to one side. It took me a while to find it, but page A24 had a six-inch squib near the bottom, with the headline: "ATM Bandit Strikes Again, Taunts Would-Be Bounty Hunter." The text described the hijacking of a teller machine in the Sunset District and noted that I had prevented an attempted theft the night before. The last paragraph reproduced a note the bandit had left on the platform where the ATM had stood:

Little Auggie Riordan,

Another ATM for me and still no
reward for you. Next time, don't bring
rocks to a tractor fight.

Your Pal,

Red

I hated it when people called me Auggie.

I spent the next hour with the yellow pages, drawing up a list
of bank branches that might be vulnerable. I wasn't finished with
Red yet.

ELECTION FRAUD FOR DUMMIES

GOING TO MEET PROFESSOR BALLOU AT STANFORD University meant getting the Galaxie 500 from the seedy Tenderloin garage where I parked it and hoping it would hold up for the drive down the Peninsula to Palo Alto. It also meant picking up my friend Chris Duckworth.

Duckworth and I had met on a case involving the theft of computer software, and from that point forward, I'd come to rely on his advice and assistance in all matters technical. He also dabbled in "show biz" as I did, performing jazz standards and show tunes in clubs, and we had even played some gigs together. One thing that differentiated us on stage, however, was the fact that he performed in drag. He was eerily convincing as a woman, and that fact had gotten him—and me—into trouble on more than one occasion. He was also chronically unemployed, "gay as a French Horn" (his phrase), a "*smart aleckus frequentus*" (mine) and tended to look up to me, so I thought of him as the gay, smart-mouthed, slacker son I never had.

Driving south on Highway 280 after picking him up at his Castro District apartment, I filled Chris in on the assignment and the discovery of Bowman's body. I finished with, "And that's where Ballou comes in. I knew I wouldn't be able to make heads or tails of what he said, so I figured you could be my interpreter."

I glanced over at Duckworth and watched him smirk back at me. He was wearing a funky, three-quarter length leather coat with French cuffs and had it wrapped tight around his slender torso to compensate for the anemic performance of the Galaxie's heater. He ran his hand through his close-cropped blond hair. "Your interpreter," he repeated. "Wouldn't that be like explaining the Hegelian dialectic to my cat?"

"How do you think your cat would do with the infield fly rule?"

"I told you, I only went to that baseball game to see the men in tight pants. Besides, I don't actually think this is such an arcane topic."

"Oh yeah?"

"Well, it strikes me that these machines are computers like any other. You collect data via the screen, process it and store it on disk or some other form of memory. That means they can be hacked like other computers."

"There's gotta be some kind of security."

"Sure, just like there's gotta be security on the FBI Web site. That didn't stop someone from putting a picture of J. Edgar Hoover in a dress on it."

"I've always wondered who that someone was." I looked over at Chris again, but all he did was make a coy zip-my-lips gesture.

The classic postcard shot of Stanford University is the view down Palm Drive to Memorial Church and the sandstone- and red-tiled roofs of the buildings in the Quad. What the postcards don't show you are the parking enforcement officers who swarm the oval drive in front of the Quad like Brazilian army ants. I was twice dissuaded from parking in a juicy faculty and staff spot by a helmeted minion with a triple-decker ticket book, so I settled for a cozy plot of asphalt in the alley behind the Organic Chemistry building that was every bit as illegal, but more discreetly so.

Professor Ballou's office was—appropriately enough—in a building named after Microsoft founder Bill Gates. The outside of the building was a nice blend of modern design and the California Mission-inspired architecture that dominated the campus, but going down a hallway past dozens of miniscule offices with frosted glass doors, I was reminded of the documentary I saw on Japanese capsule hotels. You would have thought Gates could have sprung for an extra floor in his building to give everyone a little more elbow room.

Ballou was in number 434 and his office was every bit as small as the others. He'd shoehorned in a desk, a computer and a couple of guest chairs, but as the Borscht Belt joke goes, if he had any cockroaches in there, they'd be hunchbacked. Ballou himself was small—only a couple inches taller than Chris. He looked to be in his mid-forties, had dirty brown hair running to gray at the temples and a prominent schnoz with a defined crease running through the tip of it. He wore rimless glasses with thin silver bows, a black turtleneck and a pair of wrinkled khakis. He shook Chris' and my hands when they were offered, but had trouble making eye contact. He gestured awkwardly at the guest chairs and then dropped into his own in front of his computer like he was returning to asylum. I had a feeling he didn't get out much.

His fingers scuttled along the keys of the computer keyboard. "Excuse me," he mumbled. "I want to bring up my notes for the meeting."

"Mrs. Lee gave you the background, then?" I said.

"Yes, of course." He glanced furtively at Chris. "But she didn't say there would be two of you."

"Chris is my part-time assistant. He often helps me with technical matters. He'll keep everything we discuss in confidence—as I will."

"All right," said Ballou into his lap. "What would you like to cover first?"

"Maybe you could just explain how touch-screen voting systems work in general. I'm afraid I don't even have a very good handle on that."

Ballou brightened, happy to be on familiar ground. "In concept, touch-screen systems are not that much different than traditional systems, except that the votes are stored electronically. Each polling place is equipped with touch-screen machines, which are the equivalent of voting stations in paper-based systems. The machines run software that displays the ballot and captures the voters' selections. The only difference is that instead of punching a hole on a paper ballot, the voter touches the appropriate place on the screen to select a candidate. The votes are then written to nonvolatile memory within the machine, and when the polling place closes, the memory is removed from the machine and taken to a central server where the votes are tallied. Some vendors' machines—such as the ones being used in San Francisco—also print a paper audit trail for each vote cast."

"You don't make it sound particularly insecure or error-prone. What are the problems?"

"A touch-screen voting machine is just a computer—a specialized kind of computer, but a computer nonetheless. Erroneous outcomes could happen for a variety of reasons, including software and hardware errors, procedural errors, security holes or hacks installed into the voting machines."

Chris held his hands palms up and looked over at me. "What did I tell you?"

I waved him off. "Let's get more specific. Exactly how would you go about changing the outcome of an election?"

Ballou glanced at his computer screen and then used the mouse to scroll text down. "I'm afraid there are many, many different ways, but I'll try to focus on a few of the most likely. First, starting at the polling place, when the memory is removed from the computer, a corrupt poll worker could alter the results for the precinct before turning them in. It's much easier than ballot box stuffing because you only need to change one number and there's no need to steal or forge ballots."

Chris squared a book on the corner of Ballou's desk titled *Python Cookbook*, which I assumed had nothing to do with eating snakes. "But taking that approach would mean you'd only affect the votes for one precinct," he said. "You'd have to corrupt a whole lot of poll workers to really impact an election."

"That's right. If you want one-stop shopping, then the best thing to do is to wait until all the votes are loaded on the central server. If you can gain access to the network where the election management system runs, then results for the whole election are at your fingertips. It's not dissimilar to a student who wants to cheat in school. It's more efficient to hack into the university system to change the grades for all your courses than to go to the trouble of cheating on individual exams in each class."

"But if I'm trying to catch someone who used that method, who am I looking for? Does it have to be someone in the Elections Department?"

Ballou bit his lip and shook his head like I should have known better. "No. It would help, of course, but once you put the votes on a network, you have the same security issues you would have with any other computer application. The hacker could be someone outside the Elections Department who suborns an employee—or simply tricks him into giving up his password—or it could be someone who has no contact with department employees at all, but finds a vulnerability in the system and exploits it."

"So you're saying election results could be hacked this way as a result of negligence, with no actual complicity on the part of Elections Department employees?"

"Absolutely. Most security breaches are the result of negligence. Failure to password protect an account, for instance. But we haven't even touched on the easiest—and most insidious—way to rig an election."

"Changing the programming of the touch-screen computers." blurted Chris.

Ballou looked over at Chris with a surprised look of geek admiration. "Very good," he said warmly.

Chris beamed back at him. "Thank you. The setup you gave made it seem obvious."

I felt like the bus boy at a lunch conversation between Einstein and Newton. "Okay, now that we've concluded the mutual admiration portion of our program, you want to explain exactly what you mean? You're saying the touch-screen machines run software?"

"Weren't you listening earlier?" said Chris. "You need software to display the ballot, capture the vote and write it to memory."

Ballou nodded. "And think how easy it would be change the vote someone cast before you write it to memory. You don't even have to be crude about it—like forcing every vote to be for your candidate. You could decide what percentage you want him to win by and change just enough votes so that he wins by that amount. You could even be sensitive to what precincts he's strongest in, changing the most votes in those and fewer votes in precincts where he is weaker."

"But it's exactly because Padilla did so well in Chinatown that Mrs. Lee thinks the election was rigged."

Ballou shrugged. "What I described would be a more sophisticated approach. It doesn't mean someone didn't take a brute force one."

"I have to ask the question I asked earlier—who would the someone be?"

Ballou pushed his keyboard back and made a steeple with his hands. "Now it gets interesting. Sticking with the scenario where the programming of the voting machine is subverted, the obvious choice would be someone associated with the vendor who built the machines. It could be an individual programmer who was paid to make the changes, or if you go in for bigger conspiracy theories, it could involve executives at the top. And, like the other scenario, there's also the possibility that someone at the Elections Department changed the code, or someone completely unaffiliated hacked into the network and made changes."

I leaned back in my chair and tried to swing one leg over the other, but there wasn't enough room in front of Ballou's desk. I dropped my foot to the floor again, frustrated. "Inking fingers like they did in the Iraq elections sounds better. Don't these programs get tested to make sure they work properly?"

"Yes, of course. But there are at least two problems. The first is that a smart programmer would know how to make the code behave properly under a test scenario and only alter votes during a real election. The second is that the software is often changed after it's tested—to correct bugs, for instance—and it's often not retested, or retested fully, before it's installed on the machines. There's a certification process that should be followed for updates, but the fact of the matter is, in the rushed period before an election, last minute changes are made and installed on the precinct machines without following process. It wouldn't be hard at all for someone to slip in a changed program on some or all of the machines." Ballou glanced down at his watch and raised his eyebrows in what seemed an overly dramatic gesture. "I'm afraid I'm out of time. I had to squeeze you in today. Yesterday I had you down for a full ninety minutes."

I nodded. "We've got more than enough to go on. If we do have reason to suspect the election was rigged by altering the software, how could we determine for sure?"

"If you can get a copy of the program that runs on the touch-screen computers, I could determine if it's been programmed to change votes."

"Source code or object code?" asked Chris.

"Source code would be better. Now, I really must go. I have a database class to teach." Ballou stood and reached down to grab a windbreaker from his chair. He shrugged it on.

We scrambled to stand with him and threaded our way out of the office to the corridor. "One more thing," I said. "Who's the vendor who supplied the machines to the city?"

"CVT. Columbia Voting Technologies. They're in South San Francisco." Ballou turned and started trotting down the hallway.

"Wait," said Chris. "What kind of memory do they use to store the votes?"

Ballou slowed and glanced back at Chris. He frowned. "They use flash memory. Some machines use flash cards like digital cameras. I believe the CVT machines use USB drives because they're formatted like regular disks. Now goodbye." He darted around a corner and disappeared from view.

I stood in the hallway thinking, jangling the Saint Apollonia medal in my pocket. I felt Chris' eyes on me. "There's some special reason you asked about the memory, isn't there?"

He nodded. He reached both hands into the front pocket of his crazy leather frock coat and pulled something small off another object. He held it up for me to see. "Look familiar?"

It was a plastic cap about the size of a Chiclet. "It looks like the pen cap I found in Bowman's hand."

He brought the other object out of his pocket. It was a three-inch-long, fob-like item with a square metal tip—a square metal tip that looked like it was meant to be covered by the cap. "This is a flash memory USB drive. I use it to transfer files between computers. The cap protects the USB connector when it's not in use." He paused. "Bowman was holding the memory from a voting machine when he died."

HAIL, COLUMBIA!

I DIDN'T WANT CHRIS TAGGING ALONG FOR WHAT came next, so I ferried him back to the city and then pointed the car south again to the worldwide headquarters of Columbia Voting Technologies. Pam, their friendly and garrulous receptionist, told me they were located in an industrial park on the Bay just a half mile past Candlestick Point. I parked the car at the extreme edge of the lot and stepped out to look across the water. The wind was up, making the choppy, silt-laden surface look like burnt sugar frothing in a pan. I watched as a windsurfer in a full wet suit scudded across the chop, leaving twin wakes that appeared to open the Bay like a zipper. He hit a series of bigger waves, bounced once, twice, then exploded into a pinwheeling mass of sail, surfer, spray and board. I waited to make sure he was able to haul himself out of the drink, mentally crossed off windsurfing from my list of life experiences, then turned to follow a path edged with fleshy ice plant to the main entrance.

CVT rented space in a five-story building of steel and tinted glass that looked like the passenger decks of a cruise ship. Their reception desk was located on the fifth floor, and from the looks of it and the space around it, if the Final Jeopardy category was interior design, the answer was, "What are burnished metal, ash wood and a boat load of baby spots?" I went up to the desk and leaned my elbows on the burnished metal inlay. A pudgy woman with a *Bride of Frankenstein* streak in her frizzy brown hair looked up and smiled across the desk at me. "You must be Pam," I said.

"That's right."

"I called earlier to get directions."

She smiled even wider. "And it looks like they worked. You really can't miss our offices once you know to get off on Sierra Point Parkway."

"You are so right."

We grinned at each other moronically. She was the first to break the clinch. "Who are you here to see?"

I knew from my old experience on the metro beat for the *L.A. Times* that reporters often fared better in getting access. "I'm with a San Francisco paper and we're doing an article on touch-screen voting machines. I was hoping to talk to someone about your products and the experience of providing voting machine technology for the last election."

She started nodding before I was halfway through with my spiel. "We've been getting a lot attention from the press lately—both because of the election and because of our new product release. I can see if Sanjay Jain is available to talk with you. He's our senior director of communications."

I figured Jain for a PR flunky, but that was to be expected since I billed myself as a reporter. I'd start with him and see how far I could get. I smiled again. "That would be wonderful."

Pam grinned back at me and picked up a glossy folder with the company name and logo printed on it from a thick stack near her elbow. "Here's our press kit. Why don't you take it with you to the conference room behind me and I'll see if I can get Sanjay to come and speak with you." She stood up and winked at me. "And if Sanjay isn't available, I'm sure I can find someone who is. After all, we wouldn't want those good directions of mine to go to waste, now would we?"

I agreed what a tragedy that would be and walked around the desk to a small conference room with a burnished metal door. Inside was a burnished metal table and several chairs that looked like they'd been taken out of the cockpit of the space shuttle. I settled into the one farthest from the entrance and began perusing the material in the folder. I'd made it through the first page of a press release trumpeting the use of CVT machines in the San Francisco general election ("San Francisco voters were treated to a new voting experience at the polls yesterday …"), when a slick-looking Indian guy in khakis and a pressed cambric shirt materialized in the doorway. "I'm Sanjay," he said, and offered his hand. "I understand you're doing a story about CVT."

I stood to greet him. "That's right."

He waited for me to say something more, and when nothing more was forthcoming, sat down carefully in the other chair. "I thought I knew most of the reporters with the *Chronicle*, but I don't believe we've met."

"I'm not with the *Chronicle*."

He was trying to be polite, but the strain was peeking through. He pursed his lips in a crumpled line, and said in a measured tone, "Then would you mind identifying yourself and giving your affiliation?"

"Sure. August Riordan. I'm with the *China Free Press*," I said, naming Leonora Lee's paper.

He frowned. "That's a Chinese language paper."

"My stories are translated."

"Okay … Do you have a card or some other credential?"

"No, I don't, but you can call my boss if you like. Her name is Leonora Lee. You might have heard of her."

He ran his hand down the front of his shirt, smoothing the already smooth fabric. "Yes, I know her. She's the publisher. You work directly for the publisher?"

"That's right." I nudged the folder on the table. "Say, I was just looking through your press kit. Congratulations. If I'm not mistaken, the *Chronicle* took the lead for their article on the new voting machines directly from your release."

He gave a smile that somehow managed to look proud and guilty at the same time. "Yes, they did. I'm sure it was just a coincidence. I know the guy who wrote the article did a lot of solid research before he filed it."

"We were thinking of a slightly different lead. Something like, 'Community leaders questioned the legitimacy of the results of the general election today, raising concerns about touch-screen voting technology.' Of course, it'll probably sound a little different in Chinese."

Jain gave me the sort of strained, embarrassed look you see on the faces of people waiting for their dogs to do their business in public parks. "May I ask who these community leaders are and what basis they have for their concerns?"

"I'm sure you have a good idea. Chinese community leaders concerned about the disparity between the preelection polls for their candidate and the results recorded by your machines."

He pursed his lips again. "You can't do a hack job on us just because your candidate polled better than he did in the election. Polls are notoriously fallible. Half the elections in the country would be in dispute if variation from preelection polls were a legitimate basis for contesting them."

"Half the elections in the country aren't punctuated with the murder of the elections director."

Jain lurched forward in his chair and nearly crawled across the table. "Wait a minute. You're not going to try to tie his murder into this. There's nothing to indicate it was in any way job-related, much less election-related."

I picked up the folder again and patted my thigh with it. I almost hated to tell him. "Bowman was found with the memory from one of your machines in his hands. Or more precisely, the protective cap to that memory. The person who killed him evidently took the other piece."

He slumped back into his chair. "You're bluffing. None of the reporters I've talked to said anything about that."

"Your buddies at the *Chronicle* wouldn't know. The police may not have figured it out either. But it doesn't matter. I know. I'm the one who found him."

"I see."

"Look, Sanjay, contrary to the impression I may be giving, I'm not out to do a hack job on you guys. I don't particularly care who wins the mayoral race. My concern is ensuring the elections are fairly run. If you can demonstrate to me and my readers that your systems worked properly in the last election—and will work properly in the upcoming runoff—then I'll get off your back. And so will Leonora Lee."

He looked at me carefully. "And just how would you propose that we do that? It isn't as if the software hasn't already been thoroughly tested. The results of the tests and the city's certification of them is up on their Web site for anyone to see."

"That may be, but I understand that changes are often made to the software in the rushed period before the election. What I want is an independent review of the software *as installed* on all the precinct machines."

"And who would do this independent review?"

"Professor Ballou at Stanford University."

He gave a sickly smile. "Of course. And if we don't agree to the review?"

"A front page article in the *China Free Press* with the lead I recited earlier, highlighting the CVT connection to Bowman's murder."

Jain held his face in a neutral expression, but movement under the table attracted my attention. His leg was not so much trembling as jumping. "Stay here," he said finally. "I'll be back in a minute."

Jain got up and closed the door carefully behind him, but the guy who burst through it ten minutes later didn't look—or act—anything like him. He was tall and balding with a hard-looking pot belly like a frozen turkey under his shirt. His arms seemed to hang almost to his knees and his hands were big and roughened—as if from manual labor. His clothes were well made, but fit him the way a sandwich board fits a carny barker. He stared at me with bulging bloodshot eyes and brought a calloused finger up to an inch or two from my face. "You tell that desiccated Chinese cunt that she can shove that fish wrap of a newspaper up her ass. I've had all from her I'm going to take."

I looked from the dirty fingernail pointing at my nose, to his enraged red face, to the doorway behind him where Jain stood quailing. He followed my glance and reached back to yank the door closed. "Pay attention when I'm talking."

I pushed my chair back against the wall, as much to get his finger out of my face as to give myself maneuvering room. "The way you bellow, it's hard not to pay attention. The trick would be in ignoring you. Are you in media relations too?"

With his finger hanging in midair, he didn't seem to know what to do with his hand. He dropped it awkwardly to his side. "No, I'm not in media relations. I'm the goddamned CEO."

I flipped through the folder Pam had given me until I found the company backgrounder. "A Mr. Alvin Dosher, it says here."

"It's Al Dosher. Nobody calls me Alvin."

"That's right. Alvin is the guy with the chipmunks, isn't he?"

He reddened even further. "Leave the chipmunks out of it," he said tightly.

"Sure thing. I'm going to take a little flyer here. Is there any chance you were referring to my boss, the publisher of *China Free Press*, in your earlier remark?"

"Of course, you moron."

"You mentioned you've had all you're going to take from her. If you don't mind my asking, what exactly have you taken so far?"

The question seemed to enrage him further. He drew in a ragged breath, clenched his fists as if he were going to come at me, then abruptly changed his mind. Tension dropped from his shoulders and he yanked over a chair to sit down. "Are you really that ignorant, or are you just putting up a front?"

I shrugged. "Pursuit of knowledge is the asking of questions."

"She's been on my ass since the city first put out a Request for Proposal on a touch-screen voting contract. Hectoring us in public meetings, pulling strings with the Elections Commissioners to reject our proposal, calling me personally to make veiled threats—trying to get us to withdraw from the bid process."

"I guess she really doesn't like touch-screen voting."

He shook his head. "You really are ignorant. What she doesn't like is *our* touch-screen voting. The software from her own company she likes just fine."

"Lee has a company that manufactures touch-screen voting machines?"

"Bingo. Her company, Accurate Systems, also responded to the RFP. But the Elections Commission selected us instead. So far, she hasn't used her newspaper on us, but I guess if she can't win the contract outright she aims to drag us through the mud until the city switches vendors."

The Dragon Lady failing to tell me she had a voting systems company was an interesting omission, but Bowman was still dead and there still seemed to be issues with the election. "I told Mr. Jain that I'm not interested in a hack job, and that was true. I'm interested in getting to the bottom of things. If you've got nothing to hide, why not do as I suggested and let Professor Ballou examine your software. That would be the quickest way to clear your name."

Dosher snorted. "Our name doesn't need clearing—and Ballou is on record as being vehemently opposed to all touch-screen voting technology."

"It's not about whether he likes the technology. It's about whether the software is crooked. Those are two different things."

Dosher ran a hand over his ruddy face and then stared at the table. "The software contains trade secrets. We can't risk them getting into the hands of competitors."

"You think the guy who is opposed to the technology is going to help other touch-screen voting companies by passing along trade secrets?"

"Ballou consults for the Dragon Lady," he said, but he spoke with less conviction.

"How about this," I said, and started to scoot my chair back toward the table. I never made it.

A piercing scream came from somewhere outside the conference room. Then the booming sound of a shotgun being discharged. There were more screams accompanied by running feet. Someone very near the conference room shouted, "Where is he?"

The answer—if answer it was—was a shrill cry that rose in tone and volume until it ended abruptly with a hollow clubbing sound. A moment later, the door to the conference room swung open. I was ready.

Standing in the doorway was a dumpy guy with crazy hair and a blotchy red birthmark on his neck like a spilt bottle of mecurachrome. He was dressed in jeans and a company t-shirt and carried a pump action shotgun at port arms. A nylon belt with pouches bulging with extra shells hung at his waist. He leveled the shotgun on Dosher. "Instant karma time, asshole."

Dosher sat bolt upright in his chair, seeing only the muzzle of the shotgun. He licked his lips to say something, but couldn't force the words out. There was only a pitiful gulping sound.

The guy with the shotgun laughed. "I'll always remember you just this way." He brought his finger to the trigger.

I put a 9mm slug from my Glock automatic under his left armpit.

He staggered back against the doorframe, blood spreading across his shirt like breath fogging glass. He looked at me with a stunned expression and tried to swing the gun toward me. His knees buckled then and the motion became an almost languid plunge into the carpet. The shotgun bounced from his hands as he hit and skidded to within an inch of my feet.

Dosher had jumped so hard at the sound of my shot that he had knocked his chair over backwards. He lay on his back trembling, running his hands over his face and neck to see if he was hit.

I nudged the shotgun well out of reach of the dying man, and set the Glock down on the table with trembling fingers of my own. The acrid smell of cordite hung heavy in the air and my ears rang from the pistol shot like cicadas in summer. "Who," I said, "was that?"

Dosher brought his arms to his side and hugged himself. He closed his eyes. "That was my chief engineer."

HOW NOW?

I SAT ON A STOOL IN A DIVE bar called the How Now? in down-town South San Francisco. It was dim and pleasantly cool inside. The only other customer in the place was in conference with a quart bottle of Bud and a tabletop Junior Pac Man game along the faux-brick wall behind me. The bartender—a rail thin character with a flattop and scythe-like sideburns—put a shot of bourbon down at my elbow. I reached for it with still trembling fingers and sloshed some of the liquor onto the cigarette-scarred wood.

The bartender laughed. "We can get that for you in a sippy cup if you want."

I gave him a tolerant smile and told him it wouldn't be necessary. I had come to the bar to decompress after my session with the South San Francisco cops. The good news was they weren't charging me with anything and they hadn't made the connection to Bowman's murder in the city. The bad news was they impounded the Glock and my cover as a reporter on a Chinese language paper had been blown all to hell with the CVT people. And far from being appreciative for my having saved his life, Dosher was furious at being duped. When he finally thought to ask how I came to be carrying a concealed weapon, Jain had to stop him from slugging me when I copped to being a licensed PI.

But with the things I gleaned from Dosher before he rushed me, and information I collected from Jain and the detective assigned to the case, I was able to piece together a coherent picture of what happened. It went something like this:

The chief engineer's name was Geiberger. He had worked at the company for three years, leading development of the software that controlled CVT's touch-screen machines. Last September, just before the product was to be released, he'd quit over a dispute with Dosher about stock. He claimed Dosher had cheated him out of thousands of shares he was due; Dosher and venture capitalists who funded the company said not. Despite siding with Dosher, the board made a token offer of additional shares, but it wasn't enough to convince Geiberger to return. Over the intervening weeks, he bombarded Dosher and the board with phone calls, e-mails and letters arguing his position, but he'd never returned to CVT headquarters, much less threatened anyone.

All that changed when he outfitted himself with a shotgun and ammo, pulled around to the back of the building and parked by the rear exit where smokers often stepped out for a cigarette break. He must have blocked the door from closing when the last smoker returned inside, waited until everyone was off the stairwell and crept up to the fifth floor. He went first to Dosher's office, fired the shotgun at his empty desk chair and then charged through the building searching for him.

Pam's was the scream I heard from inside the conference room, the clubbing noise Geiberger hitting her with the butt of the shotgun when she was too terrified to answer his question. (Jain had hid behind a sofa.) I found her woozy, but not too badly injured after I pulled Dosher to his feet and walked him out into the lobby. She was the only one besides Geiberger who'd been hurt.

I knocked back the shot of bourbon and signaled the bartender for another round. He disengaged himself from a *Daily Racing Form* he'd been annotating with four different colored inks and reached for the bottle of Ten High. He grinned at me as he poured and I could see him working up to another sippy cup remark when my cell phone rang. The number was blocked, but I had a pretty good idea who it would be.

"Hello, Mrs. Lee," I said without waiting for her to identify herself. "I gather you got a phone call from the South San Francisco cops."

"Yes," said the Dragon Lady, surprised. "They told me what happened. Was what you did really—really necessary?"

"I think if you ask Dosher he'd say it was pretty damn necessary. And the next shotgun shell probably had my name on it."

"Have you ever killed a man before?" Her voice was unusually quiet.

"Yes."

The line was silent for a moment. Then she said, "Where are you now?"

"Having a bourbon tranquilizer."

"I see. Do you think this is in any way related to the election fraud?"

"If there's anyone who would be in a good position to rig the software, it would be the chief engineer. And if he had a grudge with the company, what better way to get even than to sabotage the election and have CVT take the blame? The problem with that theory is he'd have to publicize the fraud for CVT to get in trouble. Instead, he seems to have been focused on a much more old fashioned way of getting even."

"You're assuming his motive was simply to get revenge. Maybe it was to get the compensation he felt he was due. Did you consider that he might have been trying to extort stock or money from the company with the threat of exposure? Perhaps Dosher refused to pay and only then did he try to kill the man."

I was impressed in spite of myself. I guess the Dragon Lady didn't get to be the Dragon Lady by being dumb. "That could be," I allowed. I took a sip of bourbon from the shot glass and watched as the bartender frowned and pointed at a crudely written sign taped to the mirror behind the bar: no cell phones. I turned my shoulder to him. "I'll tell you one thing I didn't consider—that you had your own touch-screen voting system company. Seems like something like that might have come up in our first conversation."

"Don't get too far up on your high horse, Mr. Riordan. I'm against touch-screen voting and always have been. I have always felt there was a risk of election fraud, and just as importantly, I have always felt it had the potential to disenfranchise the Chinese community—especially the older, non native-English speakers in Chinatown—because of their discomfort with technology and the challenges of ballot translation.

"When the Elections Commission first passed a motion to investigate the systems, I fought it. When I lost that fight and they voted to put out an RFP, I decided that if I couldn't prevent use of the technology, I would at least ensure the vendor selected had a workable solution for Chinese. So I formed my own company and put in a bid. But I lost that battle, too. The commission endorsed the director's recommendation of CVT—even though their proposal was $100,000 over ours and didn't incorporate full ballot and audit trail translation. They claimed we lacked experience in the application area."

"So here we are."

"Yes, Mr. Riordan, so here we are. Two people have died since you started the investigation, and we still don't have an answer. What are your next steps?"

She didn't sound so darn quiet now. This was the old Dragon Lady back with a vengeance. "I saw in this morning's paper that the Green Party is having a rally at New College. It's being co-sponsored by the San Francisco Tenants Union, and I figure it'll give me a good opportunity to scope out Padilla and his supporters."

"Very good. My daughter has a question for you."

"She does?"

"She asks if you're still planning to perform at Shanghai 1930 this evening?"

"Yes—yes I am."

"I never understood my late husband's fascination with jazz—and I understand Lisa's even less. But it seems to have worked in your favor, Mr. Riordan. I've asked Lisa to give you something. Remind her if she forgets."

"Sure," I said, but she'd already hung up.

I pushed the rest of the bourbon aside and stood. The bartender looked up from his racing form and mumbled something about "freaking cell phones." I put what I owed him on the bar and then snapped an extra ten under his nose. "Let me see you smile," I said.

He obliged me. He had beautiful teeth, but they weren't indigenous to his mouth—which put him in company with me. I dropped the bill on top of the racing form and sauntered out of there. My world seemed a much better place now that Lisa had confirmed a return visit.

NEW COLLEGE OF CALIFORNIA

SAUSALITO EST. 1971

THE GREEN BERETS

T HE NEW COLLEGE OF CALIFORNIA WAS LOCATED on Valencia in the Mission District of San Francisco, and from the looks of things, didn't have a thousandth the endowment of Stanford University. This was perhaps understandable since their founder was a hippy priest from the 1970s and not a railroad robber baron from the 1890s. Situated in an area with commercial businesses that ran the gamut from a hat shop to a garage to Pon's Oriental Restaurant, the college was housed in a pair of fake English Tudors on opposite sides of the street. The Tudors were painted a jarring turquoise with pink trim and had a lot of what smarmy realtors might euphemistically label "deferred maintenance." They looked like a couple of Easter eggs that had fallen from the basket.

I wrestled the Galaxie into a parking spot near the corner at 18th Street and walked up the east side of the street to the larger of the two buildings. A young Hispanic guy wearing a backwards baseball cap stood in the doorway. He had a pencil mustache that drooped past his mouth like an escaping trail of ants. He took a long drag on a cigarette and watched with narrowed eyes as I came up the sidewalk. When I stopped in front of him, he nodded and blew smoke over his shoulder. "You here for the rally?"

I said that I was.

"You're late," he said, and stubbed out the butt on the waffle sole of his Chuck Taylors. "We started fifty minutes ago. Besides, the theater's full. The fire marshall won't let us bring any more inside."

It didn't take long for me to fall back to my old tricks. "I'm with the *China Free Press*," I said. "I understand there's a press conference after the rally. You wouldn't want me to miss that, would you?"

He tore open the butt and shook out the few remaining grains of tobacco, folding the paper into a tiny square. "You don't look like you'd be writing for the China anything, man. But I'm just the security guy." He pushed the square of paper into the watch pocket of his black jeans. "Go inside and park it on the sofa near the front window. I'll get someone to talk to you."

He stepped back to let me enter and gestured towards the narrow lobby that ran along the front of the building. I went over to the sofa he indicated and sat down. The arched ceiling above me was criss-crossed by oak half-timbers and I could see fixtures where chandeliers once hung, but they'd taken those down and put up a bank of dusty fluorescent lights that made constant humming noise. Across the way were double doors for the theater, and on either side of them, a pair of what I guessed could be called expressionistic paintings. One looked like *The Scream* on a Schwinn bicycle and the other like an orange cactus with goiters. Overall, the ambience of the place was about as soothing as tinfoil on tooth fillings.

The amplified but indistinct voice of someone giving a speech leaked through the double doors, and I killed the next fifteen minutes alternatively trying to decipher what was being said and amusing myself by pushing the tip of my shoelace in and out of the holes in my wingtips. Finally a small door marked "Stage" at the far end of the lobby opened and an individual wearing a skirt and combat boots walked through. If that wasn't cause enough for cognitive dissonance, the fact that the individual was a man, was sporting a beret, a full beard and didn't have any bagpipes, provided ample catalyst. As he marched purposefully across the lobby to where I was sitting, I had to conclude that—unlike Chris—he was simply a guy who liked to wear skirts, as opposed to a guy who occasionally liked to look like a girl.

He came to parade rest a few feet from the couch, and I stood quickly to greet him. "You're the journalist, then," he said gruffly.

"That's right."

He asked me for what paper and I went through my spiel about working for the *China Free Press,* having my stories translated and reporting directly to the publisher. He didn't seem particularly impressed.

"We haven't had much coverage of our candidate by the Chinese language papers," he said.

"You haven't had many rallies in Chinatown, either."

He frowned and combed his fingers through the front of his strawberry-colored beard. "True enough. I'm still not sure we can let you in. You're not on the press roster. I'm going to have to kick this upstairs." He pulled a walkie-talkie out of a bag-like thing that could only be referred to as a purse and strolled out of earshot. He spoke briefly, listened for a what seemed like an interminable time and then nodded his head sharply. As he walked back my direction I could hear him say, "Understood—on a choke chain," before he clicked off.

He shoved the walkie-talkie back into his bag. "You can go in for the press conference," he said. "But you'll have to sit in the back and Padilla isn't likely to call on you since he doesn't know you." He stepped forward, getting uncomfortably close. It was the first time a guy in a dress had tried to bulldoze me. "And we expect you to write a balanced story. Kathleen says your paper isn't exactly simpatico with our platform."

"Who's Kathleen?"

"The boss lady—the campaign manager. Come on. We'll wait in the back until the rally breaks up."

He lead me through the double doors to the back of the theater, where we stood beside a TV cameraman from a Spanish-language station who was filming the doings. Up on the dais a guy in overalls was making an impassioned plea about halting gentrification of the Mission District. Padilla was seated at a table beside him. He wore a rumpled suit and had a frizzy Prince Valiant haircut, which apparently was his way of distinguishing himself from the polished, *GQ* look of Hunter Lowdon. Hovering off in the wings was a woman wearing another black beret, combat boots and a t-shirt with the famous photo of Che Guevara from 1960, but she had opted for jeans instead of a skirt. She had a long, horsey face, wavy red hair and eyes that seemed to be continuously flitting around the room, measuring and assessing the crowd's reaction to the speaker. I figured her for Kathleen, the boss lady.

The guy in the overalls went on for another twenty minutes or so, winding the crowd up for the climax of his speech, where he shouted, "And that is why the San Francisco Tenants Union is endorsing Mike Padilla for our next mayor—*para nuestro alcalde próximo*. Vote for Padilla and stop condominium conversions. Vote for Padilla and provide a place for working people to live!"

The crowd didn't disappoint. The applause was loud and enthusiastic. A group of people stood up in the middle section—perhaps a little too smartly for it to be spontaneous—and the rest of the theater was soon on its feet. Padilla got up from the table and the guy in the overalls grabbed his hand and raised it like the referee in a boxing match. The two of them basked in the mass adulation for another minute or so and then Padilla leaned into the microphone and thanked everyone for coming. He closed by urging everyone to "get out and wake the sleeping giant in San Francisco."

Security staff materialized to herd people out the doors, and judging from the enthusiastic look on everyone's faces, I was probably the only one in the audience of young progressives who found it amusing that the Green Party candidate mentioned giants, given the risk of invoking the jolly guy who hawked canned corn nibblets. But maybe that was a generational thing.

When enough of the crowd had passed so that we had some hope of maneuvering up the aisle, my escort led me to a cordoned-off section on the right that still had people sitting in it. He unhooked a velvet rope to let me into the fifth and final row of the section and guided me by the arm to a seat beside an older black woman who was killing time by knitting a cap. He piled into the seat next to mine and yanked the hem of his skirt up enough so that he could rest a combat-booted foot atop his knee. I didn't like to think what sort of nibblets he was exposing. "Making yourself comfortable?" I asked.

"That's right. I'm sticking with you the whole time." He turned away from me, combing his beard in a nervous gesture while he watched the staff wheel the podium off the stage to a spot in front of the cordoned section.

Padilla disengaged himself from a group of supporters lined up to shake his hand and joined Kathleen, who was busy at the podium putting papers down and adjusting the microphone. She glanced at him briefly as he came up, nodded and turned back to address the reporters. "Okay. Let's get started people. You'll have twenty-five minutes with Mike. There are no prepared remarks, but of course we're expecting you to dig in on the Tenants Union endorsement. Mike will call for your questions and no more than one follow-up is allowed. Everyone good with that?"

There was a collective murmur of assent from the thirty-odd reporters. Kathleen gave a brusque nod and turned to put a hand in the small of Padilla's back. She edged him up to the microphone, and before he'd even had a chance to grasp the sides of the podium, there were five urgent calls of "Mike!" from the front row.

I glanced over at the woman to my right, who continued blithely with her knitting. She felt my eyes on her and looked up with a smile. "No use getting your bowels in an uproar. He doesn't take many questions from the peanut gallery."

I smiled back at her. "Wish I'd brought *my* knitting."

The opening pitch wasn't exactly a softball. It came from a *Chronicle* reporter who asked Padilla how he responded to the charge his policies would actually cause fewer units of affordable housing to be built in San Francisco by making it infeasible for for-profit developers to get through all the planning hurdles. Padilla handled it smoothly by citing a study in Vancouver Canada where similar policies resulted in a twenty percent increase in low-income housing over a five-year period. The next question was another toughie from the San Jose paper about Padilla's position on homelessness. Padilla parried it and the reporter's follow-up adroitly, and after taking a few more serious questions from the print media, finally wound down to a series of almost laughable queries from the TV people. My favorite came at the end from a vapid-looking guy with hard yellow hair: "What color would you paint the interior of the new homeless shelters you're proposing and why?"

Kathleen actually winced when she heard it and sidled up behind him to whisper something urgent in his ear—most probably a direction to close things down. Up until that point, I had no idea what I expected to accomplish by being at the conference, but I decided to take a flyer. Padilla asked for a final question and I shot my hand up along with a couple of TV reporters. You could almost see the wheels turning as Padilla looked back and forth between the hyper-groomed women from channels 4 and 5 and the guy in the back with a rumpled suit like his own. He picked me.

"August Riordan, *China Free Press*," I bellowed. I could feel the bearded guy in the skirt tensing up beside me as I spoke. "Some in the Chinese community have expressed concern about the legitimacy of the results of the general election due to the use of touch-screen voting technology. Does the unfortunate murder of Elections Director Bowman add weight to these concerns?"

Heads jerked around to look at me. Kathleen's face got stony and my skirted escort put his combat boot down heavily. Padilla was too savvy to show a reaction, but I didn't think it was a coincidence that he took the opportunity to sip from a water glass before answering. "The murder of Director Bowman *was* unfortunate. But as a member of the San Francisco Board of Supervisors and a candidate for mayor, it would not be appropriate for me to comment on an on-going investigation. As for the election, we are quite satisfied that the results reflect the will of the people of San Francisco. Green Party poll monitors were on site at all precincts and observed no significant voting irregularities."

"Follow up," I shouted and immediately felt the heel of the guy with the skirt digging into my toe. "Doesn't today's shooting death of the chief engineer of CVT—the city's touch-screen voting machine supplier—only serve to heighten the controversy surrounding the results?"

A frisson of surprise ran through the reporters and many of them yanked out cell phones and began dialing frantically. Padilla looked nonplussed for the first time. He opened his mouth to speak, thought better of it, and then took another sip of water. Kathleen had almost crawled up his back by the time he managed, "I'm not familiar with any such report, and my earlier response about not commenting on criminal investigations still stands."

Simultaneous cries of "Mike!" came from at least six reporters, including most all of the print guys. Kathleen bulled her way to the microphone. "Sorry," she yelled. "Sorry. That was the last question. Thank you." She hustled Padilla off to the right and around the stage to a door at the back. With no candidate to badger, the reporters turned on me. Some stepped over the rows of chairs to get at me, others jumped the velvet rope and did an end-around to reach me from behind. It was like being in the middle of a rugby scrum with information about the shooting—and not the ball—being the thing everyone wanted. I gave a brief explanation—leaving out the fact that I was the shooter—answered a few shouted questions and then abruptly twisted out of my seat.

The guy in the skirt grabbed for me, but I managed to avoid him. I made it under the velvet rope, out the back of the theater and almost through the front door of the school when I felt a hand dig into my shoulder.

"Hold it."

I turned to find Che Guevara and Kathleen staring at me. Che looked friendlier. "I just got off the phone with the South City cops," she said. "They told me about your involvement. Then I remembered why your name seemed so familiar when Roger called me on the credentials check. You were also the one who found Bowman."

I took her hand by the wrist and pried it off my shoulder. She was a big, strong girl. It was like dislodging a limpet. "None of that matters. There are still a lot of unanswered questions hanging over the election."

"Don't think I don't know a dirty tricks campaign when I see it. Mike Padilla is going to change this city, and I'm not letting bastards like you stop him. Consider this a warning." She reared back and kicked me in the shin.

I yelped and reached down to rub the tenderized flesh. When I looked up again, she and the guy in the skirt were standing over me. Seeing them side by side with their black berets, black boots and black looks, I realized that they must be brother and sister.

But it wasn't hard to understand why she wore the pants in the family.

SHANGHAIED

"IT'S *THE* COLOR OF THE SEASON," SAID Chris Duckworth. We were sitting at a table in the bar of Shanghai 1930. The topic under discussion was the electric blue of his cheongsam dress.

"If it's the color of the season, how come I haven't seen it anywhere?"

Chris gulped at his Singapore Sling and shook his head in frustration. We were performing that night as the "Cassandra Q" quartet—Cassandra being Chris' drag queen name and the Q standing for you know what—and Chris had gone all out for the event. His dress was a tight, slinky number with a dragon embroidered down the front and slits up the side longer than Wilt Chamberlain's inseam. He'd paired it with dangling lapis lazuli earrings and a matching bracelet and anklet of lapis beads. He wore a black wig cut in a short bob and had done his face up like a porcelain doll's: a pale white foundation, shockingly red lipstick and a beauty mark painted high on his left cheek. In spite of my chiding him about the dress, I had to admit he looked good. Too good, in fact. It would be all too easy to mistake him for a beautiful female torch singer who'd stepped off the screen from a 1930s movie.

He returned the drink to the table and plucked out the little umbrella to twirl around in his fingers. "It might be you haven't seen the color because you didn't go to the opening night of the opera, attend any theater or look at the covers of any fashion magazines."

I smirked at him. "Wait," I said, "I take that back. I did see it on a magazine cover."

"See, I told you. Which one?"

"*National Geographic.* On some monkey's butt."

He threw the little umbrella at me. It bounced off my chest to the floor. "I should have seen that one coming," he said. "Now explain to me why I saw *you* on the nightly news for the second day running. The sound on the TV in my dressing room was down so I couldn't hear what they were saying."

It was times like this that I missed cigarettes the most. I craved the opportunity to go through the little dissembling motions of pulling the pack out and shaking a cigarette loose. "I'll tell you," I said after an awkward pause. "But you're not going to like it." I explained to Chris how I'd gone to visit Columbia Voting Technologies, how I talked to the CEO and how I ended up shooting Geiberger. By the time I finished, Chris didn't need the foundation to make his face look pale.

"My God, August. When did all this happen?"

"A little after I dropped you off. Why?"

He stirred his drink, avoiding my eyes. "I was supposed to have a job interview with them this afternoon, but they phoned me up to reschedule. Now I know why."

"A job interview? Don't tell me that you just happened to pick CVT as the ideal place to end your unemployment eligibility."

Chris brought his hand to his chest in a girlish gesture and coughed. "I looked up CVT right after you called me to talk to the professor. I saw they had an opening for a temporary QA engineer on their Web site, so I decided to apply. I *do* have to make at least a token effort to find a job to keep my unemployment benefits, and if I actually landed it, I thought I could—"

"Meddle in one of my investigations again."

"No. Help you figure out how the election was compromised. If an engineer at CVT was responsible, what better way to find out than to go undercover?"

"You nearly got killed the last time you went 'undercover,' as you put it. If you'd been on-site today when Geiberger showed up, you might have been hurt too. This isn't a game, Chris. I appreciate your help, but you've got to clear these things with me first. You hear me?" I was almost shouting by the end.

He stirred at his drink listlessly and said, "I hear you," in a near whisper.

"All right then." I took a big slug from the bourbon and soda in front of me and rattled the rocks around in the glass as I stared at a poster on the wall by the entrance. It was a painting of four girls playing mah-jongg in a whorehouse. After a while I brought my eyes back to Chris. "So," I said in a tone that I fought to keep solemn, "do you think you actually have a chance of getting this job? And the election is only five days away. Would they bring you on board quick enough for it to do us any good?"

Chris grinned so wide I thought he was going to crack his makeup. "It's a temporary position. They're hiring a bunch of people to bang on a new release and they want them to start right away. I'm more than qualified   I've temped on lots of QA gigs. And with today's, ah, incident, they're not likely to have many applicants."

I wasn't really very worried about the physical risks of Chris taking the job. With Geiberger dead, the likelihood of further violence was low, and the fact of the matter was, I needed the help. "Okay, sport, let's give it a whirl. But if you land the job, promise you'll keep me posted on anything you find, and be careful. Nothing illegal. No plumber's squad stuff—just what you learn from working there and talking to people."

Chris nodded like one of those bobbing head dolls. He quickly steered the conversation away from CVT by asking me what I'd learned in the afternoon. I filled him in on the doings at New College, including my encounter with the skirt-wearing campaign worker and the kick in the shin I received at the steel-tipped toe of his sister.

He laughed, and said, "That's what you get for pigeonholing people into our culture's rigid two-gender system."

"Exactly the lesson I drew from the encounter."

He glanced down at his jeweled Longine watch. "So where is this Chinatown cutie of yours? It's show time."

"Her mother said she was coming. She didn't say when."

"Her mother? Did she also say you had to have her home by ten?"

"Bite me."

"Careful what you wish for. I'm off to powder my nose. That will give you boys plenty of time to get set for my grand entrance."

I watched as Chris rose from the red velvet chair and sashayed through the checkerboard maze of tables to a door that opened in the frosted glass wall behind the bar. Blue lights shown from behind the wall, suffusing the many bottles of liquor on the chromium shelves with a bewitching glow. The rest of the room was lit in a ruby red by a series of wall fixtures that looked like over-large tulip blossoms bursting to open. The bandstand was across from the bar, near the entrance to the dining area. The other members of the Cassandra Q Quartet—Tristan Sinclair on piano and Sol Hodges on drums—were loitering by the Baldwin baby grand as Hodges pecked out a melody with one hand while clutching a highball glass in the other.

Sinclair smiled as I came up and tipped his trademark pork pie hat in a schmaltzy gesture. "The bass man cometh. Hey August, what do you call someone who hangs around with musicians?"

I glanced over at Hodges, who had stopped pecking at the piano and was looking up at me with an expectant grin. "A groupie?" I said.

Sinclair laughed. "Sure," he said "A groupie."

"A drummer" was the answer he'd been looking for. Sinclair had an endless store of drummer and percussionist jokes, often impugning their musicianship and/or their intelligence, and he never tired of telling them when he played with Hodges. The truth was Hodges was the best musician of the lot of us, leader of a serious band called Distant Opposition and a composer and arranger in much demand for movie and commercial work. Both he and Sinclair were playing the gig that night as a favor to me and Chris. They certainly didn't need the work.

Hodges gunned the rest of his drink and set the glass down on the piano near the music stand where he knew it would annoy Sinclair. He pinched the triangular "flavor savor" beard beneath his lower lip and nodded toward the back of the room. "Better play the intro before Cassandra there pops a falsie giving us the high sign."

Sinclair took his place on the piano bench, and Hodges settled in behind the drum kit. I carefully removed my Italian Alberto Begliomini double bass from its resting place, wiped off the strings with a cloth and half sat, half leaned on a high stool sandwiched between Hodges' kick drum and Chris' microphone. Hodges counted off the tempo and we began an extended contemplation of the intro to the Nick Drake song "Day is Done." Drake's version could best be categorized as folk, but Chris so liked the haunting, downbeat lyrics of the troubled British singer/songwriter that Hodges had done a slow swing arrangement of the tune with dissonant, Mingus-like, altered harmonies.

Chris threaded his way through the bar tables to the bandstand with a pouty expression on his face, turning his head in time to the music so that one dangling earring and then the other lay flat against his neck. He didn't exactly look Chinese, but somehow still managed to exude an air of mystery and exotic lands. He stepped daintily onto the riser, moved to the side of the piano, and in a show-opening ritual he had developed with Sinclair, adjusted the lid prop to bring the top open to its widest position, enlarging and deepening the baby grand's sound. Sinclair nodded his thanks and Chris slid over to the microphone just as we came to the head. He sang the opening lines, "When the day is done / Down to earth then sinks the sun," in a sweetly plaintive contralto that ensnared the audience, pulling them away from their drinks, their conversations and their people-watching.

He held them entranced through the bittersweet close and received an enthusiastic round of applause that began after a moment of near silence, during which the audience seemed to snap out of it and collect themselves. Chris bowed modestly and called immediately for the Gershwin tune "Love Walked In." Hodges' arrangement was more up-tempo than the original and left plenty of room for improvs. Sinclair did eight bars of intro by himself and then Hodges led us in for a chorus of the melody. Chris came in to sing the first two stanzas of the lyrics, pausing dramatically with his hand to his ear after he sang, "My heart seemed to know that love said, 'Hello!'"

I shouted "Hello!" back and he finished the stanza to laughter and scattered applause. Sinclair took a chorus with long, melodic runs and some nice left hand vamping, but instead of passing it off to Hodges or me as expected, he ploughed right on for another. Hodges made sure to wrest control from him on the next chorus and did a very sophisticated and restrained—for a drummer, at least—solo, showcasing soft rolls and cymbal accents. I was up next. I had originally intended to take it easy—simply "walking" the bass through the changes—but I abandoned the notion when I caught sight of a pair of elegantly-trousered legs descending the curved staircase that led down from the restaurant entrance on Steuart Street.

It was Lisa Lee, resplendent in a black pantsuit that was made up to look like a men's tuxedo with a cut-away jacket and a fancy waistcoat whose color could only be described as electric blue. To say I had butterflies was an understatement   they were more like mastiff bats. Lisa looked straight at me as I began the solo and my fingers suddenly felt damp and sweaty on the fingerboard. Moisture is the bane of all bass players because it increases resistance on the strings, making it harder to reach notes predictably. In spite of my nervousness, I nodded and smiled at her, imagining I was one of my heroes, George Duvivier, playing on the well-regarded 1962 Carol Sloane recording of the same tune.

I tried for nice phrasing, not an all out chops-fest. I worked in some syncopation to add interest: going off the beat at times and relying on Hodges and Sinclair to keep time without stepping on my solo. I threw in some call and response to carry me through the middle measures and added double-stops—playing notes on two strings simultaneously—to fill out the sound.

It came out much better than I had any right to expect. Applause after a bass solo is as rare as hens' dentures, but I got some. Chris made a point of stepping aside with his arm extended to acknowledge the effort, but more importantly, Lisa stood by the foot of the stairs throughout, nodding in time to the music, smiling up at me.

As pleasant as that was, I was more than a little relieved when Sinclair came back in with the melody and the pressure was off. Chris repeated the middle stanza of the lyrics, giving me the chance to shout "Hello!" once more, and then finished the tune to a nice round of applause. As Lisa moved to a table in the second row near the center, he leaned back to whisper, "Is that your little moon cake?"

"She's not my little anything yet," I said. "And keep your inappropriate cultural references to yourself."

"A thousand pardons," he said with a leering smile that I knew from long experience meant trouble. He turned back to the microphone. "Thank you very much. I'm Cassandra and you're listening to the Cassandra Q Quartet. And now, as a special request of our bass player August Riordan, we're going to play a little number for a friend of his who just arrived. From Frank Loesser, composer of *Guys and Dolls,* here is 'On a Slow Boat to China.'"

Hodges, who'd been listening to our whispered conversation, laughed out loud.

I glared back and forth between them. "You boys are as cute as a couple of discarded hypodermic needles," I said, but it was wasted breath.

Hodges hurried into a count-off and shouted, "No intro." Chris belted out the opening line, "I'd love to get you / On a slow boat to China," dispensing with the usual four bars of piano. I felt the color rise in my cheeks and looked over to gauge Lisa's reaction, but her expression was hard to read under the glare of the spotlights. She didn't look angry, but she didn't look exactly joyous either.

Chris finished the lyrics and scatted another chorus. Sinclair came in for a solo and then it was my turn. I mixed it up a little by grabbing the bow out of its holster and interweaving bowed and plucked lines. Then Chris came back in to trade fours. He scatted four bars, the piano came in for four, followed by Chris again and so on until all of us had a turn. After the final exchange with Hodges, Chris restated the lyrics, investing them with a sultry, warm tone that was particularly insinuating given the subtext.

But if Lisa was angry that—by implication—I wanted to get "her all to myself alone," her reaction was not what I expected. As the rest of the audience gave us a very enthusiastic round of applause, she sat at her table dabbing at her eyes with a napkin.

The remainder of the set seemed to go by quickly. In keeping with the theme of long distance travel, we followed up with Bart Howard's "Fly Me to the Moon," and finished with an unusual jazz arrangement of Brian Wilson's "In My Room." Lisa applauded politely, and even smiled at me at one point, but "Slow Boat" had definitely steered her off course.

Chris announced a break, and I attempted to stretch out the chores of wiping down the bass and putting it away as long as possible to delay my encounter with Lisa, but Chris was oblivious. He grabbed the instrument from my hands, leaned it into the corner and took me by the arm.

"Come on, big boy," he commanded. "Introduce me."

CINDERELLA'S SLIPPER

CHRIS CLUNG TO MY ARM FOR SUPPORT as we stepped off the riser, playing at the helpless female in wobbly heels. Lisa watched us approach her table with an unreadable expression, then rose to greet us. "Lisa," I said. "I'd like you to meet C—"

"Cassandra," put in Chris quickly, extending his hand. "I just want to say how much I admire your vest. It's a fabulous color."

Lisa glanced at Chris' cheongsam, then down at her vest. She laughed. "It *is* a fabulous color. It's a pleasure to meet someone with the same good taste in clothing."

"And in men, too," said Chris, winking broadly. "By the way, August was just describing a magazine where he saw some exotic creature modeling the same color. You'll have to ask him."

Lisa looked hesitantly at me. "Yes," she said. "Yes, I will."

"Well, I'll give you two some privacy. I see Jimmy's already got my Cosmo set up on the bar. Hope to see you again soon, Lisa."

"Yes, same here …" Her voice trailed off as she watched Chris go by in a Mae West-like medley of swaying hips, heaving bosom and wafting perfume. She frowned and looked back at me. "Is she trying to make me jealous?"

"No, not exactly. Why don't you have a seat and I'll explain."

She dropped into her chair and folded her hands on the table, all business-like. I fell into the seat beside her. "Well?" she said.

"Not to put too fine a point on it, Cassandra there is winding you up. She is really a he."

"What?"

"Our singer is a man. His real name is Chris Duckworth. Cassandra is just his drag name."

Lisa turned slowly in her chair to look behind her, like the heroine in a slasher movie checking to see what is in the back seat. Chris sat at the bar with the Cosmo in his hand. He raised it jauntily in a toast. Lisa twisted back. "Oh my god. I remember seeing something about a 'gender illusionist' on the restaurant Web site, but it completely slipped my mind. He's like the guy in *The Crying Game*. Better even."

"It *is* a little disconcerting." We looked at each other across the table and I was struck again by her disarming beauty. If left to my own devices I'm sure I would have produced something lame in the "gosh, you're *real purty* ma'am" line, but her comment about *The Crying Game* had reminded me of her own tears. "I'm sorry about our tune selection when you walked in. The guys thought it would be funny, but I can see how you might feel it was insensitive."

She made a brave little smile, shook her head and then looked down at the table. I watched as she blinked back more tears. "Don't apologize," she said finally. "I haven't heard the song in five years and—and it has strong associations for me. I'm glad you played it. It was nice to hear it again."

"Associations? May I ask what they are?"

She looked up at me and smiled gamely again. "It was my father's theme song. He always sang it at the start of each of his shows—although not nearly as well as Chris." She stopped suddenly and reached over to touch my shoulder. "How rude of me, August. I meant to tell you straightaway how great you guys sound. I really enjoyed your solo on 'Love Walked In.' And the bowing on 'Slow Boat'—woohoo! Very impressive."

I grinned like a trained chimp. "Thank you, but Hodges and Sinclair are the only ones with chops. I'm just a journeyman by comparison."

A waitress appeared from behind us with two drinks. She put a glass of white wine in front of Lisa and a tumbler full of something amber by me. "What's this?" I asked.

Lisa picked up her wine. "It's a toast to a great performance."

We touched glasses and I took a sip from mine. I could have sworn it was my favorite bourbon. "This tastes like Maker's Mark. How did you know?"

"It is and I didn't. I just know that my dad always had a glass between sets."

I nodded, and tried to ignore the little voice that was telling me that being a father figure to her wasn't a healthy thing for either of us. "You must miss him a lot."

She cupped her hands delicately around the wine glass. "I do. I was always daddy's little girl. I've never been as close to my mother. She's—well—you know how she is."

"How about your father and her? How did they get along?"

"There's a good question. I've often wondered what their early years of marriage were like. By the time I came around, they had slipped into a pattern of mutual—mostly benign—neglect. My mother stayed busy running her businesses and making lots of money, and my father futzed around his club."

"So he didn't help in building the Lee family empire?"

"No, he wasn't much of an empire builder. The truth is, he wasn't much of a jazzman either. You called yourself a journeyman, which was very modest. My father loved the music, but if our family didn't own the club, I realize now he never would have been invited to sit in. Of course I had no clue about that when I was a young girl. I simply thought he was the greatest."

"Maybe he was the greatest."

She smiled. "In other ways, yes. In the ways that mattered most."

"How did your mother and father ever hook up? I mean, I know opposites attract and all, but there have to be limits."

"Would you believe me if I told you that my mother was the talented one? That she was a singer in a nightclub in Hong Kong where my father was head waiter?"

"No."

"It's true. My father became her manager, and after managing he was promoted to husbanding. They raised a nest egg from my mother's earnings, immigrated to the US and my mother went into real estate. She was well into her forties by the time they had me, and already very successful. I'm sure she would have never taken time off for children if she hadn't been."

"But she told me she didn't understand your father's interest in jazz. Why would she say that if she herself was a singer?"

"It's only a means to an end for her. A product she can sell—like most things. But you should hear her sometime. I have an old 45 rpm record she cut in the 1960s, and boy, could she knock your socks off."

"It must be in your genes, then. You should come up during the next set and belt out a tune or two with Chris."

She hitched her thumb back at Chris. "I doubt there's room enough on one stage for that diva and me. Besides, I can't stay for the second set. My mother is a diabetic and I have to be home to give her insulin shot before bed."

"Really? That has to cut into your social life."

"Did you mean social life or sex life?"

I gulped. "Feel free to interpret the question as broadly as you like."

"Let's just say being the Dragon Lady's daughter has more impact on activity with the opposite sex than the fact that mom needs an insulin shot at night—at least in the Chinese community."

"Scares them away, does she?"

"One guy told me he'd rather eat at the grizzly bear enclosure at the zoo than come to our house for dinner."

I laughed. "There's a certain merit in his viewpoint."

I steered the conversation away from her mother then, eager to use what little time we had to get to know her better. She told me she got her undergrad degree at Berkeley and then had gone on to Stanford to get her MD. She was taking a year off before doing her internship and residency at Johns Hopkins. The news about her academic achievements, coupled with the other tidbits she let drop—such as the fact she was the captain of a champion rowing team at Berkeley and was volunteering at the free clinic—made me realize she was an entirely different person than I thought.

When I commented how blown away I was by all her accomplishments, she just shrugged and said, "Asian kids are expected to perform."

Chris effectively put an end to the conversation by tapping on the table with a bejeweled finger. "Curtain in five minutes," he announced, and sashayed past us to the stage, where he began sorting through a stack of arrangements with Hodges.

"I better go. I don't want to leave in the middle of your first tune," said Lisa.

"I don't want you to leave period. But at least let me walk you to your car."

I escorted her up the curved staircase to street level, where she stopped under the club awning and turned to face me. "I'm just going to catch a cab, August. But I'm glad you offered to walk me out. It gives us a chance to say good night."

I didn't need an engraved invitation. I leaned in to kiss her and she met me partway. Her lips were soft and yielding and still pleasantly cool from the wine. She took me by the elbow, and we held the clench for what seemed like an impossibly long time until an auto honked at us from the street. It was one heck of a first kiss.

"Wow," I said, "you don't fool around, do you?"

She laughed. "I told you—we Asian kids perform. Besides, I feel bad about leaving. The truth is my mother can give herself her own damn shots, but she told me what happened today—what you had to do at that company."

I started to say something, but she waved me off. "You don't need to explain. I'm sure what you did was necessary. I just don't think this is the most auspicious day for a first date. Bad relationship *feng shui*, if you like. I came because I very much wanted to see you play and because—" She snapped her fingers. "Damn it."

"What's the matter?"

"Mother wanted me to give you something and I left it on the chair. I meant to surprise you with it. Will you run back inside and grab it? That's the first thing she'll ask me about when I get home."

"Okay," I said. "What is it exactly?"

"Oh, you'll recognize it. Just come back here when you have it. I want to be sure before I go." She grinned impishly. "And that'll give us another chance to say goodbye."

I didn't care if she had left hot coals for me to carry back bare-handed, I was now a man with a mission. I pushed through the club doors, jogged down the staircase—ignoring Chris' shouted, "Hey August, get the hell over here"—and strode up to the table. There was a small, red plastic wallet on her chair, wedged between the cushions. I flipped it open to find a credential for the *China Free Press* made out in my name with an old photo of mine pasted in.

I had to hand it to the Dragon Lady: she was always thinking. It would be a whole lot easier not to lie about the affiliation.

I shoved the credential in my back pocket. Chris was glaring at me from the stage, so I gave him a cheery wave and mouthed, "Back in a minute." I took the stairs two at a time, announcing, "August Riordan, ace reporter," as I stepped outside.

The problem was the person I said it to wasn't Lisa, but a homeless guy with a shopping cart. He had parked the cart in front of the door and was looking fixedly at a single black pump on the sidewalk. Lisa's black pump.

A MISMATCHED PAIR

I REACHED DOWN FOR THE SHOE AND HELD it up to the homeless man's face. "Where's the woman who goes with this?"

The question seemed to startle him. His rheumy eyes grew wide and he huffed a withering breath of Night Train and stale vomit in my direction. I twisted away from him and scanned the area. To the north, at the intersection with Mission, a cab turned right and pulled away from view. I couldn't see well enough to tell if Lisa was in the back seat, but I felt a keen nip of disappointment at the thought she would leave without waiting for me to return. To the south, there were no cabs and only a few pedestrians, none of whom looked the least bit like her.

I looked back at the pump in my hands, thinking maybe that I had been mistaken in assuming it was hers. It was hard to believe she would get into a cab with only one shoe. I saw the homeless man approach me again in my peripheral vision. A rough hand tugged at my sleeve. "What's that?" he asked. I rounded on him, ready to vent my frustration with a few choice expletives. But when I turned completely to face him, I saw he was pointing a jittery finger across the street.

There, in a narrow alley between two buildings, a pair of figures struggled silently in the shadows. One was unquestionably Lisa. The other was a slight Asian man—not even as tall as her—with his hand around her mouth. He was trying to drag her further into the darkness, but she was fighting him for all she was worth, ramming him into the wall of the building and attempting to spear his insole with the heel of her remaining shoe.

I flashed across the street, narrowly avoiding a collision with a motorcyclist on a Harley. With his curse still ringing in my ears, I came skidding up to the pair. Neither was aware of my presence, Lisa's exertions having torqued them around so that both their backs were facing me. I had no time to think. I simply struck out with the only thing at hand: Lisa's spike-heeled pump.

I brought it down hard on the crown of the little man's head. He yelped and involuntarily reached for his scalp. Lisa took the opportunity to twist free, and it was only then that I saw that her assailant held a knife in his left hand. She had been very brave—and very foolish—to resist him to the extent that she had. With Lisa gone from his grasp, he leaped up, pirouetted in mid-air and landed smoothly in a triangle stance. It didn't take an expert to recognize he had some flavor of martial arts training, and from the way he now brandished the knife, snaking it back and forth with his shield hand in near-hypnotic movements, I figured he'd done more than peel apples with it.

He grunted and spat a paragraph of Chinese at me. He finished with something heartfelt that sounded like, "*sei gweilo,*" repeating it twice for emphasis. I didn't think it was a compliment.

"Get the police," I shouted to Lisa. I didn't want her in harm's way and despite my size advantage, I wasn't liking my chances with the guy.

He underscored the point by lunging forward to slice at my jacket when I made the mistake of turning to see that Lisa was following instructions. The damage was limited to Sears Roebuck and not August Riordan, but I needed to be much more careful. I threw Lisa's shoe in his face to distract him, drew back, and then reached down to my ankle. I yanked my own knife out of its sheath and came into a stance that approximated his.

That froze him. We held the tableau nearly a minute, blood pounding in my ears, chestfuls of air passing through my lungs at a rate approaching hyperventilation. Finally, the ache in my hamstrings overcame my fear of his knife-fighting skills. I said, "If you're feeling froggy, little man, then go ahead and jump."

I don't know if he understood the words, or registered the challenge from my tone, but jump he did. He feinted to my left and then flicked the blade down and to the right, coming in below my elbow for a rapier-like stab at my ribs. I was too slow to parry the thrust, managing only to twist enough to have the knife point puncture the flesh on my side, rather than coming hard under the rib cage. I slashed down with my own knife as he pulled back, scoring a long cut across the back of his hand.

Lisa's scream behind me told me that she hadn't departed as I'd asked. My side blossomed in fire and I couldn't stop myself from reaching across with my left hand to staunch the wound. That was the opening he was waiting for. He came at me, grabbing for my shoulder and bringing the knife in a short, vicious arc for the middle of my belly.

I rolled my shoulder and leaned to the side, avoiding his grasp and causing him to miss with the knife. He thudded into me, our feet became tangled and we then both fell over like a toppled supermarket display. I landed on my back with the little man's belt buckle in my face. I lost my grip on my knife and heard his clatter along the asphalt behind us. He squirmed over me, trying to retrieve it, but then Lisa came up to kick it out of reach.

That really got him going. He wriggled and scratched and gouged, finally making me so mad that I forgot about trying to reach my own knife and lifted him so I could get my feet planted firmly in his gut. I launched him off me, flinging him into the air like a human cannonball.

He bounced off a brick wall and landed with a satisfying whump. I scrambled up, but he was on his feet almost as quickly. He was having no part of the tussle now. He turned and sprinted up the alley. I yelled at Lisa again to get help and ran after him. I went out of pure mule-headedness, and regretted it almost immediately. I wasn't sure where he was leading me and my side radiated pain each pounding step I took.

We ran through a maze of dumpsters, past a fenced transformer and in and around tall stacks of wooden pallets, my longer strides chewing up the real estate between us. I was almost on him when he broke left into the mouth of an intersecting alley. Idling a few yards down was a van with its rear door open. He shouted something in Chinese and another small man standing in the cargo section of the van answered. He dove for the van as it began to pull away, landing with his legs dangling over the side like a swimmer on a raft.

I took two bounding steps forward and grabbed for those legs. I got hold of the right one—and for the briefest moment felt the acceleration of the van wrenching him out of the grasp of the man in the cargo area—when *my* grip slipped from his knee to his foot. His shoe came off in my hands, the van screeched away and I rolled into a pile of soggy fiberglass insulating material that someone had dumped in the alley.

There was no question of getting a license plate or even a good description of the van, so I picked myself up, brushed off as much of the pink fiberglass as I could and retraced my steps to the entrance of the alley on Steuart. There I collected my knife and the Chinese guy's and put both in my pocket. I also found Lisa's pump in two pieces, the heel having come off when I clobbered the Chinese guy with it.

I was holding both pieces of shoe along with the Chinese guy's black slipper when Lisa came running barefoot from across the street, bringing Sol Hodges with her. She took one look at me and wrapped me in a hug.

Hodges stood to the side with an amused expression on his face. He nodded at the shoes in my hands. "Got anything in a brown oxford?" he asked.

Lisa insisted on taking me to an emergency room to have my side looked at. As it turned out, it was nothing very serious: a punctured love handle requiring a tetanus shot and some clever bandaging. The ER doctor also recommended stitches, but I wasn't in the mood to be further traumatized.

I decided it wasn't a good idea to let Lisa go home by herself. We caught a cab in front of UCSF Medical Center and directed it across town to her mother's house on Russian Hill.

"What does *sei gweilo* mean?" I asked her after I had maneuvered my bandaged self into the most pain free accommodation I could make with the lumpy cab upholstery.

Lisa pursed her lips and stared blankly out the window. "It's not a pleasant expression. Cleaned up a bit, it means dirty white devil."

"Hard to be dirty and white at the same time."

"You know what I mean."

"Does my being white have anything to do with this?"

Lisa smiled and reached down to take my hand. "I don't see how, August. He may have followed me to the club, but I can't imagine he knew that I was going to see you."

"Which leads to the obvious question …"

"Why did he try to abduct me? I've no idea. Our conversation was pretty brief. It pretty much boiled down to, 'Come with me or I'll cut your throat.'"

I squeezed her hand and then reached to put my arm around the back of the seat. I brought my head within a few inches of hers and put some gravitas into my voice. "You are one courageous girl, but what you did was foolish—both in resisting him and staying around to help me. It's lucky you weren't seriously injured."

"You're the courageous one. I don't think he ever intended to hurt me. I think his job was to bring me back alive."

"For what?"

She looked me square in the eye, smiled ever so slightly and shook her head.

I flopped back in the seat. "Yeah, you already told me. You've no idea. Had you ever seen the guy before?"

"No."

"Did he say anything about where he was taking you?"

"No."

"I wonder if your mother would have better answers to those questions?"

"She may, but I've got a feeling this one is going to catch even my mother off guard."

Lisa turned out to be right. The Dragon Lady lived in an ersatz Italian villa made of pink marble that was layered into the hillside near the corner of Greenwich and Leavenworth. She had a great view of Coit Tower to the west and even better one of the bay to the north. We went through an ornate metal gate covered in ivy, then down a short marble walkway to the left wing of the house. Lisa barely had her key to the lock when the door swung open. I wasn't sure which was more scary—to catch the Dragon Lady with her hair up in curlers or to see the tears that were streaming down her cheeks. Lisa and she exchanged a good two minutes of high-speed Chinese, then she pulled Lisa by the arm into the house. A moment later, she stepped back outside, closing the door behind her.

She dabbed at her eyes with a tissue she took from her housecoat. "Thank you for bringing my daughter home safe to me, Mr. Riordan."

"You're welcome. I wonder if you can tell me, though, why it is she was ever in jeopardy."

The Dragon Lady set her jaw and swallowed. "I do not know why, but I will make it a priority to find out. If it affects your investigation, I will tell you."

"And if it doesn't?"

"I will deal with it myself."

"Hey, here's a thought—maybe you could hire a private eye to investigate."

"Good night, Mr. Riordan."

I went back down the path, through the gate and onto the street. Floodlights at the base of Coit Tower lit it up like a kind of shining beacon, but the wreath of cypress trees encircling its base seemed dark and clutching.

I got back into the cab and rode home.

SURE-FIRE SELLER

THE NEXT MORNING I STOPPED BY MY friendly neighborhood police station to report the assault, which in my case meant visiting the one on Eddy Street in district J: San Francisco's seedy Tenderloin neighborhood. I stood in line between a twitchy guy in a NASCAR windbreaker and garden clogs who filed a report for "grand theft by a prostitute" and a woman in a waitress uniform who told me that someone had stolen a thirty-gallon plastic barrel of vegetable oil from the back of her cafe. My turn with the desk sergeant generated a stifled yawn and five minutes of typing on a beat-up computer whose worn keys were haloed with greasy black grime. I reported the barest details about the crime, not identifying Lisa or mentioning my employment with the Dragon Lady.

I stood on the sidewalk in front of the station considering my options. Some, like methamphetamine and oral sex, were suggested to me by the denizens of the Tenderloin trooping by me, apparently undaunted by the proximity of the police. Others, like paying a visit to the remaining mayoral contenders from the November election, Alan Chow or Hunter Lowdon, I came up with myself. In the end, I decided to visit Chow since I particularly wanted his perspective on the election, and I also hoped he would be able to provide insight into the motives for last night's kidnap attempt. He had to know Chinatown and the Dragon Lady's place in it better than me.

I had done enough research on Chow to know he owned a gift shop on Grant Avenue in Chinatown called The Oriental Eye. When I inquired for him at the shop, the sales clerk directed me one block west to a narrow building on Waverly Place that might best be described as "multi-use." On the bottom floor was an herb shop, floors two through four appeared to be offices and the top floor and the balcony were given over to apartment dwellers and their possessions, including a line full of laundry snapping in the breeze and a screen of towering bamboo trees in a cast-iron planter. The door leading upstairs had a lock on it, but someone had propped it open with one of the cobblestones that had proved so handy in my battle with the ATM thief.

Chow's office was on the second floor. Inside, I found a pear-shaped guy with a nearly bald head, heavy black-rimmed glasses and a cigar clamped in his jaw at a forty-five-degree angle like a mortar. He could have been a Chinese Winston Churchill. He was sitting at the reception desk with packages piled around him on the floor, the desk and most of the horizontal surfaces within reach. He looked something like the pictures of Chow that I'd seen in the paper, but the glasses and the cigar threw me for a loop.

"We don't accept vendor samples in the morning," he said when I hesitated. "Come back after two when my secretary is here."

"I'm not selling anything."

"Then all the buying's done at our shop—a block over on Grant."

I advanced to a spot in front of the desk. From this proximity, the smoke from his cigar had all the subtle bouquet of smoldering insoles. "I'm not really buying either. I'm working for Leonora Lee. She hired me to—"

"Yeah, yeah. Investigate the election. She told me you might come by."

"I wanted to ask you a few questions. Can you talk now?"

"Sure." He took the cigar out of his mouth and waved it around vaguely. "That is, if you don't mind talking while I work. I've got about three month's worth of samples piled up—courtesy of the time I wasted on the election. Now I've got to go through them and see if I'm missing out on any sure-fire sellers. Not that it's very likely. There are just so many kinds of back scratchers we can pawn off on you unsuspecting round-eyes."

I pulled up a flimsy director's chair and set it down in front of his desk. "Round-eyes, huh? I heard a different term last night."

Chow set his cigar into an ashtray fashioned out of an abalone shell. "That doesn't surprise me. I believe the term 'round-eyes' was made up by a member of your race. Mao, on the other hand, was actually more concerned with your noses. He called Caucasians *da bi zi*, which literally means big nose."

"So did we big noses steal the mayoral election away from you?"

He laughed and leaned down to pick up a small box from a pile to the left of his desk. "Now there's a loaded question," he said when he straightened up. "Do I think the results were fishy? Absolutely. Particularly in the Chinese precincts. But there's no way I was going to win the election outright, so I'd be hard pressed to say it was stolen from me. And I'd be even harder pressed to assign blame."

"If you didn't think you could win the election, why did you run?"

He tore open the lid of the box he was holding and prized out a clear plastic globe filled with liquid. He held it aloft, swirling the contents as he did so. "A Great Wall snow globe. How about it? Would you buy one?"

I shook my head.

"Neither would I." He returned the globe to the box and tossed it into a discard pile on the other side of his desk. "Why did I run, you said? I'm surprised at you. I ran because the Dragon Lady wanted me to. And to help me build a base for future elections—maybe a go at a seat on the Board of Supervisors."

I nodded and watched as he leaned over to pick up another package. "You said the results were fishy. Say for the sake of argument that the election was fixed. Mrs. Lee is convinced one of Padilla's supporters is responsible and suggested that real estate and housing would be the primary motive. I understand it's a hot issue in San Francisco, but what makes it worth this amount of effort and risk to get your candidate into the mayor's office? Can the mayor actually influence things that much?"

He picked up the cigar and clamped it in his teeth again. "I can tell you one thing that might make it worth it—Hunter's Point. In the next term, the mayor and Board of Supervisors will select a contractor to redevelop five hundred acres of land from the ship-yard—five hundred acres in a city with some of the highest priced real estate in the world. Current plans call for construction of twelve hundred homes and a twenty-thousand-square-foot neighborhood retail center in the first phase alone."

I knew Congress had authorized transfer of the former naval shipyard at Hunter's Point to the city, and I knew the Navy had been spending millions to clean up the pollution and toxic waste that remained from their operations, but I didn't realize the clean-up was nearing completion. "That would be a lot of affordable housing for the Padilla camp, assuming you agree with the Dragon Lady's assertion that they are the ones who finagled the election."

Chow puffed a fresh cloud of smoke into the atmosphere as he fought with the strapping tape that sealed the carton he'd selected. It opened with a loud rip, and he slumped back in his chair with a winded look. "His people would be the obvious choice, sure. I don't think Padilla himself would get involved, but there are some real zealots involved in his campaign."

"Like his campaign manager, Kathleen whosits?"

"Kathleen Willmott. Zealot isn't the label that first comes to mind for her."

"Really? What is?"

"Bitch."

I reached down to rub the bruise on my shin, which didn't help my shin any, but sure made the cut in my side smart. "She does seem pretty dedicated to Padilla's cause, though. She has got to qualify as a zealoty bitch at least."

"Yes, but she knows where to draw the line. I don't think she would put Padilla's whole political future at risk by doing something that far beyond the pale. A minor league dirty trick or two maybe, but not election fixing."

"Okay, then, who else?"

Chow reached into his carton and pulled out a rectangular item wrapped in tissue paper about the size of a lunch box. When I saw the handle sticking out of the top of it, I realized it *was* a lunch box. "Oh, there are a lot of choices," he said. "But I'll give you two of my favorites. The first would be *Ciudad Verde*. That translates to Green City for you round-eyed gringo types. Their goal is to stop further gentrification of the Mission District, and they're none too squeamish about the techniques they use. They start with picketing planning commission meetings and escalate all the way up to sabotage of developers' construction sites. Then you've got the Feral Collective. They're an anarchist group that is particularly concerned with the homeless issue. They maintain a list of vacant properties throughout the city so that the homeless and the poor can easily locate places to squat."

"But I thought anarchists wanted to undermine government. Why would they care about an election?"

He worked a finger under the scotch tape that held the tissue paper. "What? You don't think causing a candidate who received a minority of the votes to win the election undermines government?"

"Oh."

Chow stopped worrying at the tape and simply tore off the tissue paper. He held the box out so I could see it. It was a standard issue kid's lunch box, except instead of a cartoon show or a comic book hero, it was decorated with an illustration from an old Chinese advertisement. "Here's something a little different. The artwork comes from a 1930s poster. It says, 'Shanghai Movie Star brand perfume. Buy it anywhere.' Nice-looking girl, don't you think?"

The girl on the lunch box was pictured in her underwear, sitting demurely on a couch in her bathroom. A toddler in diapers standing next to her was passing her a bottle of perfume to apply. They both seemed pretty pleased about the prospect. "Yeah," I agreed. "She's a cutie, all right."

"Remind you of anyone?"

"What are you getting at?"

He laughed. "Have you heard the expression 'yellow fever,' Mr. Riordan?"

"Sure—it's some kind of tropical disease."

"It's also slang to describe a Caucasian who is attracted to Asian women. As in, 'He's got yellow fever.' Don't you think the girl on the lunch box looks a little like Lisa Lee?"

I felt heat rise in my face and settle in the tips of my ears which, if the burning sensation meant anything, must have been glowing like the tailfins of a '59 Caddy. I opened my mouth to speak, but didn't manage to expel any words.

"Relax. Before you go confessing to more than you should, let me just say that anytime Miss Chinatown gets attacked while being escorted by a *da bi zi*, we in the neighborhood hear about it."

"And what exactly did you hear?"

Chow tapped an ash the size of a New York cockroach into the abalone shell and left the cigar smoking beside it. "Oh, I heard that you were brave and fought off her attacker and all that. The surprising bit is that anyone Chinese would dare to attack the Dragon Lady's daughter in the first place."

"So who did?"

"A good guess would be Wo Hop To." He stared at me like we were on stage and he was waiting for me to produce a forgotten line, then he reached for another package.

"Who are they?" I said. "One of the Chinatown gangs?"

He frowned as he examined the padded envelope he had picked up. "What do you know about gang activity in Chinatown, Mr. Riordan?"

"I remember the Joe Boys and the shooting at the Golden Dragon restaurant." The shooting had taken place in September 1977 and was the worst gang-related violence in Chinatown for fifty years, with five killed and eleven wounded.

"Forget the Joe Boys. There is only one gang in Chinatown— Wo Hop To. They either absorbed or drove out of business all the others—the Joe Boys, Wah Ching and the Hop Sing Tong. They are the real deal—a professional triad from Hong Kong. The others were amateurish street gangs by comparison."

"So what do they want with Lisa Lee?"

He shrugged and picked up the cigar again. "Leonora is not without enemies in Chinatown. She is an ambitious woman and doesn't hesitate to intimidate, browbeat or otherwise bulldoze anyone who stands in her way. Wo Hop To is involved in many illegal activities—everything from fireworks, to prostitution, to smuggling of immigrants. But they also have legitimate business interests. It would not surprise me if Leonora's interests and the interests of Wo Hop To are sometimes—or even often—in conflict. They might have attempted to kidnap Lisa as a way to get leverage on her."

"How about fixing the election? Could they have pulled that off?"

Chow grinned. "Very good. I wondered if you were going to put that together. Now you understand why I wasn't so quick to assign blame to the Padilla camp. Yes, Wo Hop To might have fixed the election. They certainly have the technical sophistication to do so. In fact, they strike me as being more technically sophisticated than any of Padilla's fellow travelers. They are also much more likely to have bloodied their hands with the murder of Director Bowman, assuming it is related. But if they did fix the November election, I have to assume they are finished with that stratagem. Their goal would have been to knock me out of the running so the Dragon Lady lost face and influence. They wouldn't bother with the runoff. More risk of being caught and no real reason to favor one candidate over the other."

I put my foot against Chow's desk and leaned the director's chair back an inch or two. When I walked in here, I had only the vaguest idea about suspects. Now I had three: *Ciudad Verde*, Feral Collective and Wo Hop To. I guessed that was progress. I realized I could probably get leads on the first two organizations, but I wasn't so sure about the latter. "Okay," I said. "That makes sense. What else can you tell me about Wo Hop To? Who's the head man?"

He turned his envelope over and took hold of a little pull tab to open it. "The organization is still run from Hong Kong. But the local boss is a gigantic tub of lard with the colorful name of Tony 'Squid Boy' Wu. He owns a dim sum place over on Sacramento."

Chow yanked on the envelope tab and there was a muffled whooshing noise like a road flare being lit. Flames shot out of the opening. Chow yelped and launched the package across the room, where it bounced off the wall and landed on the floor amongst a pile of still more samples. There was a tremendous flash and then a concussive bang that pitched me over backwards. I lay on the floor as steel gray smoke roiled over me, bits of charred paper and other particulate settling all around like confetti from a parade.

Chow managed to speak first. Most of it was Chinese, but I understood the "fuck me" part.

I disentangled myself from the director's chair and stood up. There was a small fire going in the cardboard debris where the bomb had gone off. The wall near the explosion was scorched black and the air at this height had a suffocating sulfuric tang to it that made it difficult to breath. Chow looked at me from across the desk with his glasses askew and his cigar nearly bit through in two pieces. He looked frazzled, but otherwise intact.

He rose, stubbed out the cigar and hustled through a doorway to the side that appeared to lead to a kitchen or utility room. When he returned, he had a small fire extinguisher in his hands. I met him by the flames and together we stamped and sprayed them out.

Although the fire was extinguished, the smoke in the room was now thicker than ever and we had both begun coughing. I pointed at the door and Chow nodded.

By the time we made it to the ground floor, several of the building's smoke detectors were ringing and at least two sirens could be heard in the background. Chow leaned over with his hands on his knees. He spat on the ground.

"You know what I think?" I said between coughs.

"I can guess, but lay it on me anyway."

"I don't think you should stock that one."

He looked up at me with a martyred expression. "What I figured."

PLAYING FOOTSIE

I HUNG OUT WITH CHOW UNTIL THE FIRE department arrived. They couldn't get their truck up the narrow alley, so they parked it at the mouth and three of them came charging along with a hose, rubber masks clamped on their faces and oxygen tanks strapped to their backs. Chow pointed at the stairway and said, "Second floor, but the fire's out. You won't need any of that."

The taller of the three who was bringing up the rear said, "We'll see," in a muffled voice, and they elbowed through the doorway. A few minutes later, we heard heavy boots coming down the stairs and a piece of charred envelope on the end of a back scratcher appeared in the doorframe. It was followed by the tall guy who held the scratcher at arms length.

He'd pulled the oxygen mask off to reveal a shock of unruly red hair and a big red face with an even redder mark from the mask. "Here's your incendiary source."

Chow nodded. "That's right. It was sent to me in the mail. I opened it and it exploded."

"Fizzled first," I put in. "Then exploded."

"Yeah," said Chow. "After I'd thrown it the hell away."

The fireman drew his upper lip over flecked teeth like a bad Bogart impressionist. "Well, you're lucky it wasn't plastic explosive. You'd both be dead. From what you say and what I can make from the bits that are left, it was probably a black powder device. We'll bag this and bring in the bomb guys for more analysis, but I'm ninety-nine percent certain that's what they'll come back with."

I stifled a cough in the crook of my arm. "But what about the fizzling? Was it supposed to do that or was it a dud?"

"Could have been either. It might have been set up to do a quick burn at first to give you a scare, or the powder or the detonator might have been bad, which caused part of the charge to burn off before it exploded. Bomb guys might be able to tell if we can find more of the detonator."

"All this is fascinating," said Chow, "but when can I get back into my office?"

The fireman didn't care for Chow's attitude and he made sure Chow understood that, by dragging out the questioning, report writing and calling of the police and the bomb guys as long as possible. It was lunch time by the time they finally let us go, so I decided to avail myself of some of the neighborhood cuisine. The obvious choice was Tony "Squid Boy" Wu's dim sum restaurant.

I walked a block and a half south on Waverly until I came to Sacramento, which at that point was already making its calf-wrenching climb to the top of Nob Hill. The restaurant was interred in a below-ground space just before the intersection with Stockton. It went by the prosaic name of the Pearl Tea House (not Squid Boy's Dim Sum Shack as I had hoped) and was surrounded on all sides by buildings that housed Chinese family associations. To the right, the doors for the Moy Family association were open and I could see and hear elderly Chinese playing rapid-fire mahjong at seven or eight card tables positioned around the dank, linoleum-tiled room.

The vibe for the restaurant was decidedly quieter. The glass door at the bottom of the steps to the restaurant had a sign that said Open—as well as a yellow health department "Advisory Notice"—but there didn't seem to be any activity within. I put my hand to the door, jangling the little attached bell, but was hit by a sudden attack of prudence. It didn't seem the smartest thing in the world to be heading into the underground headquarters of the gang whose members had nearly fricasseed me the night before without at least a little more reconnaissance. I let go of the door, turned and went up the steps to street level.

There wasn't any place in front of the building to hang out without being painfully obvious, so I went across Sacramento to one of San Francisco's so-called urban playgrounds: a slab of concrete, some monkey bars, a few benches, all surrounded by a high chain-link fence. I settled on a bench next to a calcified drinking fountain that last dispensed water the year Nixon visited China. From there I had a good view of the entrance to the Pearl Tea House and an old guy doing Tai Chi exercises that somehow reminded me of the creaky—but coordinated—movements of the wiper blades on my Galaxie 500.

The Tai Chi guy had finished all his exercises and sat down to smoke a well-earned cigarette by the time anything interesting happened. A stretch Hummer with tinted windows pulled up in front of the restaurant. Movements inside caused the stiff suspension to shiver and then a door on the passenger side was flung open and I could see a bald head appear over the edge of the roof. The head slid from view and the limo shivered again as the weighty body attached to the head pitched out of the limo. Two heads with black hair—and presumably lighter bodies—peaked over the roof in quick succession and jumped from the limo like paratroopers. The door was slammed shut and the Hummer made a rumbling noise and surged away.

Three men stood on the sidewalk watching the limo depart. The first was a massive, sumo-sized Chinese with a bald head and stubby arms that buoyed away from his torso at a near forty-five-degree angle due to the pneumatic action of the fat surrounding his triceps and chest. He was wearing a t-shirt made from Georgia's entire annual cotton harvest and a pair of shorts that extended nearly to his ankles. His ankles looked bigger than my thighs. The gleam of a monstrous diamond ring on his right pinkie finger was visible from across the street. It had to be Wu.

Standing next to him were two other Chinese. They would have been short and slender no matter where they stood, but beside him they were pygmies. They also looked an awful lot like the guys I'd tangled with the night before.

Wu nodded at them and then did a slow rotation to face the steps leading to the restaurant. He waded down them with difficulty, the other two following in his wake like fart bubbles after a whale.

Somehow my reconnaissance hadn't made it any easier to follow them in. I stood from the bench deliberately, brushed some pistachio nut shells I had sat in off my butt, squared my shoulders and marched across the street to the Pearl Tea House. There was a reception podium near the front door, but nobody was manning it. I veered left through an arched entryway with a beaded curtain, and stepped into the dining area. It was dull, grey and utilitarian. There were a few cardboard decorations in the shape of giant firecrackers thumbtacked to the wall here and there, and a potted bamboo in the corner that looked like more like a cane pole shoved in a bucket of dirt than a live plant. A dozen round tables with paper tablecloths and cheap high-backed chairs completed the furnishings, but only one table near the center was occupied. Wu sat at that, holding a Chinese language newspaper about an inch from his face with one hand, while he reached into a vast bowl of boiled peanuts with the other. He hadn't heard me come in.

"Catching up with the *China Free Press*?" I asked when I'd gotten about a foot from his table.

He lowered the paper slowly until he could look at me over the top of it. For the first time I noticed a tattoo of a squid rippling across the folds of his fleshy neck, just below the ear. "I don't read that rag," he said. "It's nothing but yellow journalism." He had a slight British accent.

"I thought they had a pretty good article on the attempted kidnapping of Lisa Lee in today's edition. Especially the stuff about the quick-thinking, heroic bystander who saved the day."

"That's cute, Riordan. Did you think that one up while you were sitting on the park bench trying to grow some balls?"

"No, it just came to me. How'd you know I was in the park?"

"My cook was doing Tai Chi right across from you. Plus we got about ten video cameras mounted on the building pointing that way. Plus you belong in this neighborhood like mayo belongs on mushu."

"How do you know who I am, then?"

He grunted. "Sit the fuck down. You're giving me a neck ache."

I pulled out the chair across from him and sat down. He watched me with bored eyes and then carefully quartered the paper and placed it at his elbow. "I know who you are because I spoke to Leonora this morning."

"On a first name basis with her, are you?"

"When I need to be."

"Did you mention why you tried to kidnap her daughter?"

His chair squeaked for help as he leaned back in it and laced his fingers together over his mountainous gut. "I didn't."

"No you didn't tell her, or no you didn't try to kidnap Lisa."

"The latter."

"You're being over-literal. I saw those two jackdaws from last night get out of your Hummer. You think if I go back to the SFPD and add that detail to the report I filed it won't result in your ass being hauled to the station?"

"I wouldn't mention that to the police or Leonora if I were you. It's well known that *gweilo* think that all Chinese look alike. I'm sure you are mistaken."

I was working on what undoubtedly would have been a stinging retort when a door behind Wu swung open. The Tai Chi guy from the park stepped through it carrying a plate with a stainless steel serving cover. He banged it down in front of Wu along with a pair of chopsticks. Wu grunted. "Bring him some, too," he said.

The cook stayed long enough to favor me with an ardent scowl and then disappeared through the kitchen door. Wu took a napkin from the table and wedged it under the outmost of his chins. He snatched up the chopsticks and clicked them together exuberantly like they were castanets. "Do you like *fung jau?*" he asked.

"What's *fung jau?*" I tried to mimic Wu's pronunciation, but it came out like "fuck now" instead.

Wu grinned. "It's chicken—only it's a part of the chicken that the Colonel doesn't normally put in his bucket."

"The Colonel may have his reasons for that."

"Not good ones. Apart from the head—and maybe the butt—the feet are the very best part." He swept off the cover, revealing a plate piled high with brown, glutinous-looking talons. He stabbed into the pile with the chopsticks, extracted a single claw and brought it to his mouth to gnaw on.

The cook came back with another serving and set it down in front of me. He pulled off the cover and stood over me, watching as the steam wafted up. I had to admit that the spices smelled good, but I couldn't get past the fact that I'd just been served a plate of amputated feet.

The cook saw something in my face that made him cackle. "You want some ketchup with that?" he asked.

I swallowed. "No," I said. "I'm good."

The cook cackled again and returned to the kitchen. Wu leaned down to spit out some bones and dabbed his mouth with his napkin. "It takes a little while to master the proper technique for eating *fung jau*. The bones in particular—you sort of have to root them out with your tongue. But it's good practice. You tell Lisa Lee that you're a chicken feet eater and watch her eyes light up."

I slapped the table, making all the chicken feet do a little tap dance. "Everyone I meet today seems to want to make a crack about my relationship with Lisa Lee. Well, I didn't come here for that, and I didn't come for half-assed lessons in Chinese cuisine."

Wu looked at me with a mild expression, then returned to his chicken foot. He gnawed on it expertly, rotating it as he did so it was like a tiny corn on the cob. He leaned down to dispose of more bones and looked back up at me. "Why exactly did you come here Riordan?"

The right answer was I'd come about the election, but things had changed since I'd identified Wu's men. I said, "I came here to find out why you attacked Lisa Lee."

"We went over that already."

"Not to my satisfaction. I've got a knife covered with your man's fingerprints in a sealed plastic bag." The truth was I'd left it in my car glove box and I'd probably smeared all the prints. "I've also got an eyewitness who will testify about the attack."

Wu pointed his chopsticks at me with a fresh chicken foot clasped in them. "Lisa Lee won't—"

I cut him off. "It's *not* Lisa Lee," I said. "It's someone in the band who'll say whatever I want him to say."

He shrugged. "I never put too much credence in what so-called eyewitnesses say. It's surprising how often they change their stories before trial. As to the knife, it'll be quite easy to detain you here while someone searches your office and apartment."

I pushed back my chair and jumped to my feet. "Look, Wu—"

His eyes ranged over my shoulder and he said, "Grab him." I twisted round to confront my attacker, but closed on empty air. Wu's laugh rang out behind me.

"Do you think if I was going to tell one of my employees to grab you, I'd do it in English?"

He was already working on the next chicken foot when I turned back to look at him. "Sit down, Riordan," he said between bites. "We both know you're not going to the police with this."

I stood there awkwardly for a moment, then took hold of the chair and moved it to the side where I could keep my eye on the entrance and the kitchen door. "What do you mean? I went to the station house this morning."

"Yes, but my friends at the station say your report doesn't mention you having a knife, and it certainly doesn't mention anything about Lisa Lee." He gnawed some more on the foot, then came up for air. "I'll tell you what, Riordan, I'll throw you a bone—so to speak. Leonora and I were having a little disagreement. She had something of mine, and for her own reasons, was withholding it. I am not completely lacking in empathy. I understood her viewpoint—but could not condone it. I discussed the matter with her, but she was obdurate. I tried other means of persuasion—they did not work. So I decided to obtain something she valued highly."

"To trade."

"Yes, to trade. And although you prevented me from obtaining that highly valued thing, the mere threat of losing it was enough to change her mind." He smiled at me greasily. "I got what I wanted from her this morning."

"And now you two are buddy-buddy."

Wu was hoovering his chicken foot again, but he nodded and made an affirmative sucking noise.

I reached over to the bowl of peanuts and selected one. The boiled shell split open like wet newspaper. "You know, Wu, you're pretty well spoken for a thuggish gang leader. I can't remember the last time I heard someone use the word obdurate in a sentence. Probably it was a public TV show on diamond mines."

He dropped the foot he was working on into a pile of denuded claws and made a mock bow. "I read for a degree at New College, Oxford before life's other priorities gained precedence. And I am not a gang leader. I am the president of a Chinese business association."

I scooped the nuts out of the peanut shell and popped them into my mouth. I know I shouldn't talk with my mouth full, but Wu was already becoming one with his next chicken foot and didn't seem to notice. "Alan Chow says you're head of Wo Hop To, the only gang in San Francisco."

Wu chuckled. "Chow—what a doormat. I leave more personality on my dental floss than he displays all year."

"You said you tried other means of persuasion to get what you wanted from the Dragon Lady. Did that include fixing the election so her candidate lost?"

Wu stopped his grazing and looked me dead in the eye. He laughed. Shaking his head, he put the chicken foot down and wiped his mouth with the napkin. "Where did you come up with that one?"

"A footless bird told me."

"If I wanted to torpedo Chow, there'd be plenty of easier ways to do it than rigging the election. And whatever I might think of Chow personally, I'm not opposed to having a Chinese mayor. I wouldn't have tried to prevent his election to settle my dispute with Leonora."

"How about scaring him with a dud letter bomb, then?"

Wu held his face rigidly for a moment and then brought the napkin up to blow his nose. He made a thoughtful study of the results and set the napkin to the side, on top of the newspaper. "I'm sure I don't know what you're talking about," he said finally.

"Or maybe you meant him to open it weeks ago, perhaps during the election."

He shrugged. "If Chow opened a dud letter bomb during the election, it would only serve to bring him more publicity. You can imagine the headline—'Crusading Chinese Mayoral Candidate Risks Ire of Chinatown Gangs.' That sort of thing."

"And the threat of his murder might have scared the Dragon Lady into giving you what you wanted."

He coughed into a fist bigger than a truck piston. "I think you're reading the tea leaves a little too much, Riordan." He called something in Chinese over his shoulder and the kitchen door swung open to discharge the cook—this time carrying an evil-looking cleaver smeared with blood and chicken feathers. "It's time for you to go. I wish you the best of luck in your assignment for Leonora, but don't make the mistake of coming back here again or saying anything more to the police. You won't find me quite so accommodating."

The cook came up to hold the cleaver about an inch from my right ear. I leaned away from the blade. "What, no fortune cookie?"

"No cookie," said the cook. "Just the fortune—get lost or get chopped."

I sidled out of the chair and stood. I reached across the surprised cook to grab a handful of peanuts and then headed towards the exit. "Thanks for lunch," I said over my shoulder.

When I reached the beaded archway, I turned to look back at them. Wu was already demolishing his next chicken foot and the cook had taken my place across from him. His cleaver was embedded in the table near his elbow, still quivering.

I had the uneasy feeling of having been played. I tugged on my ear lobe and went quietly away from there.

PROTESTING TOO MUCH

FOR MY NEXT TRICK, I DECIDED TO follow up on the other leads Chow had given me: Feral Collective and *Ciudad Verde*. I gave Gretchen a call to help with the addresses from the front seat of the Galaxie in my parking space in the Tenderloin garage. I'd barely gotten hello out when she rode over me.

"I read about you shooting that man in South San Francisco, August. And finding the director of elections murdered. What have you gotten yourself into? You can't pick up a paper or watch a newscast without seeing something about you, the killings or their implications for the upcoming election."

I ran my finger along a crack in the Galaxie's dash. "Is 'I don't know' an acceptable answer?"

"Hardly. But if you're going to be ignorant, may I suggest that you at least pair it with caution?"

"Yes ma'am."

There was a long silence. The receiver was muffled and then un-muffled and I heard what might have been a sniff. "I'm just worried about you, August. Now what can I do for you?"

I explained about the addresses. I spelled the name of each organization and Gretchen put me on hold.

When she came back, she said, "You know, there's a feature on your new cell phone called directory assistance."

"Yeah, I thought about that, but I figured it didn't include the same tough-love butt-kicking I'd get from you."

"You got that right."

I copied the addresses as she read them off, thanked her profusely and then rumbled out into traffic.

Feral Collective was in a storefront on Polk Street with all the windows covered over by yellowing, flyspecked newspaper. The door had a ruled page torn from a Big Chief tablet laminated onto the wood with about twenty pieces of clear packing tape. "So you want to squat a building" was scrawled at the top, with these handy points listed below:

1) Look for a building that appears unused or run-down
2) Find out where the landlord lives - the further away the better
3) Break in
4) Change the locks
5) Meet your neighbors - act legit
6) Don't let the police in unless they have a warrant

The door was locked and no amount of pounding produced a response. Before I got back in my car, I peered in the window through a seam in the newspaper, looking for signs that the collective had followed their own advice in acquiring their headquarters.

I couldn't see anything but the back side of a file cabinet with a bug-eyed alien sticker.

The offices for *Ciudad Verde* were on South Van Ness near 20th Street in the heart of the Mission District. They were in a converted Victorian, and their door, too, had a note on it. This one was of a more recent vintage, was written in English and Spanish and was simply thumbtacked to the wood. The English part said the offices were closed so the staff could attend the protest at the Salaiz Bakery and urged everyone to join the fun. The Spanish part seemed to say the same thing, but employed verbiage that was a bit more *caliente*.

It appeared I was going to a protest. The bakery was about six blocks north and west, near the corner of 16th Street and Mission. I'd parked my car in the best illegal spot I could find—next to a fireplug that I'd concealed with a homeless person's abandoned cardboard box—and I wasn't eager to leave it now for the privilege of driving. I resigned myself to hoofing it.

Every intersection on the way over seemed to have a Hispanic guy pushing a little ice cream cart with oversize bicycle tires and jingling bells. After stiff-arming the first two guys, I caved with the third and bought myself an orange Creamsicle bar. I was about halfway through the bar when I heard the chanting. It was in Spanish and it was being led by a guy with a bullhorn, but my high school language skills weren't up to the translation.

The Creamsicle was completely gone and I was gnawing on the wooden stick for the last little bit of juice when the bakery finally came into view. It was a 1960s stucco flattop on a surprisingly big lot. Protestors holding signs that read "Stop gentrification!" and "*La raza por la causa!*" crowded the sidewalk in front. The guy with bullhorn stood on a stepladder directing the action.

A cop had his black-and-white parked to one side and was sitting on the hood of the car, watching the proceedings with the enthusiasm of an assembly line inspector. Further back, beyond the screen of protestors, I caught glimpses of a figure in black sitting on a lawn chair in front of the bakery. Whoever he was, he was paying even less attention to the protestors than the cop, and seemed to be fully occupied scraping mud off the heels of some kind of exotic skin cowboy boots.

I injected myself between two parked cars, looking for someone sympathetic to talk to. A Latina with the kind of figure typically only seen on mud flap silhouettes smiled in a friendly enough way, but I couldn't get her to stop her chanting and sign waving—not to mention bouncing her spiky necklace pendant about an inch from my nose. Eventually, the crush of the other protesters moved her back and to the left and she made a bye-bye sign as she was absorbed by the crowd.

I saw another chance when the guy with the megaphone stepped down from his ladder. He passed the bullhorn to a replacement and broke for a 1960s Studebaker Wagonaire to get water from an Igloo cooler set out on the tailgate. I snaked along the line of parked cars until I came up beside him.

His hair was pulled tight to his skull in a long, braided ponytail that hung down his back like a frayed bell rope. His cheeks and chin were divoted with acne scars and he had a heavy, boomerang-shaped mustache that had grown longer on one side than the other. He wore an old Ninja Turtles t-shirt with a bleach stain splashed across the front. I waved the Creamsicle stick in greeting.

"My name is August Riordan. I'm with the *China Free Press*. I wondered if I could talk with you about the protest." I was almost shouting to be heard over the demonstrators.

He looked at me sourly for a moment, sniffed, then chugged water out of thermos cup he held. "You got a credential with a little more gravitas than a Popsicle stick?"

"Creamsicle stick," I corrected. "And, yeah, I do." I whipped out the credential Lisa had given me and passed it over.

He looked from my face to the picture and back again. "You don't—," he started, but I already knew where he was going.

"I have my stories translated."

He squinted some more at the credential. "Whatever," he said finally, and handed the wallet back. "What is it you want to know?"

"Well, first off, what's your name and role in *Ciudad Verde?*"

He tried to answer, but the new man on the megaphone fired it up and rent the air with an electrified, "*Sí, se puede!*" Ponytail grimaced and waved his hands. He pointed in the direction of the police car and led me past it to the front lawn of the property next door: Our Lady of Guadalupe Cathedral. We stood on thick-bladed St. Augustine grass behind a squat palm tree, which provided at least a partial screen for the noise.

"My name is Ernesto Ortiz," he said. "I'm the associate director of *Ciudad Verde.*"

"Can you give me a thumbnail on what *Ciudad Verde* is all about?"

"Yeah, I could, but how about taking a few notes?"

I dug out a small notebook and pen. "Ernesto O-r-t-i-z," I said. "Associate director. Got it."

"Okay. *Ciudad Verde* was formed in the late 90s when rat builders were using loopholes in the city's live/work laws to build luxury loft condos on cheap land in the Mission. This resulted in an influx of yuppies and began what we call the white blight. It was a virtual colonization. It drove up land prices and rents, forced out blue collar industries, jobs and workers.

"Our organization fights the continued colonization by lobbying to close the zoning loopholes, opposing gentrification projects when they come before the Planning Commission, supporting alternative affordable housing projects proposed by green developers and working to hamstring the rat developers and the property owners who sell to them."

I wrote down the high points to keep him happy. "And the protest here—at the Salaiz Bakery. How does it fit into your charter?"

Ortiz stared at me while he ran the tip of his pinky finger over one wing of his bristly mustache. "You didn't do any research at all, did you?"

I flipped my notebook closed. "I can go do some now with a rat builder if you'd rather."

"Relax. I'll give you the scoop, but you really ought to get a little background. This isn't a parade you're writing about. The owner of the bakery is trying to sell the property for another loft condominium development. We're fighting the issuance of permits at the Planning Commission and the Board of Supervisors, but we're also letting the owner know what the people feel about his betrayal of the neighborhood."

"Who is the owner?"

Ortiz stared at me again. I put up my hand. "Apart from somebody named Salaiz, that is."

"The legal owner is Rosario Salaiz. She ran the bakery for years, but she's not the problem. It's her son, Maurice. Now that she's too old to manage the business, he's convinced her to sell out to one of the loft developers."

"But if she's reached retirement age, maybe she needs the money. What would you have her do instead?"

Ortiz shrugged. "She's got options. Sell the business intact to keep the jobs in the neighborhood. Or sell to one of the green developers. NHDC, for instance. They've proposed a project to build thirty units of affordable housing on the site." Ortiz permitted himself a sour smile. "Another angle you might want to research is Maurice Salaiz. You'll find he's a defrocked priest from this very parish." He pointed at the St. Augustine grass.

"Oh yeah?"

"Yeah. I'll give you a hint—sex scandal."

There was nothing in that for me. I let my eyes wander past Ortiz and I saw the Latina with the hot bod approach the cop and tug on his shirt sleeve. She smiled said something to him, and he slid off the hood of the car to follow her.

I looked back at Ortiz. I needed to get the conversation onto the election. "And this permit fight at the Planning Commission," I said. "How is it going?"

"It's a war of attrition. The last time the project came up for vote, our allies succeeded in requiring a number of changes in the proposal. The developer has gone back to incorporate them, but right now we don't have the votes to kill the project outright. We wouldn't be holding this demonstration if we did."

"But if Padilla wins the runoff?"

Ortiz smiled again. "That's a different story. He's promised to change the zoning laws and completely shake up the Planning Commission. The project will be stillborn the day he comes into office."

"And how much would your organization be willing to do to ensure Padilla's election?"

Ortiz frowned. "What do you mean? Everything we can, of course."

"You *have* heard the allegations of fraud surrounding touchscreen voting and the general election, haven't you?"

At first I thought the surprised look on Ortiz's face had to do with my question. Then I felt the pile driver land between my shoulder blades. I made an oofing noise and was flung facedown on the lawn. Ortiz had to dance out of my way and my forehead crash-landed about an inch from the toe of his hiking boot, my notebook, pen and half the contents of my pockets spilling out on the church lawn around me like the treats from a *piñata*.

I tried to turn over, but someone's shoe came down on my back, pinning me to the ground. Ortiz's feet went away from view. "Riordan," said a voice above me, clearly Hispanic. "You're not a reporter. We know what you do and who you're working for and you're not welcome at this event. You got me, man?" The shoe mashed further into my spine.

I said, "I got you," a little breathlessly.

"Good." The shoe lifted off my back and a hand came under my collar and yanked me to my feet. "Here's a little extra something to help you remember."

I had about a split second to register that my attacker was the young guy with the backwards baseball cap from the Green Party event at New College. Then I was more concerned about the fist coming at my mouth. I twitched my head to the side and hooked my left arm under the one that still grasped my collar. His punch spread my ear instead of my teeth. It stung like hell and I felt a white hot fury blossom inside me. I jerked him close and landed an uppercut to his diaphragm that lifted him off his heels.

I burrowed in and launched another one with even more behind it. And again. His hand fell away from my collar and he slumped onto my arm and I knew I was holding him upright for the sole purpose of beating the shit out of him. I grunted and piled another one in. I don't know how long I would have kept at it if I hadn't heard a voice at my ear. It was calm and low, but strangely penetrating.

"You've had your eye for an eye. Let him go."

I flicked my gaze to the right and saw the guy with the exotic cowboy boots standing beside me. I took a deep breath and broke the clench. The kid with the backwards baseball cap sloughed from my arm to the ground, holding his stomach. He was struggling to get his breath while at the same time cursing me in a hoarse whisper. Ortiz stood about ten yards away, at the edge of the sidewalk. He looked at me like I'd crawled out of the hatch of an alien spacecraft.

Cowboy boots bent to the ground and began picking up my notebook and the things that had fallen from my pockets. "Ernesto," he called to Ortiz. "Get over here and help Diego."

Cowboy boots stood up. "Come on, *amigo*," he said in an undertone. "Time to get going. Neither of us is welcome here."

A BURRITO FOR YOUR THOUGHTS

"**A**RE YOU HUNGRY?"

It seemed like a line from the theatre of the absurd, but I realized I hadn't eaten anything except the Creamsicle since morning. "Yes," I admitted, and let Cowboy Boots lead me down 16th Street towards Valencia. We ducked into the door of a *taqueria*. He dropped my notebook and all the crap from my pockets onto a Formica roundtop near the window.

"You pay and I'll order," he said. "Give me twenty bucks."

I flipped open my wallet and gave him twenty. I watched him go up to the counter and launch into some unintelligible Spanish, then I peeled off my jacket and hung it on the back of the chair. The left elbow was grass-stained and torn, and the right shoulder seam had separated. Another entry in the Dragon Lady's expense report. I levered my ass into the chair and began sorting through the stuff on the table. I filed most of it back in my pockets by the time Cowboy Boots returned with a couple of frosty-looking Bohemias. He handed me one and sat down in the chair across from me.

He took a long drink from the bottle, then asked, "Missing anything?"

"Yeah, unfortunately."

He reached across the table as if he were taking something from behind my ear and produced a half-dollar-sized medal with a flourish. "You don't often see Saint Apollonia medals."

"I bet that wows them on the kid's party circuit." I held out my hand for the medal. "Who *are* you anyway?" I asked.

"You really don't know?"

"Somebody who had reason to know a lot about the saints—or used to."

"That's right."

I pocketed the medal and put the Bohemia to my damaged ear while I sized him up. He didn't look like a choirboy molester, but I suppose none of them did. He was in his mid-thirties and had a handsome, regular-featured face. His hair was longish and feathery and probably required a good fifteen minutes of blow-drying to achieve its perfect, shaggy symmetry. His eyes were dark and keen—and didn't seem to go with the rest of his features. "Father Salaiz, huh? But then, you were defrocked."

He laughed. "Is that what Ernesto told you?"

"Yes. Said it involved a sex scandal."

He shook his head. "I'll be charitable and say that Ernesto was misinformed."

"So tell me the real story."

"All right. But first tell me why you're carrying around a Saint Apollonia medal. Are you Catholic?"

I looked at him for a long moment. I wanted to hear what he had to say about *Ciudad Verde*, but I hoped this wasn't going to turn into fellowship for recovering Catholics. "I'm not sure what I am. I guess I regard the medal as a good luck piece as much as anything."

"Why?"

"What do you know about Saint Apollonia?"

"She's a martyr. She leapt into the fire after having her teeth broken by pincers rather than renounce Christ. She's the patron saint of dentists and tooth disease."

"That's right. Several years ago I had some teeth knocked out in a fight. I had a partial plate for a while, but then I replaced it with implants. There's more to the story than that, but the whole experience was very unpleasant and I'm not eager to go through it again. Carrying the medal is my way of warding off a reoccurrence."

Salaiz managed to nod while taking a gulp of beer. "Is that why you went to town on Diego?"

I drew in a deep breath and let it out. This guy must have been good in the confessional. "Yeah. I was going to let it drop until he swung for my mouth. Then I was going to kill him." I took the Bohemia away from my ear and took a long pull. "How come you call them by their first names—Ernesto and Diego?"

"Ernesto I went to school with—and I performed his marriage ceremony. Diego I confirmed. Of course, all that was before—"

"Before you got booted out of the church."

"No, before my mother decided to sell her bakery. I wasn't booted out of the church. I had an affair with a nun. It was never discovered, but we both decided to renounce our vows rather than continue the deception."

"Did you get married?"

The woman behind the counter called Salaiz's name. He got off his stool. "No," he said. "She met someone she liked better." He pointed at my side. "Did you know you were bleeding?"

Salaiz went to get the food while I pulled out my shirttail and plastered my side with napkins I took from the dispenser. The tussle in the church yard had reopened the knife wound I had gotten from Wu's goon.

"Hope you like pork," said Salaiz when he returned with two baskets containing the largest burritos I'd ever seen. "It's the specialty here."

I let my eating do the talking, wolfing down almost a third of the burrito before I said anything. It was delicious. "Why did you get involved in the fight at the church yard?" I asked when I came up for air.

"When I saw Diego jump out of a car and head your way, I knew he wasn't coming to shake your hand. He's got a dishonorable discharge from the military and has a history of violence. I'm no longer a priest, but that doesn't mean I condone violence—especially violence done to someone who is an apparent ally."

"How'd you get the idea that I'm an ally?"

"I don't know who you are—"

"August Riordan—private investigator."

Salaiz dipped his head in acknowledgement. "A private investigator who is clearly no friend to *Ciudad Verde* or *their* allies."

"Any enemy of theirs is a friend of yours?"

"Something like that."

"Ortiz lied about you being defrocked. Did he lie about the situation with your mother's bakery?"

Salaiz took a hefty bite out of his burrito then hurried to wipe salsa from the corner of his mouth. He nodded as he chewed. "If he told you the same thing *Ciudad Verde* has been telling everyone else, he did. It's true my mother wants to retire. And it's true she wants to sell the property to a developer, but that developer does not plan to build loft condominiums on this site. He's built them in the past, but not here."

"Why sell to a developer at all? Why not sell the business intact?"

"You have any sense for the economics of single-store, family-owned bakery in twenty-first century San Francisco? It doesn't make money. At least not for five years, it hasn't. Mama kept the store going for so long simply because she couldn't bear to let her employees go. On the other hand, building low-cost housing for seniors, while it won't make as much money as lofts, will certainly be good for the community and will also provide a safe and manageable place for my mother to live."

I wasn't even at the halfway point with the burrito, but I couldn't eat any more. I pushed the plate aside. "This isn't adding up, Salaiz. Ortiz said his project was for low-cost housing, too. He didn't mention the senior angle, but I don't see how that could be objectionable to him. What's his real problem with your project?"

"His real problem is that his developer—NHDC—isn't building it. Take a look at this. It's a letter my mother got from the real estate broker NHDC uses. I brought it to the protest in case I got a chance to talk to the media." He took a quartered sheet of paper from his back pocket and passed it over.

I unfolded it. It was a photocopy of a letter on Nautilus Housing Development Corporation stationery. It came from a Mr. Ralph Wood and the body of it read:

> I'm writing to remind you of NHDC's interest in your property. NHDC is a respected, quality builder and they have built nearly eighty percent of the affordable housing in the Mission. More importantly, NHDC is well connected to city government and neighborhood activist groups and its projects are routinely approved with little delay.
>
> If your current buyer decides that the political climate has made their project untenable, NHDC stands ready to offer you fair market value for your property and can deliver the political juice necessary to make its alternative development a reality.
>
> Best of luck with your original deal, but don't hesitate to call me if the approval process does not pan out.

I passed it back to him. "Okay. I buy that they're playing politics to pressure your mother into selling. But why not cave? They say they're offering full market value for the property."

"One, they're not. They're offering about $300,000 less. Two, they've nixed the senior aspect of the project because they said it will add too much to construction costs for each unit. And three, their claim to have built eighty percent of affordable housing in the Mission is way off the mark. They only have about five projects to their credit. That accounts for maybe a third of the affordable housing in the neighborhood."

"Then why has *Ciudad Verde* hitched their wagon to them?"

Salaiz rubbed his fingers together in the universal gesture for money. "They've donated significantly to *Ciudad Verde* and the politicians the organization backs."

"Like Mike Padilla?"

"Especially Mike Padilla."

I took another pull on my beer and leaned back in my chair. Salaiz watched me carefully.

"If I may ask, Mr. Riordan, why are *you* interested in the sale of my mother's bakery?"

"To be honest, I'm not particularly, but I am interested in the Green Party and their mayoral candidate." I gave him a brief explanation of why I was hired, leaving out exactly who had employed me.

Salaiz smiled. "I would have guessed someone associated with the Lowdon or Chow campaign, but since I saw your *China Free Press* credential, I can dispense with the guesswork. Let me check back at the bakery. I think I might have something useful to you."

Salaiz went over to a pay phone in the corner and fed in a couple of quarters. He dialed a local number and talked briefly. When he came back, he said, "It'll just be about fifteen minutes. In the meantime, maybe you can tell me why you became a lapsed Catholic? It's never too late to come back to the church."

Coming from an ex-priest who had gotten it on with a nun, that was rich. I deflected the conversation to a discussion of the best burrito places in the Mission and had noted down about three new places to try by the time Salaiz's delivery boy showed up. He was a bean pole of a kid with the white earphones of an iPod stuck in his ears, blaring away at about 200 decibels. He handed Salaiz a paper bag without a word and turned immediately to go out the door.

"My sister's kid, Javier," said Salaiz. "Not very talkative, but he knows his A/V equipment." Salaiz reached into the bag and pulled out two DVD disks and another iPod with a small screen. "Javier's been taping the demonstration for me. These DVDs have copies of some footage I think you'll find interesting. You can take them home to watch at your leisure, but we can use the iPod now to give you a little preview."

Salaiz manipulated a wheel on the iPod and the little screen flickered to life. It showed the demonstration from an elevated viewpoint behind the protestors—most likely a second-floor window of the bakery. I saw myself talking to Ortiz and then following him over to the church yard. The camera stayed on the protestors, but then zoomed in to focus on a limo that pulled up beside the Wagonaire. Nothing happened for a several minutes, then the cop and the Latina girl walked by. The back door of the limo swung open and Diego—the kid with the backwards baseball cap—stepped out. He ducked his head back in to talk with someone, then went on his way to dry gulch me.

The camera stayed on the limo, zooming even tighter for a shot inside. At first it was too dark to see anything, then the exposure compensated and I saw a balding Anglo sitting on the bench seat, looking in the direction Diego had gone.

Salaiz paused the picture. "That's Ralph Wood, the developer who sent my mom the letter." He released the pause and the camera panned over to a red-headed woman in a black beret sitting beside him.

"And that's Kathleen Willmott," I almost shouted.

Salaiz raised the iPod like it was a winning number. "Bingo, as we used to say at our parish fund-raisers."

DOCTOR'S ORDERS

THE REST OF THE VIDEO SHOWED ME getting clobbered and stepped on by Diego, but ended before I turned the tables and began to massage his internal organs. I thanked Salaiz for the information and the DVDs and went out of the *taqueria* to walk back to my car. I had covered three blocks and was trying to shake off another ice cream vendor when my cell phone rang. I patted the bulge in my jacket. "My agent," I said to the vendor. "Excuse me."

He shrugged microscopically and pushed his cart past me, bumping over tree roots that had split the sidewalk.

"You just saved me from orange Creamsicle overdose," I said after I'd pressed the talk button.

"The thing I like about you, August," said Gretchen, "is that you always manage to entertain yourself."

"Entertainment begins at home."

"And sometimes it stays there."

"You cut me to the quick. What's up?"

"There's a Ms. Lisa Lee waiting for you in your office, and if she's any relation to the Dragon Lady, she looks—well—less dragony than I expected."

I put a hand out to lean against the purple-leaf plum whose roots were doing a number on the sidewalk. Gretchen and I had broken up more than five years ago, but sometimes it seemed like five months. "She *is* the reigning Miss Chinatown."

Gretchen made a little growling noise. "I'd heard something to that effect. Do you know if the pageant included a skimpy yoga outfit competition in addition to the swimsuit one? Or how about best headlights? Her nipples are sticking out so far that you could hang tinsel off them."

"Well, you know how cold it gets in the office."

"Yes, and that's why I don't come in wearing yoga outfits. I suggest you get over here as soon as possible. In the meantime, I'll call the super to dial up the heat."

I said, "Good idea," but she had already hung up.

I jogged back to the Galaxie 500 and barreled north on Folsom through the Mission District, turning up 5th Street to plunge across Market a block down from my office, which was in the Flood Building near the cable car turnaround.

I shared the suite on the twelfth floor with an insurance agent named Ben Bonacker, but he wasn't at his desk in the outer office. Gretchen most assuredly *was* at her desk, which was just a few feet from my office door. She sat rigidly in her chair, hammering the keyboard to her computer with a Queen Victoria "we are not amused" expression on her face. Not that she looked anything like Victoria: she had shoulder-length auburn hair, lightly freckled skin and eyes of a gorgeous cornflower blue, which, seen without makeup, looked touchingly like those of a young child. Along with her black expression, she wore a black Chanel pantsuit that I knew for a fact had set her urologist boyfriend back a couple of grand.

"Took your sweet time getting here, didn't you?" was her opening salvo.

"Had to stop for the tinsel."

That earned me a fractional smile, but it vanished quickly as she caught sight of my torn jacket and the blood stain wicking across the front of my dress shirt. "You did it again, didn't you? When are you going to stop getting yourself beat up? And don't you dare say, 'You should see the other guy.'"

"Well, you should see today's guy. Last night's guy is probably telling his secretary to see me."

She broke eye contact and laid her hands carefully on the keyboard. When she spoke again, her voice had an undertone of restrained urgency. "I told you, you need to be careful. There's something very wrong about this case."

"You're right, Gretchen," I said, and I knew that she was.

She nodded without looking up and unleashed a fusillade of typing.

"Is Lisa still in there, then?" I had to raise my voice to be heard over the keystrokes.

Another nod. "Bonacker's in there too, so you better hurry unless you want another death on your hands. Bonacker's, that is."

I smiled and turned to push the door open. Lisa sat in the client's chair across from my desk. I couldn't claim that Gretchen had described her appearance inaccurately: she was wearing a Lycra exercise outfit and had a rolled yoga mat by her feet. But she was also wearing a partially zippered warm-up, and if her nipples were protruding, it would take some more unzipping for me to see.

Bonacker sat in my swivel chair with his hands behind his head and his feet dirtying my blotter. Fat, ruddy-faced and possessing a dandelion-like nimbus of snow-white hair and beard, he winked at me as I came in the room, but continued what he'd been saying to Lisa:

"... and that's why whole life instead of term life is one of the smartest investments you make. You really should consider it. Even a youngster like you. The sooner you start, the better."

"Hey Ben," I said amiably. "As far as *I'm* concerned, the sooner you get your fanny out of my chair, the better."

Bonacker unclasped his hands and slid his feet off the desk, dragging the blotter and a pen and pencil set with him. He stood amid a cacophony of squeaks from my decrepit swivel chair and grinned at Lisa like this was all part of the Jerry and Dean act we put on for anyone who stopped by. "That August," he said when things had stopped tumbling and squeaking, "he's a son of a gun."

I simply pointed to the door.

Lisa sat with her hands covering her mouth until I'd slammed it behind him and then she burst out laughing. "He must have trotted out every slimy sales line I've ever heard."

"Yeah, Ben's a real cockroach whisperer. But forget him. To what do I owe the pleasure of your company? Not a yoga session, I hope. Because I'm much more of a Pilates man myself."

"If you've tried either, I'll eat my mat. The truth is I belong to a club on Market Street, and when I finished with my class, I realized how close I must be to your office and decided to drop by. You weren't here, but your admin was very sweet and insisted she could conjure you up."

I walked over to the desk and sat on the edge of it. Lisa had her hair pulled back with an elastic band and that—coupled with the yoga duds—gave her a wholesome, pixieish look that was quite different than the elegant tuxedoed one she had the night before. Different, but no less attractive. "Sweet," I said, "is not the first adjective that comes to mind for Gretchen."

Lisa's eyes dropped to my midsection and she frowned. "You're bleeding again."

I pulled my jacket over to cover the blood stain. "It's nothing. I got in a little tussle and the bandage loosened. A few napkins from a burrito place and I was good as new."

"Napkins from a burrito place? I should never have let you talk the emergency room doctor out of stitches. It's too easy for the wound to reopen."

"I don't like needles, and besides, this makes for a much more interesting scar."

Lisa jumped to her feet. "Take off your shirt."

"What?"

"You heard me—take off your shirt. I want to see the wound."

I vapor locked for a moment, then the nickel dropped. "I keep forgetting that you're an MD. But you can't examine me here. This is my office, for Pete's sake. What if someone walked in?"

"That's easily remedied." She strode over to the door and pushed the button lock down. "You have anything other than napkins to use as bandages? If not, we'll send your admin out for some."

I almost passed a kidney stone. "Christ no, don't get her involved. There's a bunch of junk in the cabinet above the sink. But is this really necessary?"

Lisa came back to the desk and reached over to take my jacket lapels—all businesslike. "You could get an infection if you're not careful. And look at it from my perspective. You risked your life to help me. Don't you think I'd appreciate an opportunity to do something for you?"

I shrugged out of the jacket and let her pull it from my shoulders. "All right, but no needles. The most I'll go for is some Bactine and adhesive tape."

She grinned at me while she loosened my tie. "I was planning to sterilize the wound with some booze from the office bottle."

"I'm not wasting my good bourbon on *that*. But since you brought it up, I wanted to ask you again about last night. I found the men who tried to kidnap you."

She paused while folding my tie. "And?"

"And they—or more specifically, Tony 'Squid Boy' Wu—told me that it was all wrapped up in a dispute they had with your mother. That they were trying to use you as a bargaining chip."

Lisa put the folded tie on the desk. "Did they tell you anything else?"

"Yes, Wu said he had resolved the dispute."

"There are some things my mother does that I'm not proud of, August. Associating with Mr. Wu is one of them. But you can't be a force in Chinatown without dealing with him at some point—even if your business is one hundred percent legitimate."

"And is your mother's one hundred percent legitimate?"

"Yes, and so is much of Mr. Wu's. But that doesn't mean he won't resort to intimidation. My mother is involved in a real estate transaction with him and they were haggling over the amount of a scheduled payment. Mother's interpretation of the contract called for a payment of a certain amount. Mr. Wu's interpretation required a much larger sum. My mother agreed to pay the larger number this morning."

"Then she sent you down here to tell me to lay off Wu."

"Yes—I mean, no, August." She leaned over to kiss my cheek, and then brought her finger up to smooth a frown line that was creasing my forehead. "I came because I care about you. Wu is not someone you want to tangle with. My mother was going to call you and tell you about settling with him so you wouldn't be diverted from investigating the election. Since I was coming here anyway, I volunteered to play messenger."

"So now I know."

"Yes, now you know."

"But what about the letter bomb? Did your mother tell you anything about that?"

Lisa wagged a finger at me. "You're trying to distract me. I'm done with messengering. Stand up and let's get you over by the sink. Turns out a lot of doctoring comes down to adroit use of soap and water."

I stood and peeled off my shirt and then walked self-consciously over to the sink. Lisa gasped when she saw the plaster of dried blood and *taqueria* napkins stuck to my side. She dabbed water on the napkins so they would slough off without shredding and then made little, disapproving clucking noises as she used a hand towel Gretchen had bought to gently scrub the area.

"This is much deeper than I thought, August. And the edges are already pink from infection." She swore. "And I can't keep the water from seeping into your waistband. You better take off your trousers."

"Okay, but I'm drawing the line there."

"Relax, I've seen it all before." She yanked at my belt to unbuckle it and deftly unzipped my fly. My pants fell in a bunch around my ankles like drapery at a statue unveiling. Lisa giggled. "Let me take that back. I've not seen boxers with little tommy guns and the slogan 'hot shot' stenciled on them before."

"A gift from a satisfied client."

"I'll bet. Now let's see what you're packing," she said. And when I rushed my hands to my groin, she added, "in the medicine cabinet, hot shot. In the medicine cabinet."

She pulled open the mirrored door and ducked her head behind it to rummage inside. "You're better equipped than I expected."

"I beg your pardon."

"We'll take some of this and a few of these." She set a tube of anti-bacterial ointment on the wash basin, followed by a box of butterfly closures. "And one or two of these and whole lot of this." A box of sterile dressing pads and a roll of tape appeared next to the other items. "It's too bad you don't have any of that new liquid adhesive they make to close cuts. After stitches, that would be the next best option. Hello—what's this?" She reappeared from behind the medicine cabinet door with a strip of rubbers in her hand.

"Oh," I mumbled. "Those."

"Another gift from a satisfied client?"

"No, and I'm sure they're expired by now."

Lisa grinned and examined one of the packages carefully. "No, as a matter of fact, you're still under warranty. You're covered for another five years. And the even better news is, you're covered in the magnum size."

I looked down at my bare chest, my hairy legs and my pants in a bunch on the floor, and then back up to Lisa, who was almost vibrating with mirth. If Mr. Webster ever needed help with the definition of mortified, I had some good ideas. "Well, that's certainly a relief. I'll sleep sounder tonight knowing that—and knowing that you know it too, doc."

"Well, I'm not actually licensed yet. But I can still practice on you." She squeezed out some of the ointment and dabbed it carefully around the edges of the cut. Then she used a couple of the butterfly closures to pull the edges together and pressed a sterile pad on the top. She finished by anchoring everything with adhesive tape. Nothing she did hurt, and her movements were gentle and assured—almost like they were part of a ritualized ceremony. The whole thing had a sort of hypnotic, seductive effect on me and I let myself forget my circumstances. When her hand moved over my side as she pressed the tape against my skin, I realized too late that I was starting to get an erection—an erection that the thin cotton of the boxer shorts did very little to conceal.

Any hope I had that my condition had gone unnoticed was dashed when Lisa gave me a flirty, up from under the eyelashes look as she stepped back to admire her handiwork. "Golly, it looks like you're better already."

I nearly singed the hair on my legs pulling my pants back up. I fumbled with the zipper of my fly. "Yeah, a little too good."

"Hold on," she said. "I'm not finished." She went around to the front of the desk and cleared the few remaining items Bonacker hadn't knocked off and then bent to retrieve her yoga mat. She snapped it out over the desktop like she was spreading a picnic blanket. Then she patted the middle of it. "Hop up here."

I gripped the front of my trousers like an old lady gripping her purse handles. "Sure about that?"

Lisa weaved a sinuous path back around the desk, shucking off her warm-up as she came. She put a cool hand in the middle of my chest and shoved me toward the waiting yoga mat. I retreated until the back of my thighs hit the edge of the desk and then she took her hand away and reached up to peel her leotard all the way down to her waist. There wasn't anything underneath but skin.

I swallowed and let go of my pants once more. The belt buckle hit the floor with a loud clang. "I'll take that as a yes. Aren't we worried about reopening the wound?"

She slipped into my arms. "Don't worry, hot shot. Just leave the driving to me."

The last thing I remember thinking before I kissed her was that Gretchen had been right about the tinsel.

LOGIC BOMB

CHRIS DUCKWORTH SNORTED, BLOWING BUBBLES THROUGH HIS straw into his gourmet iced tea.

"You what?" he demanded.

We were sitting at the breakfast hutch of his Castro Street apartment. I had dropped by after capping my "date" with Lisa with a casual dinner at Cha Cha Cha's in the Haight. I repeated what I'd told him about our romantic encounter.

"Where'd you do it?"

"In the office. On the desk. With a yoga mat."

"Sounds like Clue—Ms. Scarlet in the bedroom with the lead pipe. The yoga mat was a nice touch, though. What were you trying to do? Get better traction?"

"I don't know. She put it down. I guess it did prevent us from slipping off."

"Innie or an outie?"

"What?"

"Her belly button. Was it an innie or an outie?"

I thought back to my desk's eye view of her stomach. "Now that you mention it, I guess it was an outie."

"I knew it. Further proof of my theory that outies have more fun."

"Let me guess. You're an outie?"

Chris nodded and took a delicate sip of the tea, not breaking eye contact with me. "It had to have been a breeder boy fantasy come true, August, but you don't seem very thrilled about it."

I ran my hand through my hair. "You're right. I ought to be. It was fantastic. Better than I could have imagined—"

"But?"

"It was awkward with Gretchen just outside the office. She was gone when we came out, but she left a note taped to the door."

"What it'd say?"

"Get a room."

Chris laughed. "She'll get over it. And it's not like she hasn't rubbed your nose in it with her boyfriend the pee-pee doctor."

"Nose rubbing and pee are a lousy combination, but I take the point. That's not the only thing, though. As high an opinion I have of my own worth, I can't help but feel that she's a little out of my league."

"Is that what's worrying you? Then let me set your mind at ease. Of course she's out of your league. I figure she's got some sort of father figure hang-up, but why not take advantage of the situation until she finds somebody better, works through it with counseling or gets bored?"

"This is exactly the sort of sensitive, thoughtful advice I've come to associate with you. It's no wonder that whole television series are constructed around the counsel of gay males."

Chris reached over to pat my wrist and pushed the glass of tea he had poured for me further under my face. "Drink some of this," he said. "It's oolong with a blend of ginseng, ginko and guarana—all of which are good for reducing sarcasm."

I took a pull on the straw and made a face. "Tastes like air freshener in a truck stop men's room. Did you say it's got guano in it?"

"I did not say guano. I said ginseng, ginko and *guarana*. It's also infused with raspberry quince."

"Raspberry quince. That would explain the air freshener. This isn't another of your focus group products, is it?"

"You got it."

Chris had been participating in a focus group put together by manufacturers targeting products for the trendy, well-to-do gay demographic. The last one I remembered was a horrible concoction called "Gay Fuel." I didn't have the courage to ask what the tea was named. I pushed it aside. "Can you just get me a Bud or something?"

Chris got up from the table, muttering, "Philistine," and came back with a high-end lager with gold tinfoil on the neck. He plunked it in front of me and sat down. "I would get you a glass, but I figure you'd rather shake it up and speed chug it from the bottle."

"Thanks. This is fine."

"Well, while you've been making a pathetic, transparent attempt to fend off your mid-life crisis by having sex with beauty queens twenty years your junior, I've been working on the case."

"I'm going to suppress the urge to say anything about sex with queens, so go ahead—tell me what you've got."

"I've got proof that the election was tampered with."

"Proof? What kind of proof?"

Chris frowned as he stirred the cubes in his ice tea. "I guess proof is not exactly the right word, but I found out that the Columbia Voting Technologies people believe something *was* fishy with the election."

"Then you *did* get the job with them."

"Yes, and that in itself is interesting. They hired me after a one-hour interview. It was clear they were very eager to beef up their staff of quality assurance engineers quickly."

"And what are they in such a hurry to do with their new quality assurance staff?"

Chris straightened the already squared stack of floral-patterned jute placemats on the table. "That's the interesting bit. They are very worried about the upcoming runoff election. They didn't say it in so many words, but they don't think the software used in the precinct machines and in the central system is working properly. They've been testing like madmen to see if votes are being recorded correctly at the precincts, and if the central system is correctly tallying them off the USB drives taken from the precinct machines. I think they are also worried that the code on the city's machines is somehow different than the certified versions the company installed originally."

"How do you figure that?"

"For one, they've brought back several of the city's machines to test at the company lab. For another, I saw my manager trying to compare the file sizes of supposedly identical copies of a program taken from the master distribution and one of the city's machines."

"Were they different?"

"As near as I could tell from looking over his shoulder, they weren't. But there are more sophisticated ways to determine if files have been tampered with than just comparing their size. You can check the MD5—an algorithm that creates a sort of digital fingerprint for files—to see if there had been a more subtle alteration that kept the size the same but changed the instructions inside the program. He shooed me away before I saw him doing anything like that."

I took a long pull from my beer and then picked at the gold foil. "So where does that leave us? We know CVT thinks there's something wrong with their touch-screen voting technology. Do we know where they think the problem was introduced? At the factory? At the precincts? Or at the elections office?"

Chris shrugged. "I suspect they're clueless. As I said, they had us checking the city's machines, which would indicate tampering outside their purview. But they also had us testing the software from the certified master. That would indicate either a bug they introduced by negligence or malicious changes a developer on the payroll introduced on purpose."

"Wait a minute. A bug? You mean erroneous election results could have been caused by a mistake in programming?"

"Sure. It's something we've got to consider. I don't know how the murder of the elections director would fit into that scenario, though."

"I suppose someone at the company could have killed the director if the director discovered the software was flawed. The stakes are very high. If it got out that CVT had screwed up the city election, it would probably bankrupt the company."

Chris nodded and drank some of his quince infusion. "Good thinking. I guess you *are* more than just a yoga mat Gaucho."

"Right. So here's an obvious question—have you found anything wrong with the software?"

"Nope. And it's driving them nuts because the election is coming fast. They've barely got enough time to load the new slate of candidates onto the city's machines, much less diagnose and correct the problem—if it exists."

"Could this guy that I shot—Geiberger, the chief engineer—have sabotaged the software before he left? Or even tampered with it later on the precinct machines or the central system?"

"Any of that is possible. Rather than tampering with it later, inserting a piece of code into the original software to let him change the election outcome would be more likely. They call malicious functions that go off when certain conditions are met 'logic bombs.' Geiberger could have put a logic bomb in the code before he quit, and then activated it later as part of his revenge against the company."

I picked some more at the tinfoil on the beer bottle and then rolled what I harvested into a little ball that I flicked across the table. Chris frowned and snatched it up. "But wouldn't that be fairly easy to detect if you suspected it?" I asked. "Couldn't you just look through the source code, or whatever it's called, and find it?"

"You could. If it's done in a straightforward way. He might have covered his tracks."

"But now that Geiberger's dead, there wouldn't be anyone to use this logic bomb in the runoff election. If he is the one who introduced the problem in the first election, it can't be a factor in the second."

Chris got up from the table to special deliver my little tinfoil ball to the kitchen waste basket. "Not if he had a partner," he sang out.

ONLY A DAMN CATERPILLAR

I LEFT CHRIS' PLACE MUCH LATER THAN I intended. I helped him reposition the satellite dish on his balcony ("I can never get the premium channels when it's windy"), rearrange the furniture in his living room ("The ottoman may be one of the most versatile pieces of accent furniture on the market") and further reduce the inventory of his overpriced beer ("Drink more, August; I've been stuck with this stuff since those tacky boys down the hall brought it over for my Oscars party").

Since it was late enough for Red, the ATM thief, to be active, I decided to detour on my way home past some of the bank branches I had on my list to see if I might get lucky. I spent an hour camped out by a Wells Fargo branch in the Castro, gave that up as a bad job, and then put in another forty-five minutes shivering by a credit union near the Panhandle of Golden Gate Park. The cold, the pain from the cut in my side and the after-effects of drinking Chris' beer diminished my enthusiasm for the job, and after making a pit stop at a twenty-four hour gas station on Oak, I determined a nearby Bank of America branch would be my last stop.

It was just a little after two thirty when I pulled up at a red light on Divisidero at the intersection with Geary. There were no other cars stopped in either direction, and the traffic on Geary consisted of a groaning diesel bus and a guy on a bicycle riding by with no hands, singing "I am the Captain of the Pinafore" at the top of his lungs.

The moon was full and it hung low in the sky with a plume of genie-from-the-bottle fog seeming to wrap it like a boa. I looked from the moon to a fenced construction site across the street. It was next to an office tower and I decided the site was destined to be a parking structure since my B of A branch was in an identical tower cum parking facility on the opposite corner. I was musing over my experience with Lisa—and thinking that maybe Chris was right about not looking a gift horse in the mouth—when the chain-link fence erupted and a big yellow backhoe blew through it like a sneeze through one-ply.

The backhoe Evel Knieveled off the sidewalk, bounded over the island in the middle of Divisidero—gouging asphalt and raising sparks as the loader bucket bottomed out—and hopped the curb in front of the other office tower. The light at the intersection had long since changed, so I floored the gas pedal, rumbled across Geary to the accompanying clatter of the Galaxie's worn tappets and then muscled the car into the first driveway I came to after the branch.

I jumped out of the car and ran back to the bank. The backhoe was already at work uprooting an ATM situated between two columns in a concrete arcade in front of the building. There was no question it was the same guy at the controls. He had the same badly-trimmed goatee, the same cheap plastic glasses and the same monstrous physique. They say history doesn't really repeat itself, but sometimes it does stutter: once again I had no gun to threaten him with, my only permitted weapon having been seized as evidence by the South San Francisco police. I had learned something from the previous encounter, though. I learned that it was worse than useless to call attention to myself until I found an alternative weapon. As Red brought the loader bucket to the base of the ATM and gunned the motor, I ducked behind a trash receptacle to contemplate my options.

I looked up the street to the Galaxie and considered the idea of driving it back to ram the backhoe. It was a heavy car, but I didn't think it would be a match for the low-geared torque of the tractor. What was worse, Red had maneuvered the backhoe to come at the

ATM from behind, leaving the columns it sat between as obstacles for me to get around or through. I didn't like my chances with the lumbering Galaxie, especially after having to first plow through the low strip of sculpted shrubbery that ringed the building

I twisted back to look at the construction site. It was basically a big hole surrounded by stacks of construction materials, a tanker truck and some miscellaneous tractors, including another backhoe. The idea of going mano-a-mano with Red in a backhoe was appealing—especially after the crack in the paper about bringing rocks to a tractor fight—but I doubted I could get it hot-wired in time, and I knew an experienced operator like Red would be able to drive circles around me. I let my glance follow the length of the trampled fence to the corner of the lot, and there I saw it: a fire hydrant. A brass fixture with gauges was attached to it, and attached to the fixture was a coil of hose. I figured the hydrant was being used to fill the pumper truck and the fixture was the city's way of determining how much water the construction company was using.

I sprinted across the road to the hydrant. I was worried I wouldn't be able to open it, but there was a large and obvious monkey wrench clamped over a valve next to a gauge. I pushed the handle of the wrench forward slightly and the coiled hose expanded like a snake getting an enema. I yanked it closed. I'd seen how many firemen it took to haul a charged hose and I didn't want to try it solo. I sorted through the hose until I located the steel nozzle—which fortunately had its own shutoff valve—grabbed it, and then dragged it and the hose across the street to the trash receptacle, where I set it down.

I poked my head around the receptacle to assess Red's progress. He had the ATM bent at a thirty-degree angle, but there were a few stubborn bolts clinging to the base that prevented him from carrying it off entirely.

I jumped up for the dash back to the waiting monkey wrench. I confess I laughed out loud as I flung it wide open and saw the water surge through the hose. The anticipation of it carried me back across the street, grinning and chuckling to myself as I ran. When I got there, I found Red had bent the ATM all the way over, but one or two tortured bolts were still holding. He was fully absorbed in his task, cursing as he repeatedly rammed the base with the loader blade.

I bent to pick up the hose. It was like picking up a living thing. I dropped to one knee and still almost slipped in the puddle of water that had formed from the dripping nozzle. I steadied myself next to the trash receptacle, cradled the nozzle in my left hand and then grabbed its black rubber shutoff valve in my right. I waited until Red had the backhoe lined up for another run at the ATM, then called out, "The name is *August*."

He just had time to glance up from the controls, register a sort of crazed realization—and then I let him have it.

The force of the water rocked me back, but that was nothing compared to what it did to Red. He was plastered into his seat with his hands held out like a silent movie actress cowering in front of a villain. His hard hat flew off, his glasses flew off and his shirt rolled up to expose a pale roll of fat around his middle. I kept the water going until the tractor ran aground of its own accord and he was left huddled in a protective ball like a flushed spider circling the drain.

For a moment there was an eerie silence and then he snorted and hacked and coughed up at least a lungful of water. He uncurled and ran his hand down his face to stare at me, bleary-eyed. "Man," he croaked. "I could have drowned. Where's your sense of fair play?"

"You're soaking in it."

He made as if to shake his head at my unreasonableness, then flashed a grin and reached quickly for the controls of the tractor. I snapped the water again, but the loader bucket came up to block the stream. I heard the engine noise rise over the sound of the water pummeling the bucket. The backhoe advanced towards me—crawling over the ATM, mashing down the strip of shrubbery—until it was almost on top of me and the water sluicing out of the bucket was a white curtain over my head.

I sidestepped to the right, both to get out of harm's way and to flank the bucket, but dragging the hose felt like dragging an iron tail. I had barely crabwalked out of the backhoe's path when it came crashing down on the trash receptacle, knocking it into the street and disgorging soda cans everywhere. Red saw me lining up to go at him from the side and brought the steering wheel hard over in my direction.

Then suddenly it didn't matter. The water cut off and I flopped to the ground, overbalanced from leaning into the force of the stream. I heard someone yell, "Hurry up, Red," and the backhoe accelerated past me, out into the street.

When I got to my feet I found a large truck parked in the middle of Divisidero with its front tire sitting on top of the hose, cutting the flow of water. Red had pulled up next to passenger side and was scrambling out of the backhoe to hurry into the open cab of the truck. He paused with one foot on the stepwell and turned to look back at me. "Another tie, *Auggie*," he yelled. "It's now 1-0-2, my favor." He waved, flopped into the seat and the truck accelerated away before he had even pulled the door closed.

I squinted at the receding bumper for a license number, but of course they had removed the plates. I trudged back to the hydrant to shut off the valve and was busy wringing out my suit jacket when McQuaid and his partner Jerry pulled up. Jerry jumped from the patrol car to take in the scene, but McQuaid simply rolled down the window, said, "Hiya, August," and reached for his radio.

"Shit," said Jerry when he came back from his reconnaissance. "It's only a damn Caterpillar. It doesn't even have the high capacity rear bucket."

"You're right," I said grinning, still somehow buoyed by the whole experience. "A John Deere would have done a lot more damage, wouldn't it?"

MR. SLOPPY'S

THIS WAS ON THE DISPLAY OF MY cell phone the next morning when I picked it off the nightstand:

> Auggie,
>
> U shld have followed me to the Wells Fargo @ 4th + Brannan. 2-0-2 mine.
>
> ur pal,
>
> Red

I called Gretchen at the office and asked her if she'd given my number to anyone recently.

"I'm not talking to you," she fired back.

"I understand. But if you were talking to me, what would the answer be?"

A deep sigh came over the line and I could almost see her rolling her eyes. "The answer would be yes. Some guy with a rumbly voice called up early this morning and asked for it. He said he wanted to talk to you about a hose job."

"Cute. And if he has my number does that mean he can send me e-mail?"

"Not e-mail, a text message. And yes, he can. The plan I signed you up for includes unlimited messaging."

"How thoughtful."

"I figured I could use it to send you messages when I didn't want to talk to you. Like now." The crack from the receiver going down was louder than a stripper slamming acrylic heels together.

After rubbing my ear to restore at least partial hearing, I called a buddy of mine who had access to a reverse phone directory. I gave him the number Red had sent the message from and asked him to run it.

"Sorry, August," he said after treating me to five minutes of the Muzak version of "Solitary Man." "It's one of those prepaid deals. Whoever's using it forked over seventy-five bucks in cash for the phone and air time and didn't supply any personal details. You can't trace it."

I tried calling the number anyway, but nobody picked up and there wasn't any voicemail.

I got showered and dressed, woke the Galaxie from a fitful slumber and then hauled myself over to a bicycle messenger service in the glittering "overdue for urban renewal" area known as Polk Gulch. I was carrying an envelope addressed to Kathleen Willmott with one of Salaiz's DVDs inside. The note accompanying the DVD told her to call me or the video of her and Ralph Wood sitting together oh-so-cozily in the back seat of a limo after sending a goon to attack me was going to be on this evening's TV news. I also took the liberty of enclosing a flyer a homeless person had handed me while I was waiting for the service to open. It read in part:

> DON'T KEEP YOUR FAITH
> SELFISHLY TO YOURSELF.
> MAIL THIS TO ALL YOUR
> FRIENDS. THIS PAPER
> MAY BE REPRINTED AND
> DISTRIBUTED.

But instead of being a religious screed like I expected, it was essentially a compendium of bad, over-the-top jokes and puns.

If the tenor of the homeless literature could be described as tasteless and campy, at least it fit in with the rest of the neighborhood. The business next to the messenger service promoted itself as a "Tranny Costume and Shoe Emporium," and featured a window display with a female mannequin dressed in a red, white and blue bikini with cotton leggings in equally patriotic colors. She stood in front of a charcoal grill with a pair of tongs holding what appeared to be—at first glance, anyway—a hot dog. There were other, similar hot dog-shaped items strewn across the grill. On closer inspection, however, it became clear the items on the grill were anatomically correct dildos painted bright red, and the wiener she gripped in the tongs was actually a red-colored vibrator. I guess Freud's line about cigars does not apply to frankfurters.

At 10:09 the door to the messenger service was opened by a grumpy-looking Latina. She was wearing a plastic daisy barrette with two petals missing clipped in her frizzy, henna-colored hair at an angle that suggested she'd done it with one hand while riding a bicycle. I paid to have the envelope messengered to Willmott at the Green Party campaign headquarters in the Mission and then walked three doors down to a diner with the enticing name of Mr. Sloppy's.

Although it was open for breakfast, the diner served nothing but burgers, fries and chili (but thankfully no hot dogs). I ordered and paid for a chili-cheeseburger and coffee from the stubbled counterman who was hiding a quart bottle of beer in a sack behind the register, and took a seat at the Formica counter that ran along the circumference of the restaurant. I tallied three dead flies and a twitching moth on life support beside the window track before I gave up counting and slid the bleary, grease-coated glass open to get a clearer view outside. I hadn't picked the diner, the messenger service—or the neighborhood as a whole, for that matter—because of the efficient service or salubrious environment. I'd picked it because the headquarters of Feral Collective was across the street.

There were no signs of life in the storefront across the way, but with the yellowing newspapers still taped across the windows, anything short of a three-alarm fire would have been hard to detect. While I hadn't given Feral Collective much face time on my earlier visit, this time I was resolved to stake it out until something popped. It was three days and counting until the election, and apart from Chris' news about the concerns at CVT, I still didn't have anything solid to go on.

I sipped at my coffee and watched as a couple of tourists pulled up in a three-wheeled, open-topped vehicle that looked like the sterile offspring of a golf cart and a motorcycle. I recognized it as a GPS-guided, talking "FriscoCar" available for rent at Fisherman's Wharf. The idea was to take it for a tour of the city's biggest attractions—Lombard Street, Golden Gate Park, etc.—but this couple had definitely made a wrong turn somewhere. The FriscoCar agreed. "You have left the tour," it said in a nearly accusatory tone. "Some parts of San Francisco are not safe for tourists. Turn right in .3 miles."

I was tempted to add a shouted, "Better do what it says!" through the window, but the counterman came up with my order. He slid it off his oven mitt like he was dropping off a laboratory specimen.

"Plate is hot," he said. "Self-serve condiment bar behind you."

I stared down at the mountain of chili, grated cheddar cheese and diced onion piled atop the burger. "I think we've got it covered."

The burger was surprisingly good. I had a little trouble getting everything to stay in place between the two buns, but it was worth the effort—and the collateral damage to my tie. I was engaged in a mop-up operation with the last bit of the bun when I glanced across the road in time to see the door to Feral Collective swing open. The first person out was a waif of undetermined sex wearing a cowboy hat and combat fatigues. I guessed he or she couldn't decide whether to play army or cowboys and Indians. The next guy through had definitely made up his mind: he was a Canuck from the Great White North. He had on a muskrat fur hat with ear flaps and dangling tie strings, a red plaid wool shirt with leather elbow patches and a pair of billowy, green wool pants tucked into hiking boots.

Alan Chow had suggested Feral Collective as a group that possibly had the wherewithal to fix the election. If these two were a representative sample, I doubted Feral Collective could fix a bent paperclip.

I yanked my wallet out to leave a couple bucks for the counterman's beer fund, and hurried out the door, wiping my face on one of the diner's scratchy paper napkins as I went. Canuck and the soldier/cowperson were headed north up Polk, Canuck with a canvas duffle bag slung over his shoulder—no doubt to hold all the muskrat pelts he was going to ensnare—and the soldier/cowperson with hands shoved deep in fatigue pockets. I tailed them from a half block or so behind and it was easy work because they were walking quickly in their own little world, oblivious to anything on the street. It didn't take long to conclude the waifish one was a girl, based on the way she moved and the way Canuck kept skipping along beside her, blabbing and finding excuses to touch her.

We went on this way for about four blocks—passing head shops, vacuum cleaner repair services, cosmetology colleges and the other marginal businesses trying to gnaw a living off the carcass of Polk Street—until the couple reached Cedar Alley. Cedar Alley is a miserable two-block strip of pot-holed asphalt that dead-ends at Van Ness and Larkin. If not the armpit of the Polk Gulch area, it's certainly a fusty crook of folded belly fat. Of course they went down it. By the time I hustled up to the mouth of the alley, they had already stopped mid-block in front of a brick garage and Canuck was opening up his duffle bag to rummage inside it. Further down, a ring of homeless men drank fortified wine and talked in a dull buzz around a guy in a wheelchair, but paid no attention to Canuck and his friend.

A Frisbee, a carton of Camels, a sweatshirt and a monstrous pair of bolt cutters hit the ground beside the duffle bag before Canuck seemed to find what he wanted. He herded all the stuff back into the bag and then reached over to grasp the padlock on the garage door. He shoved a key into the bottom of it, twisted and the catch snapped open. After all the attention-grabbing behavior of unpacking and packing the bag, it was at this critical juncture that he decided to check if the coast was clear. He glanced furtively at the group at the end of the block—apparently found no cause for concern—then looked in the direction he had come. I ducked back behind the closest building, biting my lip to keep from laughing out loud.

I waited until I heard the door swing open and fall closed before I risked another look. The couple was gone, the door remained slightly ajar and the padlock hung open on the hasp. I sauntered down the alley, the conversation from the group at the end growing louder and clearer as I went. "I can show you scars from a horse that kicked me," said the guy in the wheelchair.

"Kicked you?" said a guy at his feet. "Shit, Tyler, the closest you been to a horse is the dog food you ate last night for dinner."

That earned a big round of laughs and a couple of clinked bottles—and continued to keep the group focused on things besides the doings in front of the garage.

The building was a three-story slag of bricks that had been whitewashed over at some point. Almost every square inch of the whitewash was now covered in graffiti, and the lattice windows on the first two stories were backed with plywood, their panes having been broken out and the letters for dirty words spray painted on the wood in the lattice pattern like a perverted crossword puzzle. The big double doors made it clear that the building had been used for parking or auto repair at some time in the past, but there was no sign with a business or owner's name. Given that the padlock looked to be a recent addition, I figured this had to be one of Feral Collective's squat jobs.

I pulled the door open slowly. It opened on a dim, cavernous room with a pitted concrete floor where dust competed with grease for bragging rights on the most square footage covered. A smashed wooden pallet and a couple of oddly shaped mounds of junk covered with canvas were the only things filling the space, and the cracked plaster walls were blank with the exception of a stenciled sign that trumpeted an hourly rate of twenty-five bucks for repairs, some half-hearted attempts at graffiti with a dripping spray can and streaking yellow stains that started about waist high and ran to the ground. A narrow concrete staircase ran up to a hole cut in the second floor, a harsh light from the opening projecting a rippled trapezoid pattern down the steps at the top.

"Where do I sleep?" said a female voice. It came from the second floor and had to belong to the waifish girl.

"There's a futon in the other room," answered Canuck. "You can sleep there."

I crept to the staircase and began going up the steps, pressing close to the wall so I would be harder to spot from above.

"Is there running water? How do I cook food?"

"There's a grill you can cook on, but no running water. It's easier to steal power than it is to get the water turned on. But there's a great unsecured wireless Internet signal from the building next door. You can surf all you like."

"You know that I don't have a computer, Roadrunner."

"You don't need one. We've got our squat server running here. The load is pretty light, so you're welcome to use it."

It appeared I was going to have to adjust to thinking of Canuck as a Roadrunner, but he didn't *look* like a Roadrunner—not even a Canadian one. I continued up the stairs to the point where the trapezoid of light fell across the steps, and then hung back in the shadows. There didn't seem to be much percentage in confronting them yet.

"That's dandy," said the girl. "But how do I go to the bathroom and stuff like that."

Roadrunner gave a sort of embarrassed giggle. "Manny will let you use the bathroom at Mr. Sloppy's."

"What if I want to take a shower? And don't tell me to do a sink bath with hand soap and paper towels at Mr. Sloppy's. The doctor said I still have to be careful with washing."

"You can come visit me. I'll let you use the shower."

"What's *that* going to cost me?"

"Hey, barter is the best form of economic interchange. There's no regulation by the state, no monopolies and no artificial pressure on prices. It encourages people to reflect on the real value of goods and services for their own needs and trade accordingly."

"From each according to his abilities; to each according to his needs?"

"No, that's Marxism. Anarchists believe—"

"Don't go into that spiel again. All I know is your needs seem to include an awful lot of blow jobs."

"Please, Casia, this is serious stuff. If you're going to stay here, you need to make a real attempt to understand anarchist philosophy." There was a muffled plopping noise like a duffle bag hitting the floor. "Kropotkin's *Conquest of Bread* is a good place to start. In chapter six, he anticipates the rise of squatting and talks about the importance of gathering and sharing information on vacant property. Here, you can borrow my copy. Just don't move the bookmarks."

"I can hardly wait."

I decided I'd better jump in before Roadrunner pulled Voronova's *Victory over Veal* out of his bag. I flashed up the last three steps, coming to rest in what must have originally been a reception area for a group of offices. Roadrunner and Casia were standing in the center of the space under a bare light bulb with Roadrunner's duffle bag between them. He was handing a leather bound volume to her.

"Who are you?" she asked in a tone that seemed to convey relief at the distraction rather than curiosity or worry.

"The owner of this building."

Roadrunner snapped his head over to look at me, the tie strings from his fur cap swinging wildly as he turned. "You are not. The owner is in Minneapolis in a nursing home."

"Correction. The former owner is in Minneapolis in an urn. I'm the heir."

Roadrunner's jaw sagged open, then he seemed to catch himself and he gave me a squinty look. "I don't believe you. You could be anybody off the street."

"Maybe. But you *are* anybody off the street. I'll make you a deal. Answer a few questions and I'll let it slide. I don't have any immediate plans for the property."

"Property is theft. And you can shove your questions up your ass."

"Good of you to concede ownership of my ass."

Roadrunner didn't bother responding. He reached down to snatch the duffle bag and bolted for a door behind him. He slithered through, pushed the door closed and jammed the lock in place from the other side.

I looked over to Casia, who smirked back at me. She pushed the brim of her cowboy hat up with a finger and said, "Man, you got a way with people."

"I also have a way with doors," I said, and strode up to the one Roadrunner had exited through. I twisted the knob and pushed hard, but the bolt held firm. I heard the sound of furniture being moved and then a window going up on the other side. That didn't leave much time. I took a step back and kicked at the jam with everything I had. The first kick punched the door open about an inch, and I could see a splinter of fresh wood along the frame. I kicked it again and the door flew open and bounced off the interior wall.

I just caught the top of Roadrunner's fur cap as he disappeared from view below the window frame. I ran over to the window, but he'd already navigated the ladder-like stairs on the fire escape and dropped to the sidewalk on Post, the street behind the building. He took off at a sprint, clutching his duffle bag and what looked like a laptop computer. Given the speed he was running, I could finally understand the nickname Roadrunner—and appreciate a little how the coyote felt.

I turned back from the window and looked around the room. Judging from the location of a power strip, the computer must have been set up on a folding metal table in the center. Next to that was a lawn chair, and next to that was a propane barbecue grill with the words "Not to be used indoors" printed in large white letters on the cover.

Casia came in from the reception area, sweeping off her cowboy hat and leaning her willowy torso into the doorframe like James Dean on the set of *Giant*. Beneath her open fatigue shirt she had on a purple beater with no bra. With the exception of a length of dark brown mane that grew from her forehead, across the top of her head and past her collar, her hair was buzz cut to about an inch of its life and dyed the color of a Golden Retriever's fur. Her nose was pierced and when she grinned at me I saw the glint of a silver stud in her tongue. I said, "I take it you don't have a place to live."

"That's right. Roadrunner was going to put me up, but that doesn't seem like it's going to work out now. Why? You got a better offer?"

"Possibly. If you can help me out. How do you know Roadrunner?"

"We got together at a *Ciudad Verde* rally yesterday and kind of made a night of it."

I perked up at the mention of *Ciudad Verde* and rallies. "A rally in the Mission for low income housing?"

"That's right."

"Are you a *Ciudad Verde* member?"

"Naw. I'm not an anarchist either. I got into town from Reno a week ago."

"Did Roadrunner talk about the mayoral election and *Ciudad Verde's* role in it?"

She leaned away from the doorframe, cocked her hips at an insolent angle and tucked her thumbs under the waistband of her pants. "Not really. Roadrunner said a voting anarchist is an oxymoron."

"Do you have any idea why he would have run away like he did?"

She smiled, and looking past the crazy haircut, the body piercings and the overtly seductive moves, I flashed on a shy little girl selling Girl Scout cookies in a shopping mall in Reno. "Well," she said, "for one, you look an awful lot like a cop, man. For two, you said you inherited the building, which I kind of doubt since Roadrunner said the owner was an old Vietnamese lady. And for three, he didn't want you to get hold of the squat server."

"That's the laptop he took."

"Yeah. It's running a Web site with a database of vacant properties for people to squat."

"Connected to the Internet via a stolen wireless signal from the building next door."

"Bingo."

I sighed and brought a hand up to scratch the stubble under my chin.

She stepped close and put the cowboy hat on my head at a crazy angle. It was about three sizes too small. "I'm not doing very well for you, am I? How'd you like to see my barracuda tattoo? I can make it wiggle like it's swimming."

She started to pull out her t-shirt, but I took hold of her hand to stop her. "Don't. I've got big issues with tattoos."

She laughed nervously. "You really are square. Let's just put our cards on the table. How about a BJ to let me crash at your place for a couple of nights?" When I didn't respond right away, she added jokingly, "I just hope you taste better than Roadrunner. That guy needs to get some fruit and vegetables in his diet."

I took the cowboy hat off and put it back on her head. "I'm very flattered, Casia, but I don't think you should stay with me. Did I hear you say something about a doctor to Roadrunner?"

She whipped off her hat again and turned the left side of her head towards me. "That's right. I'm a bionic woman. I've got titanium in my skull."

I peered into her close-cropped hair and saw a three-inch line of pink scar tissue above her left ear. "Why titanium?"

"Titanium clips, actually. Part of the cure for epilepsy. I had something called an angioma that was causing me seizures. They cut a hole in my head to take it out and I haven't had a problem since. Except for the fact I had to sneak out of the hospital when my stepdad and his drunk buddy tried to pull a train on me."

"Jesus Christ. How long ago was this?"

"Over a month."

I touched the back of my own head. I couldn't believe she was living on the street a month after having brain surgery. "Look, Casia, I'll give you a couple hundred bucks to crash in a hotel for a few nights. Just be sure you don't spend it on something else."

"Really?"

"Really." I extracted my wallet and dug out four fifties. When I looked back up at her, her eyes were rimmed with moisture. I passed the money over and she smiled awkwardly. "Try the Park View in South Park," I said. "It's best."

"Thanks, man," she said. "I couldn't do another night in a doorway." Then, after a beat, "Say, do you smell cheeseburgers?"

I was working on a response with some kind of plausible deniability when Casia stepped over to the barbecue and lifted the lid. Inside, there were long, flaky ashes like you get when you burn paper—and two charred but largely unburnt rolls of the kind of narrow, glossy paper that is used to print receipts at ATM machines and gas pumps. I picked out the least damaged of the rolls. Four signature lines had been printed near the end with the words "Precinct Judges" written beneath each. Handwritten signatures filled the lines.

Hungrily, I yanked at the end of the paper to unspool it further. The names of candidates and the numbers of propositions from the last election were printed in a continuous stream like miniature ballots as far as I went. I'd never seen the paper audit trail from an electronic voting machine, but I had to believe it looked an awful lot like this.

"What is it?" asked Casia.

"Proof that anarchists do vote—even if it's for other people."

She smiled and punched me in the arm. "That's cool—I guess. How about buying me a chili-cheeseburger at Mr. Sloppy's to celebrate. I keep smelling them and now I've got a craving."

"Sure," I said. "If you want. Never go near 'em myself."

DIAL D FOR DUCKWORTH

"H ELLO SHITHEAD," WAS THE FIRST THING I heard after fumbling open my cell phone from the comfort of my Galaxie 500. I had hiked back to where it was parked after getting a surprise hug goodbye from the suddenly sentimental Casia.

"Mom?" I said into the phone. "How'd you get this number?"

"I'm not your goddamned mother. I'd have sold you to the circus if I was. It's Kathleen Willmott."

I swung my feet onto the bench seat of the Galaxie and leaned back against the driver's side door. "Got my package, did you?"

"No, I thought I'd call to chat you up. Of course I got your package. I'm not going to let you ruin this campaign by passing that DVD on to the media."

"Maybe you should have thought of that before you sent Diego to attack me from behind. I can just see the lead now: 'Green Party campaign manager Kathleen Willmott caught on video—'"

A sound that was almost a snarl came over the line. "I did not send Diego to attack you. The fact that I was in the car doesn't mean I sent him over. You took two unrelated events and made them seem like they were connected. And don't think I don't know where you got the video. You wouldn't have bupkis if that pedophile priest hadn't hung his little DV camera out the window to film the whole thing in glorious pornovision—just like he does with the choirboys."

"Golly, Ms. Willmott, for someone who feels her actions have been misconstrued, you sure are quick to jump on the pedophile bandwagon with the padre."

"Can it, Riordan. What do you want?"

"I want to meet with you to talk about election fraud. And I want some straight answers."

"Be at Padilla campaign headquarters in an hour. Corner of 13th and Mission."

I started to ask how she'd enjoyed the homeless flyer I'd stuffed in the envelope with the video, but the line clicked off before I got the opportunity.

I rummaged through my jacket pockets to extract the two rolls of paper I'd salvaged from the barbecue at the garage. I unspooled a portion of each in turn and took a closer look at the information printed on them. In my small sample, the votes cast for mayor were spread pretty evenly, but it seemed as if Chow had garnered the most. I rewound the rolls and took a closer look at the signatures of the precinct judges. There was a Zhou, a Li, a Hou and one lonely guy named Schlomo Rabinowitz. The odds were three to one that the audit trails had come from a Chinatown precinct, but I figured I knew one person who could tell me for sure.

I opened up the phone again and kept pressing buttons until the directory of names and numbers Gretchen had preloaded for me appeared on the display. I dialed D for Duckworth and selected his mobile number.

"I can't believe it," he said when he picked up. "August Riordan called me from a cell phone. The next thing you know, monkeys will be text messaging."

"I'm already one up on the monkeys. I got my first message this morning. How'd you know it was me?"

"Gretchen text messaged your number when she got the phone for you."

"Okay, drop it with the messaging already. I got a question for you. What can you tell me about paper audit trails and the CVT voting machines?"

Chris gave a satisfied chuckle. "You name it. I've read the manual front to back. What do you want to know?"

"Well, for starters, what do they look like and what happens to them after the voting's over?"

"Hold on a sec," said Chris in a quieter voice. "I better go into a conference room." I heard the sea-in-a-seashell sound of someone muffling a cell phone and then a door opening and closing. "Okay, I'm back. I didn't want my co-workers listening to me spout off about the machines. There's been some developments here and everyone's getting very paranoid."

"What kind of developments?"

"First things first. You asked what the audit trails looked like. They're printed on rolls of thermal paper about three or four inches across. There's a window on the machines that lets you see the print-out of your votes before you confirm your ballot. Once you do that, the machine advances the paper into a take-up spool so that the next person who uses the machine doesn't see how you voted."

"And what happens to them when the precinct closes?"

"They run the shutdown procedure on each of the machines and it advances the paper some more and prints signature lines for the precinct judges. Then they open the machine to remove the take-up spool, the judges sign the roll to certify that no hanky-panky went on and they put it in a special bag that is taken to election headquarters along with the USB drives that have the electronic record of the votes from each machine."

I gave my lower lip a good chewing while I thought that over. "So the idea is that if the electronic vote is somehow compromised or disputed, they can go back to all the paper rolls and recount the votes by hand."

"That's the theory, but it'd be a gigantic pain in the ass if they had to recount all the votes that way. The printing's hard to read—it begins fading almost immediately because of the thermal paper—and when people change their mind about a vote before they confirm their ballot, the original vote is marked cancelled and another copy is printed, which makes it all the harder to tally. The bottom line is they'd never use the rolls to do a full recount. They might use them for spot checks if they had some other reason to be suspicious."

"What if you did find a way to hack the electronic vote. Wouldn't you have to fake the audit trail to cover your tracks?"

"Ideally. But like I said, it'd be very impractical to actually use them for a recount. My guess is if you were careful not to raise any suspicions, you could leave the original rolls alone and no one would ever bother looking at them."

"But if you were being thorough, you'd print phony audit trails to match your phony electronic results and replace the originals. Then you would—"

"Yeah, yeah. Destroy the originals. I just don't think it would be worth the trouble."

"Well, somebody may have. I've got two charred rolls showing votes that seem to total in Chow's favor."

Chris whistled. "Maybe I'm not the only one doing work in this partnership after all."

"It's not a partnership. Think of yourself as an unpaid intern."

"You got the unpaid part right. What's the number printed under the judges' signature lines?"

"3338, then there's a dash, then 05."

"3338 is the precinct number. It's from District 3—Chinatown. All of the precinct numbers there start with three. I made a point of checking that when I started. The 05 is the number of the particular machine at the precinct."

I put both of the rolls on the Galaxie dashboard and leaned back to admire them. They looked like the tape from an old adding machine. It was hard to believe the sanctity of the election depended on such a primitive audit mechanism. "Good," I said finally. "At least I can give the Dragon Lady news of some real progress. But you said you had developments at your end."

"Yes, I hate to one-up you, but they've determined somebody put a logic bomb in the voting machine software."

"How's it work?"

"I don't know. I'm not even supposed to know they found a problem, but I managed to sniff some instant message traffic and I saw my boss talking about it to the CEO, Dosher."

"First with the text messaging and now with the instant messages. I'm not even going to ask. Do they know who did it?"

"Not really. But the name Geiberger came up." There was a pause and then I heard the door being opened again. "I'll be out in a minute," said Chris to someone outside. The door closed and then he came back on to speak in a harried whisper. "They're having a meeting here. I've got to go."

"Okay, but find Geiberger's address for me."

"Talk about intern abuse," he said, and hung up.

IT ISN'T EASY BEING GREEN

THE GUY ON THE RECEPTION DESK AT Padilla election headquarters had his nose buried in *The Big Book of Science Fiction*.
He was wearing a t-shirt with "I Gave My Word to Stop at Third:
1987 Teen Abstinence Day" printed across his chest. My guess was
he'd been thrown out at first more times than not. I identified myself and asked to speak to Kathleen Willmott.

"A Mr. Riordan to see her bitchiness—check." He picked up
the phone, did a phony double take and brought a hand up to cover
his mouth and a soul patch that looked like a flattened spider glued
to his chin. "Oops, did I just use my out-loud voice?" He dialed a
four-digit extension, said that I was here and nodded several times
while the person at the other end of the line talked for what seemed
like an improbably long time. He hung up without saying anything
in response. "Kathleen and Kaleb are in the corner conference room.
You're to meet them there. But don't touch anything, don't talk to
anyone and don't breathe any of our air if you can avoid it."

"Got it," I said, but I was talking to the book jacket.

Willmott and her brother, who apparently was named Kaleb,
were sitting in folding chairs at the far end of a folding plastic table
when I stepped into the room. She still had her beret and he still
had his skirt. Neither of them stood.

Most of the remaining floor space was taken by boxes of campaign materials and what looked to be an envelope-stuffing assembly line with piles of flyers, printed address labels and a postage machine laid out in sequence. The walls were covered by campaign posters, scuff marks and the odd thumb tack, and there was a cinder block bookshelf along the side wall with a fish tank on top. Lettering on an index card taped beneath the tank read: "Goldie Prawn, Green Party mascot." Goldie floated contentedly above a ruined castle and a chest of treasure leaking air bubbles.

I stopped at the head of the table, basking in the concentrated glares of the Willmott family. "Nice fish," I said.

"You got thirty minutes, Riordan," said Willmott. "If you want to talk about fish that's your business."

I pulled out one of the flimsy chairs and sat down in it. "Okay, why did you send Diego to attack me from behind?"

"I told you we didn't."

"Are you saying it was his own idea?"

"On a scale of yes or no, no."

"Well, who's was it?"

Willmott looked over at her brother, who responded by biting his lip. She turned back to me. "Ralph Wood."

"The developer? Does Diego work for him?"

"Yes."

"But I saw Diego guarding the door at the New College rally. What's he got to do with the campaign?"

Willmott pushed back against her chair, provoking a loud creaking noise. "He's a volunteer."

"A volunteer who takes orders from somebody else."

Willmott started to answer, but thought better of it: not so Kaleb. "You don't know the first thing about campaigns," he said. "It's common practice for staffers to be paid by people or businesses who support the candidate."

"You mean special interests. I thought the Green Party was different. I thought they didn't follow common practice. Now I hear you've got a real estate developer calling the shots."

"Ralph Wood isn't a special interest," said Willmott. "He's working for the people building low-income housing. He's one of the few who's really fighting gentrification in the Mission."

"What's the story on Diego, then? How did he get hooked up with Wood?"

"He was hired on at one of Wood's construction jobs," said Kaleb. "One day he broke up a fight between five guys using a two-by-four, and Wood took notice. Now he works as Wood's personal body guard—when he's not helping out on the campaign."

"Sounds more like a personal thug to me."

Willmott leaned onto the table, folding her hands in front of her with exaggerated care, as if she was just barely keeping herself under control. "What do you want, Riordan? We know you work for Leonora Lee."

"I want to find out who fixed the election."

"Nobody fixed the election. You and Lee are trying to throw dust in everyone's eyes. Her candidate never had a chance of winning, but the thought of Padilla in office is making her so crazy that she'll do anything to derail his campaign."

I fished one of the paper rolls out of my pocket. "This is a signed audit trail from an electronic voting machine in a Chinatown precinct. It shows voters there, at least, picked Chow over other candidates. Whoever rigged the election replaced it with a phony roll and tried to destroy the original—but as you see, they didn't quite succeed. I'm turning this over to the authorities. Once I do, the election will be blown wide open."

Willmott shook her head. "Go ahead and give it to the authorities. I don't believe it's proof of anything. Even if it is what you say it is, you'd still have to show that the votes on it are different than the official results. It wouldn't surprise me if Chow carried at least one precinct—and there's nothing to show someone replaced it with a phony. You probably stole it out of the elections director's office. After all, you are the one who found him murdered."

She had a point. The roll by itself didn't prove anything but sloppy election day logistics. For all I knew, Roadrunner might have picked it up when it bounced off a truck, but thinking that put me in mind of him again. "Who's Roadrunner?" I asked.

"A cartoon character or the New Mexico state bird—now I know you're throwing dust. Let's get this straight. Nobody fixed the election, and no person, animal, vegetable or flightless fowl at this campaign even attempted it."

I returned the roll to my pocket and looked down the table at Willmott and her brother. They stared back, their desire to see me out of their hair palpable in the strained expressions on their faces and the way they sat forward in their chairs. "That still leaves the video," I said.

Kaleb slammed his hand on the table. "You fucker."

"Look, we agreed to talk with you," said Willmott. "What else do you want? You can't ruin this candidate's chances over something done without his knowledge or approval."

"Nobody's addressed why Wood sent Diego after me in the first place."

"Well *that* should be obvious," put in Kaleb. "You're *an asshole.*"

"Ralph is very passionate about the cause and the candidate," said Willmott. "He doesn't want you to do anything to damage Mike Padilla's chances. It's as simple as that."

"I don't think so. If you're not dirty, then he is. His response was all out of proportion to the threat. Something else is going on. Find out if he was involved in fixing the election or I'm releasing the video."

Willmott came out of her chair and clenched her hands in front of her, shaking with rage. Her face was as red and contorted as a newborn's. "You're delusional. No one fixed the election. Period." She paused, seeming to realize how overwrought she appeared and lowered herself back into her chair. "Besides, you can't prove a null hypothesis. I have no way of convincing you he didn't do it. All I can do is find evidence that he did, which would be much worse than having the media get hold of the video."

"Do the legwork. Report back and convince me that you made a good faith effort and I'll let you off the hook."

Willmott curled her lip over her upper teeth like she was going to spit them out. Kaleb stared morosely into his lap.

"Start by looking at Wood's ties to Feral Collective," I suggested.

Willmott started to say something, but she was distracted by movement behind me. I twisted around to see Mike Padilla and Ralph Wood walk into the room, all smiley and buddy-buddy. Padilla had another of his rumpled suits on. Wood was very pressed in the pant leg and very shiny in the shoes. He had on a gold pinkie ring, gold aviator-style glasses and one of those silly wireless cell phone headsets stuck in his ear. Something about the headset made me hate him even more.

The smile dropped from Wood's face like an iceberg calving when he saw me. "What's he doing here?"

I stood and walked to within three inches of him. He quailed like he expected me to slug him, but I snatched the headset from his ear and flung it across the room. It bounced off the wall and plopped into Goldie's tank, where it see-sawed its way down to the colored gravel at the bottom. "Decorating Goldie's pad," I said.

I gave him a little shove in the chest and he toppled back into Padilla, who was wearing an expression like I'd pressed a wad of gum into the family bible.

"Don't be a stranger," I said to Willmott. "In particular, don't be a stranger past three PM tomorrow. If I don't hear from you, I can still make the evening news the day before the election."

ALL THE GRASS BY ITS ROOTS

WHETHER I MANAGED TO BLACKMAIL THE WILLMOTTS into checking out Wood or not, I realized that merely by possessing an audit trail from a Chinatown voting machine, I had met the terms of my employment. At a minimum, it was proof of problems in election day procedures, and the Dragon Lady could use it to force an official investigation. No doubt she would want me to keep going to help figure out more of the why's and wherefore's, but it was time to update her so she could give me my well-deserved pat on the back—and it wouldn't hurt to do it in person in case Lisa just happened to be with her at her office in the Lee Family Association building.

They had replaced the glass in the front window of the art gallery, but the same maestro was in the alcove playing his two-stringed violin. I gave him another buck and went farther back to call for the penthouse elevator. The only problem was that the red phone was dangling by its cord, broken in two pieces like a cracked lobster claw. The elevator itself was partially open, its door sliding back and forth over and over again as it ran into something that protruded from the lower track. The something was the handle of heavy cleaver that glimmered malevolently as I yanked it out. Chinese characters were splashed in red on either side of the blade, and while I didn't know the exact translation, I was certain it wasn't a wish for long life and good fortune.

I held up the cleaver to shout at the violin player. "What do you know about this?"

He twisted on his stool, caught sight of the cleaver and then jerked around like he had seen the horsemen of the apocalypse on jet skis. He snatched up the stool and tip jar and trotted away without a word or another glance behind him.

I slipped through the gap of the closing elevator door and punched the button for the penthouse floor. I didn't know what I was going to find at the top, but I did know that all I had to deal with it was the cleaver and the knife on my ankle.

As it turned out, the only thing required was a broom.

The office was a shambles. Lisa's desk in the reception area was overturned, the stereo and office equipment on top now strewn across the floor. The pagoda-pattern rug had pieces hacked out throughout its length like the perforations in a player piano roll, and the three-foot cobalt vases that flanked the door of the Dragon Lady's office were now just three-inch piles of cobalt shards. The heavier rosewood desk inside the office had withstood all attempts at overturning, but its accoutrements, too, had been swept clear and cruel divots had been taken from the polished surface and—just for good measure—a second cleaver imbedded in the center. The delicate rosewood chair and table set had been smashed into kindling and a ceiling-high bookshelf behind the desk had been toppled.

I searched the rooms, closets and other less likely places to hide, but didn't find any sign of Lisa or the Dragon Lady. Nor was there any blood or indication of a struggle. I used the call log on my cell phone to dial the number the Dragon Lady had reached me from before, but that just rang a phone I found buried under a pile of books in her office. I knew the number Lisa had given me on the first day was also an office line, so there seemed nothing for it but a trip to their house on Russian Hill.

On the ride over I called my buddy with the telephone directory to finagle the number of the phone that went with the Greenwich address. All that bought me was a message in Chinese from the answering machine. I pulled the Galaxie to a stop in front of the single-wide garage door with a warning in three languages about towing and hustled up to the metal gate that led into the villa. It was hanging wide open. I poked my head through and immediately spotted a third cleaver sticking out of the front door. But that was locked tight with three deadbolts, and cleaver or no cleaver, didn't look like it had been breached. I rang the doorbell, but got no answer.

I walked the full perimeter of the house and didn't find any further indications of tampering or attempts at forced entry. What I did find were bars across all the ground-floor windows, alarm sensors and signs for 24/7 monitoring by a home security company.

While the cleaver in the door said they had been there, I had to conclude that the bad guys either couldn't get in or realized that the Dragon Lady wasn't home. If they had come here first, it was still possible they had found Lisa and the Dragon Lady at the office and snatched them up. But if they'd failed to find them at the office on the first try, it looked like Lisa and her mother had anticipated the threat and skedaddled.

The next question was who they were running from. I had a pretty good idea, but I figured if anyone could tell me for sure it would be Alan Chow.

I had almost as much trouble as the fire department wedging my vehicle down the narrow section of Waverly Place where he had his office. When I saw him come hurrying out of his building, I stopped trying entirely, shoved the gearshift into park and spilled out of the car with the cleaver I'd taken from the Dragon Lady's. Chow was headed away from me, but I caught up with him as he paused to light a cigar by the door of a market with smoked ducks and chickens hanging in the window. He looked up at the sound of me pounding down the alley, shook out the match in his hand and puffed a fog of grey-green smoke into the surrounding atmosphere.

"Riordan," he said with the cigar between his teeth. "Come to help me check samples?"

"You're more right than you know," I said. "How'd you rate this one?" I presented the cleaver, handle first.

He pushed his eyebrows up in surprise, making no move to take the big knife. "That's a number one blade cleaver. Cheap. Carbon steel. Costs maybe three bucks wholesale and we sell it for $7.95 in the shop. Tourists buy them by the truckload, but most are too scared to actually use it when they get it home to their kitchen. Takes a certain finesse to wield one." He gestured at the birds in the window. "Although they're great for chopping Peking duck."

"I was more interested in the, ah, customizations."

He sighed, jockeyed the cigar around in his mouth and reached over to grasp the handle. He turned it to sight down the blade. "Someone's put a pretty wicked edge on this—with a real grinding stone. Won't hold, though. Steel's too cheap."

"Come on. You know I'm talking about the characters."

"Oh, those. '*Zhan jin sha ju.*' A literal translation would be, 'Chop all with a knife,' but what it really means is death to you and your family."

"A warning for the ducks?"

"Hardly. It's a famous quotation from a Chinese emperor after a failed coup. He also said, '*Zhan cao chu gen:* Pull all the grass by its roots.' It's the oath he swore on the chief conspirator."

"Did he carry it out?"

Chow returned the knife. He took a long drag on his cigar and then pulled it from his mouth to examine the tip. "Sure. Killed over a dozen people, including the man's children and his parents."

"And what's the oath doing on a $7.95 duck cleaver in the twenty-first century?"

"It's a sort of calling card. Chinese gangs sometimes leave them behind as a threat—often to extort money from business owners. Finding one of these in your door can make you see things a little differently about paying protection."

"And which gangs would do this?"

"As I told you before, there is only one—"

"Wo Hop To. Yes, you told me. Wu's cook had a cleaver like that."

Chow grinned and flicked cigar ash into the street. "It would be the rare Chinese cook who does not. So you've been chatting with Tony 'Squid Boy' Wu."

"Yes, but he was smarter than me. I only learned what he wanted me to. I found two cleavers like this at Leonora Lee's office and another stuck in the door to her house. I was told that Wu and Mrs. Lee had been wrangling over a business deal, but that Lee had met Wu's terms. Do you know if they've fallen out again?"

A truck from the fortune cookie factory on Ross came up from behind Chow. We squeezed into the doorway to let it by. When we stepped back, Chow shook his head. "The cleaver says they're splitsville. Nobody else would leave it behind. But don't ask me what the issue between them is because I don't know."

A horn sounded behind me. I turned to find the cookie truck blocked by the abandoned Galaxie. I took a tentative step back, but couldn't resist asking one more thing. "These cleavers—they put me in mind of hatchet men from 1920s songs. But it's all symbolic, right? They don't actually use them, do they?"

The horn sounded again, longer and more insistent. Chow shook his head and clamped the cigar back in his teeth. "You're forgetting that Wo Hop To is a Hong Kong gang. There are very few guns in Hong Kong. Yes, they use them—often one in each hand. I've seen photos of men killed that way. They look like they'd been through a wheat thresher."

I ran into more parking problems on the way back to my office. There weren't any spots—legal or illegal—on my side of Market Street, so I had to settle for an illegal one in an alley behind the San Francisco Shopping Centre. I forded Market Street at the intersection with 5th and went past all the old men playing chess on folding tables near the cable car turn-around. I paused to indulge in my superstitious ritual of tapping the Samuel's Jewelers Street Clock and finally slipped into the lobby of the Flood building while a young mother herding six-year-old twin boys held the door open, yelling at the kids to stop trying to pry gum off the sidewalk with a pocket comb.

JB, the security guard behind the reception desk, nodded at the Popeye's Chicken bag I carried in both hands. "A little late for lunch, isn't it August? But you shoulda got the bucket. It's a better deal."

"Just a little afternoon snack," I said and winked at him. "I'll remember the bucket next time." The bag had come wadded up from the floor of the Galaxie and actually contained the Wo Hop To cleaver. I didn't think it would be good form to carry the knife uncovered through the streets of downtown.

I continued over to the elevators and caught a ride on an ascending car to the twelfth floor. I walked past the entrance to our suite and pulled out the key for the private door to my office.

Taking my hand away from the Popeye's bag to fish out the key was a small act that turned out to have big consequences. The paper at the bottom split and the cleaver fell to the floor. I jumped back to avoid self-mutilation and dropped to one knee to retrieve the knife. Just as I got hold of it, the lock snicked back and the door pulled open. A set of fingers wrapped around the edge, then the long barrel of a silenced handgun poked out, followed by the tousled bangs and forehead of the little man who had gotten the better of me in the knife fight outside Shanghai 1930.

Gretchen's voice came from the outer office, high-pitched and bordering on hysteria, "We told you he's not here." There was a muffled grunt and then the blowgun noise of a silenced pistol. Gretchen screamed and the little man moved to go back inside.

I didn't let him. I rammed the bottom of the door with my shoulder and brought the cleaver down on his black-slippered foot like I was tenderizing pork chops. He shrieked and reached for his wounded toes. I launched upward, bringing a hard, flat palm into his jaw as I came. I took him by the hair and beat his skull into the doorframe. His eyes rolled back in his head and I wrenched the gun from his rubbery fingers as he puddled to the floor.

The gun was some species of .22 automatic I'd never seen before. I made sure the safety was off and ducked into my office. As soon as I crossed the threshold there was another shot, and I saw Gretchen grab at her torso and pitch forward onto her desk, gazing at her assailant in the other room with a kind of languid curiosity as she fell.

Bonacker told me later that was when I began with the howling, but I don't remember now.

What I do remember is striding across my office with the gun extended at arms length. I started firing before I even rounded the corner, sending two slugs kissing into the far wall. I was only vaguely aware of Bonacker slumped on the floor by Gretchen's desk as I entered the reception area. What I couldn't fail to miss was the cook from Wu's dim sum place with a matching automatic in his hand. I don't know what he thought was coming at him, but he managed to raise the gun and squeeze a shot in my direction.

I felt something go zinging by my ear, but it couldn't have mattered less. What mattered was moving forward with the front sight bisecting his face while I worked the trigger. The first shot obliterated his left eye. The second bit an angry, red hole in his forehead as he toppled forward. I missed with the third, but advanced to stand over his twitching body as I pumped rounds four, five and six into his chest and throat. The trigger stopped working and a gigantic sob escaped from me like a trapped air bubble.

I threw the gun down and stumbled over to where Gretchen lay smeared across her desk. I lifted her carefully to find the lower half of her black turtleneck soaked in blood, a hole just below her right breast welling more. I yanked off my jacket, wadded it up and pressed it hard into the wound. I was blubbering over her when I felt movement beside me. Bonacker levered himself off the ground, one bloody hand held to the center of his gut.

"Call the ambulance," he said. "I'll do that."

I stared as he struggled to his feet and then finally thought to ask if he was okay.

He held up his left hand. The tip of his little finger was gone. He yanked out his handkerchief and wrapped it around the damaged appendage. He replaced my hands on the makeshift compress and elbowed me out of the way. "I can handle this. Just make the call."

Gretchen's phone had been knocked to the floor and I couldn't get a dial tone. I cursed and dodged around the dead cook to Bonacker's desk, where I managed to raise the 911 operator. She told me they would be there soon. I nodded, let the handset slide from my shoulder.

I was on my way back to Gretchen—one foot on either side of the dead cook—when the sound of the Jeopardy theme song emanated from his belt line. I reached down to rifle his pockets—a reignited fury making my movements clumsy—and extracted a flashing cell phone. I pressed talk and grunted into the receiver. A voice I recognized as Wu's replied in Chinese.

"Squid Boy," I said in a hoarse voice that cracked with rage.

"Who is this?"

"It's death. Death to you and your family."

There was a soft click and the line went quiet.

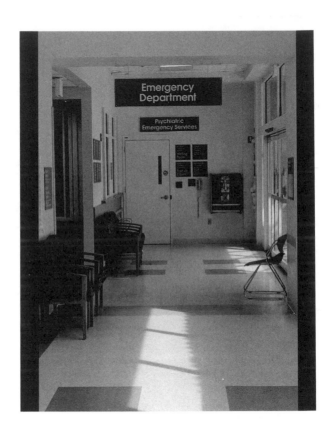

STRANGE BEDFELLOWS

I GOT SCOOPED UP BY THE COPS ALMOST immediately after the paramedics arrived, but made Bonacker promise to contact Chris before I was frog-marched to the elevator in handcuffs.

Two hours later, the handcuffs were gone but not the black feeling of despair that rebounded over me when I stepped through the sliding glass doors of the Parnassus Hospital emergency room. I stood in the entryway, clutching an old scarf of Gretchen's like a lab monkey clinging to a piece of shag carpet. A male nurse in blue scrubbies brushed my elbow going by and knocked me out of it. I pocketed the scarf and hurried into the waiting area.

A pile of well-used wooden toys in a sort of virtual sandbox was at the center of the room. Chris sat in the middle of it with a Hispanic five-year-old in bib overalls and a plaid newsboy cap. They had put a chipped wooden turkey into a wooden stove and oven combination and were busy setting the cooking temperature on an oversize dial. The kid kept spinning it all the way to five hundred, but Chris was patiently dialing it back each time. I asked, "Too many chefs in the kitchen?"

Chris muttered a quick, "Gotta go," to his friend and jumped up. The kid ignored him and spun the dial back to the maximum. "He's no chef," Chris said to me. "More of a barbequer."

Up close I could see his face was pale and his eyes red-rimmed. "How is she?"

"Okay—I mean, well, they haven't really told me."

"What have they said?"

He led me by the sleeve to a pair of hard plastic chairs by a yellowing ficus. "Gretchen had already been admitted by the time I showed up. There was no one I could ask but the admitting nurse. She didn't know anything and didn't want to leave her station, but I pestered her so much she finally went back to check. At least I assume she checked. When she came back she had a funny look on her face. She said Gretchen was with a trauma surgeon and it was fortunate that she got to the hospital as quickly as she did."

"That doesn't sound good at all, Chris. How could you possibly characterize that as 'okay'?"

"I don't know. I guess I was—Jesus, August, where have *you* been? I've been here all by myself. I didn't know what to do." He put his head into his hands and made little peeping noises, punctuated by violent shrugs of his shoulders. He was crying. The mother of the Hispanic kid glanced up from her magazine with a stony expression. I almost ripped the magazine from her hands and threw it across the room.

Instead, I pulled my chair closer to Chris and squeezed the back of his neck. "Sorry. You did fine. There is nothing to do but wait. What happened to Bonacker?"

"He left."

"He left?"

"They brought him out in a wheelchair, but he didn't seem to need it. He had them call a cab and he left."

"What the hell? Did you talk to him?"

Chris looked up at me, raw, red tracks going down either cheek. He sniffed and dabbed at the tears with the back of his hand. "Yes, of course. He said those Chinese mobsters scared the hell out of him and he was leaving town. Especially since—"

"Especially since what?

"Especially since you threatened to kill the head guy."

"I'm going to do more than threaten."

Chris blinked at me. I could tell he wanted to say something in response, but knew better than to start with me now. "You didn't answer my question," he said quietly.

"Where have I been? The cops showed up at my office right after the paramedics. I've been locked in a small room with Lieutenant Kittredge. And believe me it wasn't pleasant."

"At least you had something to do."

"Besides baking wooden turkeys?"

He smirked through the tears. "Yes, besides that. I take it he let you go without charges."

"He did, but that wasn't his original idea. I pretty much came clean with him. Told him about the cleavers and the Lees going missing—gave him most of the details on the election investigation. Even gave him one of the audit trails I got hold of. But I didn't give him any reason to think the Dragon Lady was doing business with Wu, and I didn't tell him about being attacked at the protest in the Mission."

"So he thinks Wu was going after the Lees because …"

"I told him what I believe now. The Dragon Lady must have found out something about Wu's involvement in fixing the election, confronted him with it, and then backed off when he tried to kidnap Lisa. Then she changed her mind—or he decided he couldn't trust her to lay off—and he went after both of us to stop it from coming out."

"And Gretchen got in the way."

I swallowed. "Yes."

Chris pulled a set of keys from his back pocket and held them out. "Bonacker said to give you his set of keys from the office. He wants you to pack up his stuff and mail it to him." I started to curse, but Chris put up his other hand. "You didn't let me finish before. Apart from the fact he was leaving town, the other thing he told me was he stepped into the path of the first bullet. He said Gretchen had mouthed off to the gunmen when they asked for you, and when it was clear they were going to shoot her, he dove in front of her. The bullet hit his hand."

I took the keys. "Bonacker?"

"Yes, Bonacker. He said he was too frightened to get off the floor after that. He said he was sorry."

I jiggled the keys and thought about Bonacker sacrificing himself for somebody else.

A pair of Italian loafers appeared on the edge of my peripheral vision. I looked up to see a soap opera casting director's idea of a hospital doctor. He was wearing an improbably crisp white jacket with a black and brown-patterned tie knotted in a perfect half-Windsor under his outthrust chin. His features were tanned and I would have said sculpted, but even the marble Michelangelo used for David had flaws and there weren't any on this guy. His longish brown hair was tousled in a not-quite-haphazard way and his eyes were big and bright and burning mad. His name was stitched in script on his jacket, but I didn't need to read it to know he was Dennis Drent, Urologist. I recognized him from the photo on Gretchen's desk: her boyfriend.

"This is all your fault." His voice was high-pitched and nasally. "I told her something like this would happen if she stayed working there."

I stood to look him in the eye. He had a couple inches on me, but I probably outweighed him by thirty pounds. Chris jumped up and tried to wedge himself between us. I pushed him gently to one side. "It's okay, Chris," I said. "He's right. It is my fault."

"Then why didn't you do anything to prevent it?"

"I didn't see it coming. I should have, but I didn't. I'm sorry. I'd give anything for it to be me instead of Gretchen."

Drent stared at me for a long moment. I'd never met him, but he surely knew that Gretchen and I had been engaged, and it was even possible that she had told him about the urologist jokes Bonacker and I cracked around the office. I could imagine the wheels that were turning in his head. "Everything I've heard tells me you're a reckless, irresponsible loser," he said when the wheels stopped. "And you don't even pay her a competitive salary. Not that you can afford it on the piddly stream of revenue you bring in. It's not safe for her to stay there. I'm going to insist that she find another job when she recovers."

I felt Chris tromp on my toe. He was worried I'd find "piddly stream" too hard to resist, but I was more interested in something else the doctor had said. "All right. That might be the best thing. But you mentioned her recovery. We haven't heard anything. Is she going to be okay?"

Drent stuck out his chest. "I've been supervising her care personally. I recruited my colleague, Dr. Schneider, one of the best trauma surgeons in the Bay Area, to attend to her."

This was tough slogging. "And what does Dr. Schneider say?"

"Both he and I feel she'll make a complete recovery."

Chris squealed and wrapped me in a bear hug. I hugged back. It was the first time I'd embraced a man with such passion, but I have to admit I found it emotionally satisfying.

Drent narrowed his eyes at us and I was pretty sure he added another item to his list of reckless, irresponsible and poor.

"Is she awake?" Chris asked. "Can we see her?"

"No you may not. She going to be in the critical care unit for quite a while. The bullet struck one of her ribs, broke it and lodged in her right lung. The lung collapsed and she lost a fair amount of blood, but fortunately no major arteries were damaged. She tolerated the repair surgery well. What she needs now is time to recuperate—time to recuperate without unnecessary distractions."

Chris and I glanced at each other to remind ourselves what unnecessary distractions looked like. "Okay," said Chris. "We understand. But please tell her we love her and we're pulling for her quick recovery."

"Yes, please," I said.

Drent gave a curt nod, more like he was marking a completed task than acknowledging the request. "That's done then. I suggest you go home. As I said, she won't be seeing visitors for some time." He turned and almost ran through the admitting doors into the emergency room.

"Piddly streams," I said in a fair imitation of Dent's voice after the doors closed behind him. "That's where I generate *my* revenue."

Chris flopped back into his chair. "Hush up. She needs him now more than she needs us. And she's going to be okay. That's the important thing."

"You're right," I said, and sat down. "But someday you'll have to explain what she sees in him."

"I think it's more what she didn't see in you, August."

"I'm glad we're having this talk."

"Never mind that. What are you going to do now? Shouldn't you be worrying about the one woman you still have a chance with?"

"You mean Lisa? Of course I'm worried about her."

"And you still think the best way to help her is a jihad against Wu?"

"Is that a trick question? Wu is the one who went after her and her mother. The one who shot Gretchen. Who else would I go after? Greenhouse gas emitters?"

"You might as well for all the good it will do. You say Wu is part of an international triad. He's probably already left the country. You'll never get near him. In fact, it's more likely he'll send reinforcements to finish the job on you than the other way around. The Dragon Lady didn't blow town for nothing. She knows the score."

I rested my elbows on my knees and stared down at the hospital's fetching, high-traffic cranberry Berber. "Did you forget what just happened? Wu almost killed Gretchen and Bonacker."

"And why is that? Probably because you or the Dragon Lady were close to finding out about his involvement in the election rigging. Your best bet is to find the connection."

"I know I said he was involved, but the only person we can tie to any real hanky-panky is this kid Roadrunner." I explained about getting the audit trails from Roadrunner in the abandoned garage and finished with, "But I can't see Wu and Roadrunner working together."

"Politics makes strange bedfellows."

I looked back up at him. "Well, *you* would know about strange bedfellows."

"Strange is different, not the same. By that definition, you're the one sleeping with strange people. You remember you asked me to find Geiberger's address?"

"Yes."

"Well I found it. And it seems to me that Geiberger would be the perfect sort of bedfellow for Wu."

My cell phone went off in my pocket. The caller was in the 415 area code, but I didn't recognize the number. I flipped open the phone and was treated to a brusque, "Riordan?"

"Yeah?"

"It's Kittredge. Shut up and listen."

He talked for a breathless ninety seconds. I asked him one question, he answered and then hung up in my ear.

Chris frowned over at me. "What was that about?"

"Lieutenant Kittredge doing his best to make a perfect day even better. He said that two short men wearing dark clothes and masks rushed the emergency room at Mount Zion Hospital—the hospital where they took the other Chinese guy from my office. They found his bed in critical care and put two slugs in the base of his skull. Kittredge figures Wu is getting rid of witnesses. He suggested I consider protective custody."

"My God. What about Gretchen?"

"He's going to put a twenty-four hour guard on her. But since she can't testify against Wu, there's probably little risk. There's more, though. He says they checked one of the signatures on the audit trail I gave him and it was faked. So Roadrunner had a faked roll from a Chinatown precinct and not a real one. Maybe he was going to substitute it for the real ones and didn't get a chance."

Chris shivered and hugged himself. "There goes your only solid lead. What do you think about my idea about Geiberger now?"

"I think you better give me his damn address."

THE CRAB LADY

I KNEW THAT CHECKING OUT GEIBERGER'S PLACE WOULD be a fishing expedition, but I didn't realize how much of one until I saw the words "Harbormaster Road" in Palmer cursive on the sheet of buttercream stationery Chris handed over. That turned out to be the main drag for the Oyster Point Marina, which was conveniently located on San Francisco Bay less than a mile from Columbia Voting Technologies.

I parked the Galaxie behind a row of tractor-trailer cabs with wind fairings like high foreheads. I flipped open the glove box to extract a penlight and set of lock picks I referred to as "mother's little helpers" and stepped outside. It was cold and blustery. The sun had dipped behind the thicket of sailboat masts in the marina and the roof of the darkening sky was streaked with cirrus clouds like thin-spread cake frosting. It didn't take long to determine that the address Chris had given me was nothing more than a mailbox at the harbormaster's office—and that getting the actual berth number for Geiberger's boat from the aforementioned master (whose personal space was heavily infused with the oily bouquet of diesel fuel) was admitting an interest in a dead man's property that didn't seem becoming.

I made a full tour of the walkway that led along the fourteen marina fingers—dodging goose shit and the strutting, non-migrating geese that had deposited it—looking in vain for any kind of berth directory or an obvious indicator about which of the three hundred-plus vessels must be Geiberger's. I went past the place where the breakwater abutted the land and stopped to stare out at the fishing pier that projected from the point. There was a lone fisherman at the end of the pier with a tall casting rod. He had the rod parked in a holder and seemed to be more concerned about consuming a hot dog and a Bud than catching any fish.

Watching him reminded me that I hadn't had anything to eat since breakfast. I turned back from the pier and trudged over to a combination bait shop/mini-mart that some entrepreneurial genius had set up to meet all the needs of the frustrated marina fisherman. The delaminated door on the boxy prefabricated building made an obnoxious scraping noise as I opened it. The proprietress—a stout middle-aged woman wearing a bucket hat and a sleeveless blouse that exposed flabby, salmon pink arms—seemed inured to it. She remained hunched over something she was working on behind the counter, a small TV bolted to the ceiling above her showing a bleary rerun of M*A*S*H.

I went to the cooler for a can of Tecate beer and then came up to the roller grill she had going near the register to get a dog. There were five in rotation and they all looked like they'd been cooking since Alan Alda pinched his first nurse. I selected a bun and used a set of tongs to snag a wiener near the back that seemed the least leathery. I was squirting mustard down the middle of it when the woman behind the counter finally looked up. "Wait," she said, "don't do that."

I froze with the mustard dispenser poised in midair. "What?"

She craned her neck to look at the roller grill. "Oh, that's okay. There's still enough left."

"Enough left for what?"

She laughed and brought a weathered hand up to cover her mouth. A beat went by and then she muttered, "Crab fishing," behind her palm.

"I don't see a crab bait sign. Exactly where are the hot dogs meant for human consumption?"

She laughed again. She pulled her hand away and waved me off, a lumpy charm bracelet jangling at her wrist. "Those wieners have been cooking since this morning. I would have put a fresh one on for you if you asked. I'll tell you what—that one's on the house."

I put the mustard up and went to work at the onion and relish containers. "No need. If it's good enough for the crabs, it's good enough for me. But I didn't think you were allowed to fish for crab inside the Bay."

She shook her head and went back to what she'd been working on, which I now realized was tying up a hot dog in some sort of wire mesh trap. "You can't fish for Dungeness in the Bay. Any other species is fine."

I frowned and looked out the window behind her. The sun had dropped all the way behind San Bruno Mountain to the west. "But can you fish at night?"

What I meant by the question was can you see to fish at night, but she apparently took it a different way. She looked up at me with a conspiratorial expression. "Harbormaster goes home at six. He'll never know. Even if you use a boat."

"I see. Well, your secret's safe with me." I put the dog in one of those paper trays you get at mini-marts and pushed it and the beer onto the counter for her to ring up.

She wiped her hands on her jeans and punched a couple of buttons on the register. "That'll be $6.40." While I rooted in my hip pocket for my wallet, she brought a small basket from behind her and set it on the counter. "Lemon for your beer?"

Inside the basket was a pair of ancient lemons so desiccated and pale they looked like bird skulls. I declined and handed over a five and two ones, putting the change from the transaction in her Shriners jar.

"Thank you, sir. My husband Bob was a Shriner. Couldn't wait to put on the fez and ride his motorcycle in the parades. You been doing some fishing yourself?"

"No," I lied, "I was looking at a boat."

"Larry Kosub's Bayliner?"

"Not his. But that reminds me—didn't that guy who went postal at that voting machine company have a boat here?"

The crab lady nodded and carefully lowered the baited trap to the floor. She picked up an empty one and set it on the stool by the register. "That's right. George Geiberger. But some hot shot private dick settled his hash before he could hurt anyone. Pass me another dog, will you?"

I picked out another wiener with the tongs, put it on a paper tray and slid it across to her. Being called a "hot shot" was worth a small celebration at least, so I popped my beer and took a couple of big swallows. It tasted better than it had any right to. "Did you know him?"

"I know all the liveaboards. Where else are they going to buy groceries? He moved onto the boat after his wife divorced him. You should have seen all the crap he brought with him. First time I saw someone try to stow a lawn mower on a boat. He was a bit of a loner, though. Didn't really talk to anyone. To tell you the truth, I didn't have much of an opinion about him one way or the other."

"What sort of boat did he have?"

She grinned at me. "Hoping to get a cheap price on it from the estate?"

I grinned back. "Maybe."

"It's a cabin cruiser—a little bit older. A 1972 Chris Craft Constellation, but he'd refurbished it real nice." She looked over at me, apparently expecting me to say something. When I didn't, she prompted, "Aren't you gonna ask me how big it is?"

"Of course. How big is it?"

"It's a forty-five-footer. Got a guest and a master stateroom, two heads, galley, nice salon and sun deck—the whole nine yards."

"Sounds nice. What do you think it would go for?"

"Hard to say with those older boats. If you found the right buyer, you could probably get one hundred thousand. But as part of a probate sale, where they're looking to clear the cash as quick as possible, I imagine it might go for as little as eighty."

I inhaled about half of the dog and chewed thoughtfully. "That would be more in my price range. Do you know where it's berthed? Maybe I'll sneak a peak at it while I'm out here."

"Sure." She tapped a marina map thumb-tacked to a pole by the register. "It's in the last finger—number fourteen—just out the door along the breakwater. I think it's berth number seven—somewhere in the middle, anyway. You can't miss it. It'll be the only forty-five-footer with a red canvas tarp over the aft deck."

I nodded my thanks while I wolfed down the rest of the hot dog. "What about your boat?" I asked just to be friendly. "What kind is it?"

She laughed and waved her arm at me again. "I think you got a wrong idea, bub. Mine's just a skiff with an outboard. I put a plastic lawn chair in it and string up one of those work lights mechanics use and I've got me a poor man's crabber."

I pounded the rest of the beer and threw the can and the crumpled hot dog tray into the trash. "Well, happy hunting tonight—and make sure you throw back any Dungeness you happen to catch."

She winked at me. "You betcha."

CABIN BRUISER

I WENT OUT THE DOOR OF THE MINI-MART and across the gangway to the finger that ran along the breakwater. A big cabin cruiser was tied up in berth number eight. It had a red canvas tarp covering the aft deck and—although a dinghy hanging off the stern made it hard to see—the name *Vote Boat* written in gold on the transom. No lights were on in any of the craft in this part of the harbor, and with the sun now well and truly gone, the only useful illumination came from a sodium lamp on the breakwater.

There was a short ladder hung over the side near the back of the cruiser, but the gap of oily black water between it and the dock was wide enough to swallow a shoe, a cell phone or your whole being. I lunged across and managed to get a foot on the lowest rung and a hand on the gunwale. There was a display of athletic ineptitude then—which I imagined was not dissimilar to the spectacle presented by a fat dog attempting to scamper into the bed of a pickup truck—and eventually I found myself on my butt near the door to the salon.

The memory of Geiberger and the shooting at CVT flashed through my mind. It felt odd to be on the boat of a man I'd killed. For the first time, I let myself actually consider whether the shooting had been necessary. I told the cops and Dragon Lady there was no other way, but could I have called Geiberger off with just a warning?

I shook my head to clear the thought and crawled up to the door and twisted the handle. It was locked, but the lock was nothing special and ten minutes of jiggling a pick and a tension wrench with the penlight clamped in my teeth brought a slobbery penlight, a sore jaw and an open door. I went down three steps and shone the light around. The interior had the feel of a single-wide trailer. There was a red Naugahyde Barcalounger near the door, a built-in dinette with a Formica table and bench seats, a small galley with downsized stove, sink and refrigerator, all on top of nylon shag carpet that looked like it was taken from the set from a vintage porno film. The crab lady had called the boat refurbished, but this was more like a complete period restoration. With the Naugahyde, the Formica and the nylon, there weren't enough natural materials to fill a 1970s (Styrofoam) Big Mac container.

I moved across the salon to a small stateroom near the bow of the boat. The room looked lived in, or more accurately, wrestled in. Clothes were strewn around the room and the few furnishings that weren't bolted down—a clock radio, a space heater and a wastebasket—were scattered across the floor like thrown dice. The sheets on the bed were twisted in a big grimy wad, and even though Ajax laundry detergent used to claim it was stronger than dirt, I was betting on the dirt in two falls out of three.

My first assumption was that someone had tossed the room ahead of me, but as I went through the closets and the built-in cabinets and found nothing either particularly interesting or professionally scrambled, I came to the less sinister conclusion that Geiberger was just a big slob. The last thing I did was pry up the mattress from the box springs and lean it against the wall. Underneath I found two girlie magazines and a penis pump. That ended my interest in the room.

The attached head was smaller than an airline toilet. Apart from the fact Geiberger was on blood pressure and cholesterol medication, and appeared to have been using his toothbrush to scrub the bilge, there was nothing of interest in it either. I went down a short stairway to the master stateroom, and all that changed.

Rather than the flimsy, veneered particle board that had been used to construct the door of the guest stateroom, the door to the master was made of steel, as was the doorframe. A sturdy padlock secured it. When I realized the penlight wasn't going to provide sufficient illumination in the pitch black space, I risked the overhead light and kneeled in front of the door to go at the padlock with the picks.

It wasn't particularly challenging—probably even easier than the lock on the salon door—but now that it seemed I might actually be onto something, I rushed the job and ended up snapping the end off one of my tension wrenches. I had a devil of a time getting the broken bit of wrench out of the opening of the lock, and an even harder one substituting a larger wrench, which didn't really leave enough space to maneuver the picks. By the time the lock finally clicked open, my knees were sorer than they were after a teenage visit to the confessional.

I yanked open the door and stepped inside. It was half storeroom and half office. In the storeroom category were items from Geiberger's landlubbing days, including the push mower the crab lady had mentioned and a collection of yard tools piled in the corner. But of more direct interest was a gun case filled with rifles and shotguns. The door to the case was unlocked and seven of its eight slots were occupied. I figured the final slot had to have been home to the shotgun Geiberger brought with him to CVT.

In the office category we had a computer desk and a filing cabinet, and a strange-looking electronic tablet standing on a set of legs like a painter's easel. It had to be a voting machine. The presence of an CVT logo and an ungainly printer module loaded with a thermal paper roll like the one I had taken from Roadrunner clinched it. The machine appeared to be plugged in, but if there was a power button or switch, I couldn't find it. Nor could I figure out where the USB drive was located. I had more luck getting the computer booted, but the password screen prevented further progress.

Since the voting machine looked like it would fold into a suitcase-sized package, I resolved to carry it and the computer off the boat for Chris to examine later, and switched to the sort of low-tech searching I could handle now. It didn't take long to hit pay dirt in the filing cabinet. In a manila folder labeled with the current year I found a folded San Francisco precinct map. When I spread it out on the floor, I saw notations with the letters C, P and L written in tiny script beside each of the precincts. Beside the letters were numbers ranging anywhere from hundreds to thousands. The letters were repeated at the bottom of the map, but the numbers beside them were much larger and each had a double line beneath it like a sum.

I figured that the C, P and L stood for Chow, Padilla and Lowdon and that the numbers were desired vote counts for each precinct individually and the city as a whole. But if this was a blueprint for fixing the election, someone had screwed up the plan. It showed Lowdon as the landslide winner.

I refolded the map and finished going through the file cabinet: more porn and a penis pump catalog. I switched to the built-in drawers and closets of the stateroom, finding a lot of canned goods, office supplies, expensive tools, marine equipment, fishing gear and boxes and boxes of shotgun and .30-06 shells. The last item I found at the back of the bottom drawer was a thin strongbox with a combination lock. It rattled when I shook it, but the rattle didn't sound metallic like coins. I was rummaging through one of the drawers I had searched earlier for a hammer and a chisel to prize open the box when I heard the whine of a starting motor—a starting motor for the boat I was on.

I whirled in time to see the door of the stateroom slam closed. The engines caught with a dull thrumming and over that I heard the rattle of the padlock hasp on the other side of the door. I kicked at the door anyway and got nothing for my trouble but a bruised foot.

The boat surged backwards in the water and I lost my balance and fell to the floor. Whoever was driving let up on the throttle, we drifted for a four count, and then the boat heaved forward. I scrambled atop the chest of drawers and shoved my face into a shoebox-sized porthole. I saw the last three or four boats in the marina finger go plunging by and then we were through the gap in the breakwater and out into the open bay.

I slid down from the drawers, but just as my foot touched the floor, the overhead light snapped off. I cursed and fished out the penlight. I was convinced someone would be coming through the door any moment, so I went back to the places I had searched with an eye towards scavenging some sort of weapon. My hand passed over the hammer, an oversize monkey wrench, and—ludicrously—a small chain saw in a case before I settled on a crowbar. I took a post beside the door with the bar raised above my head.

I kept telling myself that I was only going to get one chance, so I needed to make sure it counted, but I was wasting my virtual breath. I wasn't going to get any chance. The noise of the engines dropped, then they cut out entirely, leaving the boat scudding forward in the dark for a long minute until the chop sucked away the last of its momentum. I heard the sound of footsteps on the deck above me, and then a sharp clang from below, and then more footsteps and the sound of an outboard motor drawing near. I left my station by the door and scrambled up on the chest again to look out the porthole. The only things I saw were dark water and the runway lights of San Francisco Airport off to the south.

The outboard motor was held at idle, then it growled in acceleration and finally faded to a drone as it moved away from the cabin cruiser. I stayed at the porthole, strangely detached from my predicament. I was certain I was the only one left on board, but I couldn't for the life of me see what the purpose of the exercise had been. Perhaps to get me in trouble with the police for stealing the boat.

I listened to the sound of little waves slapping against the hull, and gradually I became aware of a change in the boat's motion. It was not rolling as sharply in the chop as it had been. The motion had became less pronounced, dampened in some sense. A frisson of fear shot through me. I dropped from the chest to the floor, landing in three inches of icy water.

I lashed out in a panic with the crowbar, severing the knob from the door, but doing nothing about the lock on the other side. I wedged the bar between the door and the jamb and pried. The tip of the bar snapped off. I threw what was left in the water and aimed another kick at the wooden bulkhead. It bowed slightly, but it was a long way from splintering or cracking. I whirled away from it and shone the penlight at the back of the room. The shiny, yellow plastic of the chainsaw case gleamed at me from a shelf in the closet.

I splashed through the water to the closet, yanked out the case and used it to plow the desk clear. I flopped the case down and fumbled open the latches. The saw looked grimy and disused and there were oily rags wrapped around the blade, but I heard gasoline slosh in the tank when I shook it. I held it at arm's length, gripped the starter cord and pulled for all I was worth.

There was a metallic wheeze followed by a kind of strangled hiccup. Then nothing. I kept pulling, five, ten, fifteen times, my arm getting tireder and the water getting higher as I went. It had risen past mid-calf when I slumped against the desk, both arms trembling violently from a mixture of fatigue and panic. Then I saw the diagram. It was printed on the inside of the case and when I shined the penlight on it, I could see a pair of fingers pulling a recessed choke valve on the chainsaw. "Starting position" was what it said.

At that point, if the diagram told me starting position was cuddling the blade between my legs, I would have done it. I located the valve, yanked it out and gave the cord a ferocious pull. The chainsaw snarled to life. I let it run rich to warm up, and then pushed the choke open for a leaner mix and strode over to the bulkhead to the right of the door. I squeezed the throttle trigger down and pushed the blade into the wood. The tip of it wanted to skitter along the veneer, but I leaned into the handle and the saw plunged through the particle board like it was papier-mâché. Wood chips flew like snow flurries. Directing the blade in a straight line was relatively easy, but sharp corners were harder. In the end, the best I could manage was an amorphous, amoeba-shaped hole. The saw stalled before I made the full circumference, so I had to kick at the piece I had cut to snap through the last few inches.

The water was now high enough that it was brimming over the edge of the hole. I chucked the chainsaw through it and waded back into the room to grab the precinct map, a Winchester Model 70 from the gun case and a box of .30-06 shells. The map I shoved down the front of my shirt, and the shells and rifle I clutched to my chest. I stepped through the opening I'd cut and hurried up the stairs to the salon level where it was still dry. The water appeared to be coming in from below deck, but I didn't know enough about boats to say how the bastards managed it.

I paused to feed four rounds into the magazine of the Winchester. Then I worked the bolt to get one into the chamber. For all I knew I was wasting my time, but I had to believe that if the bad guys had taken the trouble to steal the boat and scuttle it with me aboard, they would be waiting around to see how it went. And if they were waiting, the sound of the chainsaw might not exactly have been music to their ears.

I went up the steps to the aft deck and opened the door, praying that the dinghy was still there. I was already shivering from my waist-high dip in the freezing water and I couldn't face the idea of a swim back to shore. The dinghy was still hanging over the stern, and a cautious sweep of the 270-degree moonlit view available from a hunched position by the salon door didn't reveal any other craft in the water. With the cruiser sinking discernibly lower by the minute, I was tempted to jump into the dinghy and paddle for it, but I forced myself to go up the ladder to the flybridge to check out the view from the top.

The crack of a pistol shot echoing over the water convinced me I'd made the right decision. I flopped to the deck like a trained seal and patted myself furiously. Everything was still attached. I combat crawled my way up past the helm chair to the console. I counted to ten, held my breath and then slowly raised myself above the low windshield and rested the barrel of the Winchester on the Plexiglas.

There was another large cruiser almost directly ahead at a distance of a hundred yards. Its running lights were off, but I could see three men standing at the stern. Two of them were dressed in street clothes and sported what looked like 9mm automatics, while the third was wearing a wet suit and had a scuba tank on his back. Faint light reflected off the glass of his face mask, which was pushed up above his forehead, and he gripped a line that ran from the railing to a motor launch. I searched for the name of the cruiser on the transom, but it appeared to be obscured.

I eased back on my haunches and nearly laughed aloud. Yes, I was the moron who'd let himself be trapped on a sinking boat, but these were the wingnuts who'd let me get hold of a high-powered rifle and then paraded around like shooting gallery targets.

I knew that I would never be able to pick them off in cold blood. Killing the two in my office after they attacked Gretchen was one thing, shooting Geiberger another, but I didn't have the makings of a sniper. It wouldn't do to have them taking potshots at me while I made my exit, though, and I didn't like the idea of the diver scavenging the wreck after it sank.

I sighted the rife at a point about a foot above the waterline. I braced for a shot, pulled the trigger. The report of the rifle set both ears ringing and the recoil punished my shoulder, but that was nothing to the effect the shot had on the men and the boat. The bullet dropped several inches from where I was aiming, but still managed to tear into the hull. I heard—or more accurately felt—a visceral thud after it hit. The trio on the stern froze like they'd been caught in a spotlight, then dropped below the railing, one of them reaching an automatic over the top to fire blindly in my general direction.

I worked the bolt quickly and pounded the stern with another round. That persuaded the shooter to give up on the automatic and scramble towards the helm. I'd dropped two more pills into the back of the boat by the time they coaxed one of the engines to life, the other almost certainly shot out of commission. I stood and watched as they limped away to the east with the motor launch bucking and dancing in the wake behind them.

All this had taken too long. I jerked around to find the aft deck flooded and the level of the boat in the water so low that the dinghy was already floating behind it. I threw down the rifle and half slid, half jumped down the ladder to the deck below, landing with a splash in water that came to mid-thigh. I waded across to the dinghy and heaved myself into it. Yanking my knife off my ankle, I slashed at the slack lines that still secured it.

The dinghy drifted free and I watched with a morbid fascination as water crested the gunwales on the cruiser and the bow began to rise. The hiss of air escaping from the portion of the boat above water fought with the gurgle of bubbles from the submerged section. The bow rose further and soon the boat stood on its stern like a trained killer whale. A sudden suction drew the dinghy towards the cruiser and panicked me into fitting oars into oarlocks and rowing off a safe distance. At the end, the bow of the cruiser came back to a thirty-degree angle and then slid beneath the chop with what seemed to me was almost an audible sigh.

I put my back into the oars and rowed for all I was worth. If the cold and the wet weren't motivation enough, I didn't want the jokers on the other boat coming back to find me in a ten-foot dinghy. Thirty minutes and nearly as many blisters later, I came up on a skiff with a mechanics light hanging from the mast about a quarter mile from the opening of the marina breakwater. Sitting on a plastic lawn chair in the middle of the skiff was the crab lady. She was wearing iPod earphones, was bent over one of her traps and didn't hear me until I was right on top of her.

"Hey," I shouted when she looked up, "got any of those dogs left?"

A MYTHIC TALE

WHEN I GOT HOME THAT NIGHT, I fell into bed without even kicking off my shoes. I slept for ten hours straight and woke up in the same face-down, bag-of-bones position that I landed in. A hot shower and a couple cups of coffee made me more responsive to external stimuli and that was when I noticed the buzzing noise my cell phone was making. I flipped it open to find another text message:

```
Washington  Mutual.  8th  +
Market.  3-0-2.

--Red
```

Red's ATM conquests were the least of my problems now. I chucked the phone onto my pillow and went into the living room, where I found the light on my answering machine was blinking as well. The first message was from Chris:

"I found out that Gretchen is awake and doing well. You'll be pleased to know that *we* sent flowers and a tasteful card, but don't bother trying to get in to see her. Dr. Pee-Pee has got us on the no-fly list at the hospital. I'll be back at CVT tomorrow, trying to see if I can find out more about the logic bomb. I hope you did something clever at Geiberger's. Ta-ta."

I wasn't exactly sure what I had accomplished at Geiberger's, but clever couldn't be stretched to encompass it. The next message was a hang-up from a blocked number at 10:10 PM, followed by another at 10:32. The final one at 11:05 had the voice of a real person:

"August, this is Lisa. I've been calling this number and your cell, but you haven't been answering. Mother didn't want me to contact you, but I had to let you know we're safe. Things have gotten … complicated. I won't go into the details, but—but I miss you. Please take care of yourself and don't do anything foolish. I may not be able to call again for a while, but you're definitely in my thoughts." There was a pause and then she giggled. "You and your cute little ass."

There's nothing like a flattering mention of one's ass to really set you up for the day. What I didn't like was the veiled reference to the continuing threat from Wu and, given the events of last night, the nagging feeling that there were more players in the game than were listed in my program. Certainly the guys on the other cruiser did not fit the employment profile—or the work methods—I had in mind for Wu's minions.

That led me to the decision to track down the cruiser. Chris was right: Wu had probably skipped out of the country by now and my chances of finding him before the election were nil. Finding a forty-odd-foot cabin cruiser with a transom peppered with .30-06 shell holes might be a little more my speed.

I dialed the office of a big-wheel lawyer I'd worked with named Mark Richie. I happened to know he owned a yacht. I'd never been on it, but I'd spent a good percentage of my life staring at a wall-sized photograph of it while I cooled my heels in his waiting room. I clocked in another twenty minutes of wait time after his secretary put me on hold.

"August," he boomed in his usual hale fellow voice. "Sorry to keep you. What can I do for my favorite Miles Archer?"

"You mean Sam Spade. Archer was the one who got shot."

"Course I do. What's up young man?"

"I need some advice. Where do you keep your yacht?"

"I keep it in Sausalito."

"Why?"

"Because that's where I keep my house." He laughed. "Are you pondering a nautical turn?"

"No, I'm trying to track down the location of a particular boat. A forty-foot cabin cruiser."

"I'm surprised at you, August. Boats are registered just like cars. Bribe someone at the DMV like you usually do."

"I didn't get the name of the boat."

"Hmm. Name wouldn't do you any good. You need the hull number. What is this, a hit and run?"

I picked up my box of Lucky Charms from the card table and shook it idly. "Something like that. The last time I saw it, it was heading east and north from Oyster Point Marina."

"And you're sure it's not berthed there?"

"Not likely."

"Well, if you mean to check out all the marinas in the east and north bay, you've got your work cut out for you. There're about eight in Oakland alone."

"Can you take an educated guess about the most likely places for that sort of boat to be docked?"

"A forty-foot cruiser, you said. Did it look new? Well maintained?"

"It looked pretty flossy to me."

Richie made a little clicking noise with his tongue. "I've never thought about matching boat types to particular marinas before, but it's sort of a fun guessing game. You can leave out most all of the marinas north of the Golden Gate—Sausalito, Tiberon, etc. They're mainly for waspy yacht owners like me. Cruisers are more blue collar. But it sounds like your boat is one of the classier vessels. The Berkeley Marina is mixed. There's a yacht club, but there are also fishing boats and plenty of cruisers, so I'd try it. I'd definitely check out Alameda Marina, and in Oakland I'd try Jack London, Mariner Square and North Basin."

"What about San Francisco?"

"You could give Pier 39 a go and the marina near Fort Mason. There's an east and west harbor there. The east harbor, which they call Gashouse Cove, is more likely because two yacht clubs have staked out the west. But the east is still pretty prestigious. There are no open berths and the wait-list time is years." He sighed, and there was a rustling noise as he moved the phone closer to his mouth. "Of course this is all complete speculation on my part. There are easily a dozen other marinas your boat could be in."

"Your speculations are a lot better than mine. Thanks for your help, Mark."

"My pleasure. It was a good break from redlining contracts. Anchors aweigh."

I hung up then and tried giving Gretchen a call at the hospital. I got as far as the nursing station in critical care, but they told me she wasn't allowed phone calls yet and, besides, she was taking a nap. I wanted to blame Drent for blocking access, but since I hadn't given a name it was hard to see how.

The elevator in my building was out of service again, so I plodded down the four flights of stairs to the first floor, taking a mental inventory of the new aches and pains I'd accumulated as I went. The blisters on my hands and the soreness in my shoulders from rowing topped the list. When I got to the lobby, I pushed through the front door and turned left on Post to head to the garage where I kept the Galaxie. I didn't get far.

The passenger door of a black Mercedes parked on the corner popped open and an obvious ex-boxer stepped out. There was scar tissue over both his eyes, his nose was signaling for a left turn and his ears were as shrunk and misshapen as a couple of flattened chestnuts. He strode over to me, rubbing the back of his shaved head as he came. "With me," he muttered.

"You think?" I started to turn away, but he grabbed a wad of my coat, yanked me close and landed a shot to my solar plexus.

"Yeah," he said as I bent over the punch.

He steered me to the back seat of the car, piled in after me and grunted to the driver, another bald-headed cutie. The car roared out onto Post.

It took me a while to get my breath back, and a while longer to sit upright. "Where are we going?" I managed finally.

He stared out of the window at the passing cars, already bored with the whole thing. "To an opening."

"Right—what kind?"

"Garage."

I had intended to follow up on Riche's suggestions for marinas in Oakland and Berkeley first, but I remembered his description of the San Francisco marina near Fort Mason well enough when we pulled into the parking lot. The driver brought the car to a stop and undid the door locks.

"Get out," said the guy next to me.

"What then?"

"You're the detective—figure it out. But if we have to come back, it won't be for a ride."

I stepped out in a patch of rubbery ice plant littered with fast food wrappers and the string and tail from a crash-landed kite. The Mercedes reversed, did a three-point turn and pulled away.

The lot ran along the water between the two harbors. I trudged over to the eastern one, which Richie had called Gashouse Cove. It was smaller and older-looking than Oyster Point Marina, but the layout was similar: seven or so fingers with berths for several dozen boats in each. There seemed to be one of just about every kind of craft—including tugboats and fishing boats—and there were a number of cruisers.

I went over the rickety gangway for the nearest finger and started my search. The only cruiser docked in it was too small and too dilapidated. The next one over had no cruisers at all. Same with the next. But the fourth had two likelys docked next to each other. Both were large, gleaming white and angular and looked more like something that Han Solo would be flying around the outer reaches of the universe than would be puttering around the Bay. I walked on rotting planking to the back of the closer boat and stooped down with my hands on my knees, leaning out as far as I could over the water to catch a look at the transom.

Venus de Milo was written there in a sort of ersatz Roman lettering, but there were no bullet holes. As I straightened up—swearing under my breath about the twinges that still radiated from my stomach—a lilting voice sang out, "*Mister* August Riordan."

A silver-haired man with a ruddy complexion and an even ruddier Bloody Mary stood on the aft deck of the second cruiser. He waved the celery stick from his drink at me. "You're getting warm, man, but you're not hot yet."

I walked around the U formed by the berths to the back of his boat and repeated my inspection. A constellation of holes in a trapezoid shape hung a few inches above the water line, in line with the starboard propeller. A layer of white contact paper covered the name of the boat, but in the bright morning sun I could just make out the letters: H.M.S. Happy Day.

"Did you find what you were looking for?" said the man. He stood at the back railing, nearly on top of me.

"Yes."

"Come aboard, then. I expect you'll want to talk."

I looked up at him with what was probably a dubious expression. "Is anyone else there with you?"

"Just me and my vodka bottle."

A set of portable wooden steps were parked just below the boat's ladder. I managed the steps and the ladder with considerably more grace than the evening before and stepped onto the covered aft deck. It was tarted up like the Archbishop's parlor. An elegant but spindly antique table with two matching chairs cowered in the center of an oriental rug that was too good for walking on. Beside them stood a delicate floor lamp with a Tiffany shade. Further afield was a squat leather ottoman with a cutting board balanced on top. That was home base for the Bloody Mary fixings: cocktail shaker, sliced celery and a pepper mill.

My host fit right in with his eclectic surroundings. He was dressed in chinos and an untucked cambric shirt that was old and worn but crisply pressed. He wore Persian slippers with curled toes and no socks and a ratty-looking bracelet made of colored threads. But he also had a massive silver watch with more dials and sweep hands than a fighter cockpit and a pinky ring with a green stone the size of a Thompson Seedless. Up close, I could see the skin of his patrician face was more mottled than ruddy, and he wore horn-rimmed reading glasses on the tip of a pinched nose whose network of capillaries looked like the hub city in an airline route map.

He said, "Do you have any idea what it costs to restore a mangled engine on a boat like this?"

"Don't ask me. I'm into perforation, not restoration."

He fixed me with a look over his glasses and shook his head. "That's what the rappers do, isn't it Mr. Riordan? Make up smart little rhymes."

"Yeah, except they're better at it than me."

"I suppose if a man is good at perforation, he can't be good at everything. Please, have a seat." He arranged himself on one of the spindly chairs. I sat on mine like I was incubating an egg, hoping I wouldn't pulverize it.

"Could you make out the name of the boat when you inspected the transom?"

"It looked like H.M.S. Happy Day."

"Yes, and that was what brought to mind the comment about the damaged engine. There's an old riddle about boat ownership. It goes like so: What are the two happiest days of a boat owner's life? The day he buys the boat and the day he sells it. Because of the expense and bother of maintaining it, you see."

"Then it follows that the saddest day must be when a boat sinks—especially if you're on it."

"Probably. But don't confuse ownership with breaking and entering." He stirred his Bloody Mary with the celery stick. "My apologies. I've been rude. Would you care to join me in a morning pick-me-up?"

"No I wouldn't. Let's quit barbering around the edges here. Rude isn't failing to offer me a drink. Rude is trying to drown me. Who are you and what do you want?"

He gave me the faintest of smiles and sipped his drink. "Are you familiar with Sisyphus?"

I sighed and crossed my arms. "Sure. He's the one who says, 'Exit, stage left, even.'"

"That's Snagglepuss, you idiot."

"Oh. So it is."

"Sisyphus was the king from Greek mythology who offended the gods and as punishment was made to roll a huge stone up a hill in the underworld. But every time he reaches the top, the stone escapes and rolls back again, trapping him in a meaningless labor throughout all eternity. Accordingly, pointless activities are often referred to as Sisyphean tasks."

I flicked at some lint on my trousers. "Thanks for the news flash. And *your* point would be?"

"You are engaged in a Sisyphean task. By that I mean your investigation of fraud in the mayoral election."

"You call it meaningless if the wrong candidate gets elected?"

"I know that Leonora Lee hired you to investigate why her candidate lost. Let's assume there was fraud and some votes were taken away from Chow. He wasn't going to win. He wasn't going to come close to winning. He probably wouldn't have even gotten enough votes to participate in the runoff. So, the results are the same, whether or not there was fraud. It serves no purpose to investigate because the outcome will be the same. The epitome of a pointless task."

"It matters to Lee because she wanted to influence Lowdon's platform by making a stronger showing. But set that aside. If I was trying to assemble the biggest yarn ball in the world, I doubt I'd have people sinking boats out from under me. It can't be completely pointless if people will kill to stop you. So I'll ask again—who are you and what do you want?"

"The name's Calder. Arthur Calder. I represent a group of civic-minded San Franciscans who feel that the November election is best put behind the city as quickly as possible. Allegations of fraud serve only to raise concerns in the public's mind about the sanctity of the voting process. Concern that would be misplaced. The results are the results. They wouldn't have changed."

"Why don't you just cop to it. You work for CVT."

"I meant what I said. I represent a coalition of like-minded, but *independent*, individuals."

"You're full of it—no matter who you work for. But even if the fraud in the last election didn't turn out to be material, John Q. Public should damn well be concerned about electronic voting in San Francisco. And the runoff is proving to be a much closer race."

Calder settled back in his chair and nibbled on his celery stick. "We're confident we can prevent any reoccurrence—assuming, for the sake of argument, there were any problems."

I threw up my hands. "I can't believe I'm having this conversation. You tried to kill me, and you're making it sound like a League of Women Voters' project."

"And you trespassed and most likely stole property. Listen, my friend, you're in way over your head. You've no idea who you're up against. We know you showed some restraint last night. We decided to show you some in return."

A seagull screeched behind me, making me jump in my chair. Calder looked across with a dead calm expression.

"So now we've talked," I said, "one man to another. Your idea is that I fold my tent and go home. Stop digging into the election."

"That would be it."

"And what if I put the cops onto you?"

"It's your word against mine, and believe me, I'm better connected at Bryant Street than you are."

"What if I trace the ownership of the boat? Find out who you're representing?"

"The boat's in my name, so it's still your word against mine. And you can be sure that there won't be any damage the next time you see it. Nothing to link it to the incident last night."

"And if I continue to investigate?"

Calder set the drink down on the table. "I think you know what will happen. What would have happened last night while you slept in your bed if we wanted it to. But I'm a man who believes that the stick works better with the carrot." He leaned forward to pull something out of his hip pocket. He slid a fat envelope across.

I thumbed open the flap and peeked inside. It was bulging with hundred dollar bills. "That looks like a nice chunk of change."

"Yes, a nice bit. It's $15,000. You'll get another $50,000 if you stay clear until the election's over. You don't even have to tell Lee that you're quitting. Just tell her that you ran into a dead end. You can collect from both of us."

I stared down at the money for a long moment. Then I smiled. I reached under the table and took hold of the nearest leg, snapped it off. I gripped it like a club and stood over Calder, who was now trying to become one with the seat back.

"Here's another bit of Greek mythology. Remember the Procrustean Bed? And the guy who cut or stretched people to fit into it? You or any of your people come near me again and I'll stretch your ass so wide it will fit all four of these. Call it a Procrustean Suppository."

I flung the table leg into the water and went away from there.

AUGUST ALLEY

C ALDER HAD POLITICAL FIXER WRITTEN ALL OVER him. At
first blush, he seemed too well-heeled to be associated with
Willmott and the Green Party, but I was going to be very surprised
if she couldn't tell me who he was and where he fit into the San
Francisco political scene. Besides, she was overdue with an update
on her investigation into my favorite low-income housing developer, Ralph Wood. If it turned out that Calder was a crony of Wood's,
who was I to complain? Theirs would be almost the first two dots
I'd managed to connect in the picture.

I jogged across Marina Boulevard to the Safeway (nicknamed
the "Dateway" for its popularity among the young Marina District
crowd as a pick-up spot) and sat down on the curb in front of the
store. I used my cell phone to call Green Party campaign headquarters, recognizing the voice of the wiseacre with the teen abstinence
t-shirt when he answered. I asked for Kathleen Willmott.

"She's out of the office."

"Do you know when she'll be back?"

"As soon as she gets her broom out of the shop?"

"Cut the comedy. This is important campaign business."

I heard him adjust the microphone on his headset, then he came
back on in a more confidential tone. "Hey, you're the guy who came
here yesterday, aren't you?"

"What about it?"

"I don't know what you said to them in that conference room, but you should have heard the yelling after you walked out."

"I have that effect sometimes. When's she coming back?"

"Nobody knows. She missed a neighborhood breakfast event this morning. All us chickens figured it had something to do with your meeting."

"You mean she quit?"

"Or was fired."

"I'm sure there's some other explanation. Look, you got a cell phone number for her?"

"Nope. Strictly need to know. Only the campaign big wigs have it."

"How about an address?"

"That I can do. Everyone has one on file." After a little rummaging, he read off an address in North Beach on—of all places—August Alley. "That's good for both her and her brother. Now, since I gave you the address, are you sure you don't want to tell me what went on in the conference room?"

"Very sure," I said, and hung up.

One of the few uses I'd made of the Internet was to look up August Alley when I'd heard that such a place existed in San Francisco. So, while I'd never been there, I knew exactly what and where it was: a tiny, one-block alley between Union and Green streets. The only significant reference I found to it on the Web was a "spoken word" album called *Beatsville* released by Rod McKuen in 1959. On a track called "R.S.V.P." with bongo drums bonging in the background, McKuen begins his description of a beatnik party with the line, "Kranko's having a party at his pad on August Alley." I made a mental note to relay the cultural significance of her "pad" to Willmott when I found her. I was sure she'd be a big fan of McKuen's effort, if for no other reason than her choice of headwear.

I flagged a cab at the corner, and we took Bay to Columbus and then turned right onto Green, where the driver pulled into a head-in spot on the hill rising towards Mason and the Powell-Mason cable car line. Bells from a passing cable car and the clock tower of nearby Saints Peter and Paul Cathedral rang as I stepped out of the cab. It was twelve o'clock.

The neighborhood was a mix of Victorians, fake Victorians and blocky buildings from the 60s that weren't fooling anyone. August Alley itself was clean and neat, the modest, well-maintained houses along it jammed shoulder to shoulder. I went along a narrow sidewalk, past a brightly colored girl's bicycle with teal and silver fringes hanging off the handles, and up to a sawed-off "pocket Victorian" with the requisite number.

It was painted blue with white trim, and a redwood fence ran from the back of it to an apartment building next door, enclosing a miniscule backyard. A frost-bitten orange tree with stunted fruit grew in the yard, dropping a harvest of curled leaves onto the sidewalk. There was no one else in the alley, but the sounds of a hammer and a circular saw filtered down from construction going on in the top floor of an apartment house at the corner with Union. I went up two concrete steps to the door and pressed the buzzer. It didn't produce any sound I could hear. I wadded up my fist and banged on the door. No soap. I stepped back to examine the front of the house. There were no windows facing the alley, but I could see the convex bubble of a skylight cresting over the edge of the roof line.

I was fantasizing about climbing onto the roof to peek in or pry open the skylight when a car appeared at the Union Street entrance to the alley. It was a plain American sedan driven by a stocky guy with a buzz cut. He went by without glancing my way, but I caught sight of a light bar in the back window as he drove past: one of the new SFPD "stealth" cars. I tracked him until he turned left onto Green and then gave my attention back to the house. If the Willmotts weren't home to talk to, I would be just as happy to toss their place, especially if the local beat cop had just finished his patrol.

I considered my options. The skylight idea was too *Mission Impossible*-ish. Picking the lock was out—I'd left the picks at my apartment—and there was no mat for a key to be left under. That left boosting myself over the fence and breaking a back window, which I figured was just about my speed.

All that figuring came to naught when I decided to knock on the door again for safety's sake and came to examine the rather unusual doorknob. It was painted white to match the house's trim and was in the shape of a fist holding a short rod. There was no lock built into it, so it turned freely when I twisted it. The door opened just as freely—the deadbolt hadn't been set.

I slipped inside and locked the door behind me. The front room had a fireplace and a flat panel TV with a cluster of furniture—sofa, easy chair and coffee table—orbiting in front of them. A door on the right led off to the small kitchen and a darkened hallway opened at the back. The ceiling was high and there was a sleeping loft along the rear wall, reachable only by a rickety-looking ladder. Light came in from two skylights: one near the front door and another, larger one that looked like it could be opened for ventilation over the loft.

I crossed the room and prowled along the hallway. The first doorway I passed opened into a bathroom. The second led to a spare bedroom being used as an office, and the third, further down the hall, was closed. I spied a stack of documents in the office beside an industrial-strength shredder and decided to make that my first port of call—after checking out the final room. Despite all my earlier knocking, the idea that Willmott could still be home sick in bed worried me, and I certainly didn't want her surprising me while I ransacked the place.

I crept up to the door of the last room and teased it open: I needn't have worried about Willmott being sick. The two people inside were permanently immune.

A sleigh bed with slats in the headboard and footboard dominated the room. Willmott's brother lay face down, curled over a pile of pillows in the middle of the bed. His hands were cuffed together around a slat in the headboard. He was still wearing his skirt, but the back of it was flipped up to reveal his bare buttocks. Willmott lay hunched on top of him, with her thighs against his backside. She was naked from the waist down, except for the leather harness of a strap-on that projected out from her pelvis to be thrust in the only place it could be thrust. Her beret had fallen off and lay upside down on the floor beside the bed.

Both had been shot in the temple at close range. Blood and brains from Willmott were splattered over the bedspread, carpet and bedroom wall. A tighter pool of gore congealed around her brother's head, a triangle of light from the bedroom window jabbing into it like a knife.

There were other grim touches—like the open can of Crisco shortening on the nightstand and the ball gag in the brother's mouth—but the one that made me go numb was the Glock 19 on the carpet near the door, in just the position someone might ditch it after he or she had finished with the dirty work. I got down on my haunches and flipped the gun over with a pen to examine the serial number on the slide. It was my gun—the gun I thought was in the evidence locker at South San Francisco Police Headquarters. No doubt the log would show that I had signed it out. And no doubt the ballistic tests would conclude that it had been used to kill both Geiberger and the Willmotts.

I brought my hand to my forehead and squeezed. That was when the pounding began—not in my head, but on the front door. "San Francisco Police Department," someone shouted. "Open this door immediately."

I hesitated only an instant before snatching up the gun. I doubted there would be fingerprints on it other than mine, and I didn't want to make the case against me any stronger by leaving it behind. The only question was how to make my exit. The front door was out. I figured there was another door off the kitchen, but they were probably swarming that one just as hard. I thought of my original *Mission Impossible* fantasy with the skylight and ran into the front room. I scurried up the ladder to the sleeping platform, and then pulled the ladder up behind me, shoving it against the back wall. If I stood on the bed of the platform, I could easily reach the skylight, which, as I hoped, was hinged.

I popped open the latches, took a bounce on the bed to get a running start and chinned myself up to the edge of opening. I slapped a forearm onto the asphalt roof tiles, and half pulled and half pitched the upper half of my body onto the roof as the sound of splintering wood came to me from below. I slithered the rest of the way out onto the roof and pivoted on my belly to lower the skylight back to the closed position.

To my left was the end of the roof and the miniscule backyard. I could hear more cops down there, smashing the glass of a door or window. To the right, however, was the flat roof of one of the 60s buildings. I crawled to the edge of the Victorian's roof, risked getting three-quarters upright and then leapt across the two-foot gap. I landed squarely on both feet, but rolled immediately onto the gravel, skinning the bejesus out of my palms and spotting my jacket and pants with tar.

I elbowed and kneed it over to the back edge of the new roof and looked over. Somebody's carefully raked Japanese rock garden filled a ten-by-ten plot between the house and low wooden fence, and beyond that was another 60s vintage house that fronted Mason Street. I looked at the drop to the ground and grit my teeth. There was no way I was going to jump from that height in cold blood, so I lined myself up along the edge of the roof and then dangled my feet over the side. I slid more of my legs off and then suddenly the rest of me snapped down like a clock hand and I just managed to grip the edge of the roof to prevent a free fall to the ground. I dangled like that for a beat—gravel burrowing itself into my grasping fingers—and then I let go.

I landed hard on the back of my heels and then fell backward to enjoy a deep tissue rock massage on my ass and shoulders. I bit my lip to avoid screaming aloud and arched my back to get a hand under my ass to rub my throbbing tailbone. A burp of siren from another cop car coming down the alley put an end to this moment of self-indulgence, and I scrambled to my feet and limped over to the back fence. This I hopped with relative ease and then I made my way uphill across an ill-kept backyard populated with children's toys, high weeds and hidden deposits of dog shit, to a gate that opened on Mason.

There were no cops and very few cars or people moving in either direction for several blocks. I half jogged, half walked south on Mason until a cable car overtook me. I flagged it down and rode it back downtown, a little Chinese boy eating a pork bun staring at the bloody scrapes on my knees the whole way.

I went first to my apartment to clean up and change clothes. I grabbed more ammo for the Glock and took all the mad money I had out of its hiding place. I was in and out in about twenty minutes. I wasn't sure if the cops were already after August Riordan proper or just the guy who had surprised—or forced—the Willmots in a tableau of incestuous, S&M sex and then blown their brains out with a (soon to be identified) 9mm gun, but I didn't like the odds either way.

I decided to risk one more errand before going to ground for the day, and that was to talk with Chow. He wasn't at his office on Waverly Place, but he loomed lively, large and loquacious behind a glass case in his store on Grant.

He finished ringing up the sale for a pair of $8.95 Kung Fu slippers, passed them in a plastic bag to a fifteen-year-old kid with blackheads and a black duster, and said, "Ah, Mr. Riordan. I am seeing you more than I see my own grandkids. But I'm happy to be able to see you at all—especially after what I read about your run-in with the Wo Hop To gang. It is not often that one chops the choppers and lives to tell about it."

"You don't know the half of it. That was three disasters ago."

"Do tell."

"I'd rather you do the telling. Do know a guy named Arthur Calder?"

He nodded and reached down to straighten a row of Buddha ashtrays on the counter top. "He's a windbag asshole. He's also the head of something called the San Francisco Home Builders League."

"Which does what?"

"It's a trade group of contractors and construction workers. It's pro-development and is rumored to have its fingers in the Department of Building Inspections, where it uses its influence to expedite the review and approval of its members' projects. It also backs political candidates that are sympathetic to its cause."

"From what I understand of your and the Dragon Lady's politics, he would be an ally, but you just called him an asshole."

"Yes, a windbag asshole. The League gave some money to our campaign just to hedge their bets, but their main friend in politics is the current mayor, Charlie Hill."

"And since Hill has hand-picked Lowdon to be his successor, it follows that Calder and the League must be friendly with him, too."

Chow smiled and patted the head of one of the Buddhas. "Yes, that's true as far as support for development goes. Lowdon is definitely behind more housing for the middle class in San Francisco. But he's got a touch of the reformer in him, and I don't think he cares for the shenanigans alleged to be going on in the Inspection office. Still, when all is said and done, Calder and the League are going to be behind Lowdon—and they're probably expecting that Lowdon's allegiance and debt to Hill will hold him in check when it comes to shining sunlight into places that it doesn't belong."

I picked up one of the ashtrays. The ashes were meant to go in a pond that opened before the squatting Buddha. "A place to cool your tired butt" was written at the bottom. I laughed. "The more I learn about politics in San Francisco," I said, "the more I want to move to Des Moines. How about a guy named Ralph Wood? Do you know him?"

"Another asshole. But an asshole for the other side. He and Calder are mirror images of each other. They both want to build stuff and make money. The only difference is what they build—low-income housing or yuppie lofts."

"If they are so much alike, could they get past their differences and work together?"

Chow shrugged. "It's possible they could make a deal. But one or the other would have to turn his back on their current political allies."

"What about Wu. Whose side would he be on?"

"He has no sides. He works for himself and whoever pays the most." Chow reached across to take the ashtray from my hands. "And as much as I like seeing you, Mr. Riordan, I must ask that you not stop by any more. I can tell by your questions that you've dropped yourself in a pot of trouble. It worries me that you ask about Wu only as an afterthought. Ignore him at your peril."

PIZZA PARTY

AFTER FINISHING WITH CHOW, I CAUGHT THE number thirty Stockton bus to Lombard Street near Van Ness Avenue where a lot of the cheaper tourist motels were located. I picked the Golden Gate Motor Lodge and asked for a room for three nights from a clerk who was spelunking his mouth with a bent paperclip. I spoke in halting English and gave my name as Ronald Olson, allowing him to overcharge me fifty bucks when I held my wallet open and professed uncertainty about the right denomination of bills to be used for payment. "All the money is green," I said. "In Sweden we have different colors and sizes."

"But only one kind of meatball," said the clerk.

He gave me a key for a first-floor room next to the ice maker and the concrete stairwell. Inside was a carpet with the sort of pattern you see when slime mold grows on split pea soup, and several badly done imitations of the paintings of the kids with big eyes. There was also a bed with a sagging mattress that enveloped your butt like gel in a dental mold and a TV with one of the color guns on the fritz. The stains on the ceiling looked worse than most peoples' garage floors.

I sat on the bed and watched a magenta-colored newscaster from the local station read the evening news. The murder of Kathleen Willmott and her brother was given big play. They showed a clip of Padilla giving an emotional tribute to them, followed by a promise to dedicate the election victory to their memory. He lambasted the current administration—and by implication Lowdon—saying that they were ultimately responsible for the Willmotts' deaths because of insufficient focus by the SFPD on major crime. He ended with an impassioned plea for voters to turn out tomorrow for "Kathleen and Kaleb."

Then came the part I was dreading. They showed a clip of what looked like an impromptu news conference given by Lieutenant Kittredge. He stonewalled most of the questions—"Was the murder politically motivated?"; "Is there a connection to the death of Elections Director Bowman?"; "Can you comment on rumors regarding S&M paraphernalia at the crime scene?"—and gave only the barest sketch of the circumstances of the bodies' discovery. However, when asked if there were any suspects, he replied, "No active suspects, but we want to interview private investigator August Riordan as a person of interest."

Even if the ballistics hadn't come back yet, there was plenty to tie me in: my call to campaign headquarters and my cab ride to the crime scene, for openers. And that didn't even factor in the possibility that I'd been ID'ed by the patrol cop who drove by the house.

I mashed down the power button on the lunch box-sized remote that went with the motel's Paleolithic-era TV and excavated my butt from the mattress. I didn't need to hear any more. What I needed was to compare notes with Chris and to get some food.

I retrieved a well-thumbed Yellow Pages from the laminated nightstand and flipped it open to the pizza listings. A bunch of clipped toenails fell out. That put a dent in my appetite to the extent that I refrained from ordering a large, but didn't stop me from getting a medium double-meat Stromboli. I was too paranoid to phone Chris from the hotel—and I had turned off my cell phone to avoid being tracked by it—so I walked to a corner gas station and used a pay phone. "August," Chris shouted into the receiver when he realized it was me. "Do you know you're a wanted man? The police are looking for you."

"Oh really?" I said. "Then it's a good thing I'm calling from a pay phone on my way out of town. Now go find another and dial this number." When he rang back, I explained I was kidding about leaving town and gave him directions to the motor lodge, emphasizing that he be very careful not to be followed. I hung up then and went to the station mini-mart to get a six pack to go with the pizza.

The pie arrived well before Chris did. I was working my way through my third slice, orange grease from the pepperoni coating my fingers, when he knocked at the door. I wiped my hands on the complimentary shoe buffer provided by the motel and let him in. He was dressed in a dark blue pea jacket with a matching watch cap.

"You were supposed to make sure you weren't followed," I said, "not dress up like a character from *On the Waterfront*."

"I was trying to be less conspicuous."

"It *is* better than a spangled Elvis suit." I rebuttoned the door and pointed to the pizza and beer on the bed. "Grab yourself a slice. You longshoremen must work up big appetites."

He looked down at the congealing pizza like he was taking in a frog on a dissection tray. "Gross, August, you know I don't eat processed meat."

"It's free range sausage."

"I'm not touching it."

"Have a brewski, then."

He pulled off his watch cap, folded it and set it carefully down on the nightstand. "Being a fugitive hasn't improved your sense of humor. Is there coffee?"

"There's a coffee maker and a tray of fixings on the vanity, but I'm not sure I'd recommend it."

He walked over to the vanity and reached a timid hand out to pick up a plastic spoon. It was stuck to the tray. He shivered and sat down demurely on a wobbly straight-back chair with a furry orange seat cushion. "You should give yourself up, August. Jail would be preferable."

I slumped onto the bed and grabbed another slice of the pie. "You may have a point."

"So?" he asked. "What the hell is going on?"

I filled him in on the events since I'd seen him at the hospital, including my adventure on Geiberger's boat, the debacle on August Alley and my conversations with Calder and Chow.

"So?" he asked. "What the hell is going on?"

I laughed. "I have some ideas. Tell me what you found out at CVT and maybe we can piece it together."

"Happy to. But I'm afraid all I'll be doing is supplying another piece that doesn't quite fit. I told you they figured out there was a logic bomb. I got an engineer on the staff—a very cute engineer, by the way—to open up about the details. Problem is, they've only got part of it figured out."

"Well, tell me what they have figured out. And keep your fantasy life to yourself."

Chris stuck his tongue out. "Remember that I told you a logic bomb is a malicious bit of code that's hidden in the regular software?"

"Yeah."

"Well, just like a real bomb, it needs a sort of trigger. Turns out the trigger for this logic bomb is in the ballot definition file, which is really just a list of candidates and propositions formatted in a special way that the voting machine can read and display on its screen. When that file has the trigger set for a particular candidate, the logic bomb goes off and the machine will ensure that the candidate receives a majority of the votes registered on the machine's memory, regardless of how the votes are cast. If it's not set for any candidate, then the machine works the way it's supposed to, recording votes accurately."

"Why not just build a preference for your candidate in the logic bomb up front? Why go to the trouble of separating the trigger out in the ballot file? Seems indirect."

"Because if you do it this way, you can use the bomb over and over again to rig elections. All you need to do is set the trigger in the ballot file for the candidate you want to win before the ballot's loaded onto the machines. You don't have to reprogram the software on the machines, which are subject to a lot more scrutiny than the ballot and may not be updated between elections."

"All right. I get it. But you just talked about changing the votes on the USB drives. Does the bomb change the votes on the audit trail, too?"

"It's very clever about that. Sometimes it does, which risks the voter noticing the discrepancy. But the engineer told me that only about three out of every hundred voters notices if there's a difference between the votes cast and the votes printed on the audit trail. Other times it *doesn't* change the vote on the audit trail, but as I told you before, the chances of someone discovering a discrepancy by unspooling one of those little rolls and manually counting votes is pretty low. Either way, the logic bomb makes sure enough votes are registered for the selected candidate."

"And they're sure Geiberger was the one who did it?"

"Yep. He's the only one who had the skill and access to pull it off."

I threw a rind of pizza crust back into the box and looked down at the remainder a little queasily. "So what's the problem? Sounds like they've found the smoking gun. What don't they know?"

Chris smiled and put his hands into the pockets of his pea jacket. He tipped his chair back against the wall. "They haven't figured out how the ballot is secretly marked, and because of that, they don't even know that the logic bomb was triggered during the November election. When they looked at the old ballot file, they couldn't tell which, if any, candidate was secretly flagged to win."

"So this is all hypothetical?"

"It's real enough. But since they aren't certain it was used, they are not about to go public with the problem. And it seems to me it's entirely possible it *wasn't* used. You said you found a precinct map on Geiberger's boat with election totals that had Lowdon as the clear winner. Maybe that was Geiberger's real plan, but he got tripped up somehow."

I nodded and guzzled what was left in my current can of Bud. "I've got a theory about the precinct map. I think Geiberger was approached by Calder to fix the election, and I think Calder's original instructions were to make sure Lowdon won hands down. Then Calder began to worry about Lowdon cleaning house at the Department of Building Inspections and he decided to switch sides. Chow said Calder and Wood were mirror images of each other. I think Calder approached Wood and made a deal to divvy up the development at Hunter's Point. Then they told Geiberger to fix it so Padilla got enough votes to force a runoff. They knew it would be too obvious to have him win in the general election, but they figured it would be okay to have him squeak by in the runoff."

"How do you explain the Willmotts' murder and your being set up for it?"

"Willmott must have done what I asked and started checking into Wood's involvement in the election fraud and found something. Wood found out and decided she and her brother had to go. They framed me for it to get me out of the picture, too."

"But why did Calder also try to kill you on Geiberger's boat?"

I grinned at him. "I knew you were going to ask that. I'm pretty sure the thing with the boat only happened because I was snooping around. My guess is they were going to sink the boat that night anyway to destroy whatever evidence Geiberger might have left behind. But when I didn't take the bribe Calder offered, they decided to tie me into the doings at August Alley. Either that, or Wood acted without consulting Calder. He's definitely the more hardboiled of the two."

Chris pursed his lips and raised his shoulders in a gesture that signaled it was remotely possible. "Fine. But explain Bowman's murder—and Wu. How does Wu fit into your unified theory of mayhem?"

I crumpled up the beer can and threw it at the trash can in the bathroom. It sailed high and landed with an unholy clatter in the tub. "Beats me."

"And you haven't fit Roadrunner into it either."

"I know." I rose from the bed with an airy belch and false display of sangfroid. Chris made a face. I walked over to where he was sitting and levered his chair off the wall. "Pull your watch cap on and let's go," I said. "We're going to find Roadrunner and make him fit."

LADY PSYCHIATRISTS' BOOTH

C HRIS WAS A MEMBER OF A CAR-SHARING cooperative that allowed members to rent cars by the hour, picking them up and dropping them off from "pods" in their neighborhood. Chris had selected a green Toyota hybrid with the collective's logo on the side in big, yellow letters, and the fact that the car was so conspicuous and that he insisted upon driving didn't do a great deal to aid my digestion. I felt the Stromboli rising as he asked, "Where are we going?"

"To South Park. I told Casia—the girl who was with Roadrunner—to stay at an SRO there. I'm hoping she took the advice and she can tell us where to find him. Apparently they hooked up for at least one night so she must know where he lives —or square "

In San Francisco, South Park isn't a rude cartoon show made with paper cut-outs: it's a south of Market neighborhood that has seen more than its share of ups and downs. In the 1800s, the oval park at its center had been ringed with the houses of the city's elite, but the 1906 earthquake and fire had leveled all that. After it was rebuilt, it became home to a motley collection of warehouses, machine shops, sleazy hotels and bars. Then came the dot-com bubble and burst, pitching the neighborhood through another cycle of prosperity and decline. It has since recovered to some extent, but none of the fancy restaurants and venture capitalists from the dot-com era have returned, and the SRO hotel I'd recommended to Casia—the Park View—while less unsavory than most, was not exactly pulling the neighborhood up.

Chris insisted on creeping along Van Ness until he got across Market, so it took us the better part of a half hour to get to the park. We found a spot by the curb that ringed the oval of grass, eucalyptus trees and playground equipment and wedged the car in between a beater pickup full of recycled cardboard and a late model BMW. It was a perfect microcosm of the neighborhood. The hotel was on the far side of the park, but as we cut across the dewy grass, I spotted a pair of dark figures lounging on a swing set just beyond a circle of light thrown by a street lamp.

The taller figure was more rumpled-looking and had a bandana wrapped around his head so that it peaked like the pope's hat. He was smoking a cigarette, and as he took a drag, the orange glow from the butt illuminated a scraggly gray beard and a nose like a new potato. The other figure was more slight, was sporting a cowboy hat, and just at that moment, had his or her head tipped back to drink from a bottle wrapped in a paper bag. I caught the camo pattern on her sleeve and I knew it was Casia. I called her name.

She brought the bottle down with an audible slosh and raised her hand against the glare from the street lamp. "Who's that?"

We stepped closer. "It's your old pal, Ovaltine."

"The dude from the garage. What's Ovaltine got to do with it? Isn't that some kind of laxative?"

Chris and the guy on the swing laughed.

"Before your time," I said. "Forget I mentioned it. We wanted to talk with you privately."

Casia exchanged glances with the bearded pope. He said, "Don't talk to them if you don't want to, sweetheart."

"It's okay, Walt. He's my—what you call it—benefactor." She passed the bottle over. "I'll see you back at the hotel. Maybe we can play another game of Canasta."

Walt lurched out of the swing and would have done a face plant if I hadn't caught him under the arms. "Thanks, man," he mumbled. "Just knock on my door when you're ready, Casia." He shuffled off into the night, coughing like a Soviet tank starting up.

Casia grabbed the chains of the swing above her head in a maneuver that was vaguely exhibitionistic. "So, who's your friend?"

"His name is Chris."

"Well, Mr. Ovaltine, my earlier offer still stands. But I'm not into three-ways."

Chris emitted a kind of strangled gasp. "I sincerely hope you're talking about light bulbs."

"What's with him?"

"Another vote against three-ways. But we didn't come for that. We came to ask some more questions about Roadrunner."

Casia let go of the chains. "That jerk-off again?"

"That's the one. Have you seen him since the garage?"

"Yeah, he helped me store some stuff in a locker at the bus station when we first got together. He was waiting for me when I went to retrieve it."

"What'd he want?"

"He wanted to know what happened after he disappeared down the fire escape. And he wanted to convince me to go back to the building to squat."

"To which you replied?"

She laughed and hooked her thumbs under the arms of her beater t-shirt. "I told him to go fuck himself—that I was now a proud resident of the Park View hotel. As for what happened after he left, I told him you bought me a cheeseburger."

"You didn't mention the paper rolls we found in the grill?"

"Hell no."

I wasn't sure I believed that, but it didn't really matter. "Look, Casia, we're trying to find him. I was hoping you could tell us where he lives."

"I only stayed with him the one night. He had a basement room in a house near that penis tower thing."

"Coit Tower," put in Chris.

"Yeah, whatever. It was dark when we got there and I don't think I could find my way back."

"Do you remember a street name?" I asked.

"No, I wasn't paying attention. And man, we did all kinds of twists and turns to get there. The only street I remember was Columbus."

"That's way down at the bottom of the hill in North Beach."

"Yeah, we were having a drink or three at a bar there, and then we walked up to his house."

"How about the name of the bar?"

Casia took her cowboy hat off and dropped it in her lap. She ran her hand over the streak of dark hair. "I don't remember the name, but I remember the booth we sat in. It had a little sign over it that said, 'Booth for Lady Psychiatrists.' Roadrunner said it was his favorite place to have a drink because women always come up and try to psychoanalyze him."

"That's Vesuvio. Is that a hangout of his?"

"Seems like. The bartenders all knew him, and he also told me a favorite writer of his drank there."

"That would be Kerouac. Okay, Casia, that helps. Can you think of anything else that would give us a handle on him?"

"I know where he works."

"Works? I didn't put Roadrunner in the nine-to-five category."

"Ha. You're right about that, man. It's more of a volunteer thing. He told me he helps out at the Bicycle Advisory Committee."

That rang a faint bell for me, but I couldn't place it. "What the hell's that?"

"You got me. A bunch of people making suggestions about bike lanes and shit."

"I wouldn't think anarchists would stay inside the lanes."

"No, and he told me he doesn't even own a bike."

"Okay. I think we'll go with the Vesuvio lead. Thank you again."

She smiled up at me. "Thanks are appreciated, but I could sure use a little something more to keep me in cheeseburgers. I spent the first installment like you told me. I'm prepaid for four nights at the Park View, but that didn't leave much for food."

"Especially after going in on the Mogen David."

She giggled. "That was Walt's Mad Dog. I was just having a little nip to be sociable."

I brought out my wallet to extract another hundred. I also took out a business card and a pen and scratched Chris' cell phone number on the back. I dropped the card and the money into Casia's hat. "There you go. Give me a call at the number on the back of the card if you see Roadrunner again. Don't use the other numbers because they don't work. And go easy on the Mad Dog—alcohol can't be good for you."

"No worries there," rasped a voice out of the darkness. "I'll monitor her consumption." Walt shuffled back into view, a yellow-toothed grin opening a ragged gap in his beard. "Sorry to eavesdrop, but what kind of friend would I be if I abandoned her to you two?"

"A fair question, Walt," I said. "A fair question."

December had been dry so far, but about five minutes after we got back into the car, it began to rain—hard. Vesuvio was smack dab in the middle of North Beach, and with the rain, the hubbub for the eight PM show of Beach Blanket Babylon at Club Fugazi and the generally impossible parking situation, there was no legal place to put the Toyota for blocks. It was also not lost on me that the Willmotts' "death house" (as the TV news called it) was less than a half mile away, and it wasn't the brightest idea in the world for me to be endlessly circling the neighborhood like a lost dog—or a maniac killer.

I finally directed Chris to pull the car up Jack Kerouac Alley, which ran between Vesuvio and City Lights—the publisher and bookstore that first printed beat poet Allen Ginsberg's *Howl.* It was illegal to park anywhere along Kerouac, which left plenty of space for us and made it possible to pull almost right up to the door.

Chris switched off the Toyota. Over the sound of the rain drumming on the roof, he said, "What's the plan, boss?"

"Go in and look for him, what else?"

"Maybe I should do it. I'm not wanted by the city and county of San Francisco."

"True, but you don't know what he looks like and I doubt you can inspire the same forthrightness that I can. Just keep the battery warm—or whatever it is you keep warm on these wind-up cars—and be ready to go if I come running out."

He reached over to touch my arm. "Okay, but promise me you'll go easy. You been doing too much punching, chopping, shooting and generally butch stuff lately. In fact, here's a little Broadway theater exercise to get in touch with your feminine side before you go. Complete this phrase—Little Orphan ..."

"Annie get your gun. See you, Chris."

I jumped out of the car and ran over to the Roman mosaic that spelled out the name of the bar beneath the overhang by the door. Inside, it was warm and muggy, the water from patrons' coats and umbrellas steaming up the place like an orchid hothouse.

Roadrunner was nowhere to be seen downstairs. I elbowed my way up to the bar to get a pint of Anchor Steam, taking in the artifacts on the wall behind—a black cat with glowing electric eyes and a W.C. Fields quote about thanking the woman who drove him to drink—while a barmaid with fantastic gelled bangs like fins from a prehistoric fish poured the beer.

I paid and took the beer up a narrow staircase to the second floor, which wasn't much more than a wide balcony overlooking the floor below. There were tables along the balcony railing, windows that looked out on Kerouac Alley and Columbus, and two booths: one near the landing of the stairs and another—the one for lady psychiatrists—across the way near the front of the building. Neither of the booths was occupied and the only other person upstairs was a nerdy guy reading a book. I walked along the railing to a table just past the second booth and sat down facing the windows that looked out on Columbus. Anyone approaching the booth would get a (hopefully unrecognizable) view of my backside, while I would see his or her reflection in the window. But once someone sat down, the booth wall would prevent either party from observing the other even though we would only be a few feet apart.

I sipped my beer and shuffled a stack of coasters while the rain caromed off the window like thrown pebbles and no one new came up to the second floor. I was down to suds and backwash at the thirty minute mark, and had given up shuffling to flip the coasters into the chair across the table. At forty-five, I'd lost all the coasters to wild flips and was wrestling with the decision to go downstairs for another beer. On the one hand, I didn't want to risk having to confront Roadrunner downstairs, but on the other, I wanted the beer and I figured it wouldn't hurt to check in with Chris.

The reflection of a muskrat fur hat rising over the staircase banister decided for me. Roadrunner stepped onto the landing in his full Great White North regalia, juggling two pint glasses of beer and a boilermaker shot. I hunkered down at my table to make myself less conspicuous, but I needn't have bothered. He walked over to the booth with a jaunty and supremely self-absorbed gait, and with much clinking of glass and kicking of wooden benches, ensconced himself therein.

The glasses of beer interested me. Maybe he knew from experience that there was no table service upstairs and had come well-stocked, but maybe a friend was joining him. I decided to wait before bracing him. The wait paid off almost immediately, when I heard someone else on the staircase and I caught sight of Diego, the kid who had dry-gulched me at the *Ciudad Verde* demonstration. I watched him in the window as he sauntered across the checkerboard linoleum, shaking the rain from his baseball cap as he came. His eyes slid across the back of my head without recognition and he stepped into the booth without exchanging a word of greeting with Roadrunner. Then, over the sound of the ambient bar chatter, he spat, "What the hell is this, *pendejo?*"

"Beer."

"It's Coors, isn't it? I told you last time I don't drink that shit."

Roadrunner said something I couldn't hear and then Diego said, "What?"

"I said I'm sorry."

"Never mind. Are you ready for tomorrow?"

"Yes. As long as they haven't changed the network."

"Why would they?"

"No special reason. But with all this craziness going on, they might have done an audit or something."

"I doubt it, and if I were you, I wouldn't mention it again."

There was a longish pause. I assumed Diego was taking a drink of the beer he didn't want. "Can I ask you a question?" said Roadrunner finally.

"I guess. Just hurry the fuck up."

"The talk at 13th Street is that Kathleen and Kaleb were killed in bed having sex."

"So?"

"So I remember you joking that she probably buggered him up the ass."

"Yeah?"

Whatever Roadrunner said was too soft or inarticulate for me to catch. Diego came back strong:

"That's another thing you shouldn't mention again."

I figured this was my cue. I stood from the table and took a quick step around the corner to face the booth. Roadrunner was sitting in the back, cringing like he was expecting a blow. Diego sat on the outside, but was leaning inward in a menacing way. As Roadrunner caught sight of me, puzzlement and then shock flickered across his face like bad acting in a silent movie. Diego jerked around to see what he was reacting to.

I tapped the sign above the booth. "Evening, ladies."

Diego made a move to stand. I mashed down his shoulder and flicked open my jacket. The butt of the Glock peeped out. "I think maybe you've seen this before. I reloaded it. It's got all fifteen in the magazine and it still works."

"Fuck you."

"Given what I just learned about you, Diego, I'm going to take that threat seriously. In fact, Roadrunner, step out of the booth. I think you and I need to find someplace a little less hostile to talk."

"Me?"

"Yes, you."

"Don't do it," hissed Diego.

Roadrunner froze. He opened his mouth, but no words came out. He just managed to take hold of the edge of the table and squeeze.

I pulled the Glock from its holster and held it down by my side. "Everything is unraveling, Roadrunner. Diego's going to ride the needle at San Quentin. You are, too, unless you do something to separate yourself from him and Wood. And me—I'm desperate. I don't have anything to lose at this point. I'll shoot you both right now if I have to."

Most of what I said was bullshit, but Roadrunner didn't know that. He looked at Diego and then he looked at me. He unlatched himself from the table and started to slide my direction. Diego got agitated and would have reached across to stop him, but for the up close and personal experience I gave him with the muzzle of the Glock.

Roadrunner was going slower than poured Play-Doh. I nearly had him at the edge of the booth when I felt a tap on my shoulder.

It was my turn to act surprised: Wood stood behind me with an open cell phone to his ear.

"Yes, I'm still here," he said. "Please hurry. He may even be armed." He put his hand over the speaker. "Would you like to talk to the cops, Riordan?"

I realized I should have paid more attention to the whiskey shot. I hesitated only an instant, then slapped the cell phone out of his hand. I strode towards the stairs, reholstering the Glock as I went. I giant-stepped down them two at a time. A siren started very loud and very close, and by the time I reached the bottom, a cruiser had screeched to a stop right in front of Chris' Toyota. A female officer jumped out and ran to the door.

I rushed forward to meet her. She entered the bar in high color, water spotting her glasses. "Are you looking for Riordan?" I asked.

She nodded curtly. "That's right."

"He's upstairs in the john."

"Okay, thanks. Please stay here."

I nodded, but as soon as she went past, slipped out and ran to the Toyota. I jerked open the door to find Chris in a state that frantic didn't even begin to describe. He gestured wildly at the cruiser. "Police," he mouthed.

I dove into the seat and slammed the door closed. "Skip the closed captioning. Just get the hell out of here."

For all the mute hysteria, Chris responded like a champ. He shoved the gearshift into reverse and we crawfished out of the alley onto Grant. He shot down Grant to Broadway, where he flung the car left through an amber light and sixty seconds later we were in the Broadway tunnel, heading for the far side of Russian Hill.

BYE-BYE WI-FI

"WHAT I DON'T UNDERSTAND IS WHY WOOD came up to you after he called the cops. Why not wait for them to surprise you instead of doing it himself?"

Chris and I had driven to the car-sharing collective to exchange the Toyota for a VW bug. After another argument over who was going to drive, I was sitting behind the wheel with the motor off while he sulked in the passenger seat.

"Because he didn't want the police to bag Roadrunner. Better to stampede me off than risk Roadrunner spilling his guts." I patted the steering wheel. "You know, this is only buying us a few hours. They are going to tie the other car to you eventually—even if no one got the plate number."

"I know."

"Well, thanks for sticking with me. I didn't mean to drag you into this." I reached over—a little tentatively—to pat his shoulder.

"You can't drag a drag queen. Now stop with the *Steel Magnolias* sniveling and let's figure this thing out. So you think Diego killed the Willmotts. And Roadrunner mentioned a network—which sounds very promising."

"Yes, and something Casia said clicked for me. The place she said Roadrunner volunteered—the Bicycle Advisory Committee. I know where it is. It's downstairs in city hall, right next to the Elections Office.

Roadrunner was stealing wireless Internet at the abandoned garage. Is it possible he tapped a network at the Elections Office and got access to the server where the election management system runs?"

"Sure. Then I'd be right about Geiberger's logic bomb not being used—it was Roadrunner all along. We can call the Elections Office tomorrow before they begin tallying the votes and tell them to check. If they find a security hole, they can close it—or maybe even lay a trap for Roadrunner and catch him in the act."

I wrung my hands on the steering wheel. "I wish we had something a little more definite. They're not likely to take an anonymous tip very seriously. And the hole may be hard to find. I mean, they could do an audit and miss it, couldn't they?"

Chris nodded. Someone had put a plastic daisy in the flower holder in the VW. He plucked it out and twirled it between his palms. "If there's a wireless network at the Elections Office, I could try to hack into it myself. The problem is proximity. Most wireless routers can only transmit to computers a few hundred yards away, and that's inside buildings. We'd be trying to reach a router in the basement of city hall from outside—unless you want to try sneaking in."

"Well, I'm sure the guards at the security checkpoint would be happy to see me."

Chris sniffed at the daisy, then smiled. "I'm sure they would. But maybe there's a better way. I've got a friend with some equipment. Let's see if we can borrow it."

Chris replanted the daisy, retrieved his cell phone and made a call. I understood the "hello, Jerry, this is Chris" part, but he could have been speaking in tongues for all I got out of the stream of techno-babble that followed. His "right, see you in fifteen" was more my speed, though, and when he hung up, he directed me to an apartment on Carl Street in Cole Valley. While I double-parked next to another bug of 1970s vintage whose bumper was secured with twisted coat hangers, Chris ran up the steps to the apartment and retrieved a black duffle bag and a five-foot antenna that looked like it could be used to tune in sitcoms from Mars. He threw these into the back seat and we took off.

We barreled down Oak to Franklin and then hung a right on McAllister. We had a bad moment at the intersection with Van Ness when I gunned the motor to beat a yellow light and then thought better of it. We ended up a few feet over the line and a cop car pulled up beside us. I could sense the driver's eyes on me. It took all my acting experience from Miss Dyer's fourth grade reenactment of *Valley Forge* (I was a drunken Hessian soldier asleep on guard duty) to look over at the car and give a sheepish sorry-about-that-officer grin. The cop behind the wheel wagged a finger at me and went back to sucking his Slurpee.

We made it across Van Ness without further incident and pulled around to the Polk Street side of city hall. It was still raining and it was getting late, which meant there was zero foot traffic, but everything in and around the vicinity was lit like a nighttime shuttle launch. The base and dome of the building were fitted with floodlights, and the glass doors of the entrance and various office windows shone with a blinding florescent light.

Chris unzipped the duffle bag and removed a hefty laptop and a tangle of cables. A power supply came next and then an adapter to plug into the car's lighter. He wired everything together and plugged the adapter into the car. Then he reached back to the antenna and strung a cable from the end of it to a socket on the side of the computer.

"Is that thing going to work from the back seat?" I asked.

"I hope so. If not, we may have to hold it out the window."

"Swell."

Chris booted the laptop and brought up a program called Bye-Bye Wi-Fi. He twitched the laptop's internal mouse around the screen, clicking buttons here, selecting menu options there. After about five minutes worth of machinations, he pronounced himself ready to begin.

"What do we do?"

"I already see several wireless networks, but I think we should get a general lay of the land before we try to hack in. Make a circuit of the building, driving as slowly as you can, and I'll see what networks I can pick up. After we get the full list, we can attack the ones we think are most promising."

City hall is boxed by Polk, Grove, Van Ness and McAllister. It would be easy enough to drive slowly on Polk, Grove or McAllister because they are low-traffic streets bounding Civic Center Plaza, but Van Ness would be another matter. We'd either have to park or buzz along at twenty-five or thirty in order not to get run over.

I pulled the shift indicator into drive and took my foot off the brake. We prowled down Polk, just rolling forward at idle speed. Periodically, Chris would glance up to see where we were, but mainly he kept busy pasting information from the Bye-Bye Wi-Fi program into another window he had opened on the laptop screen. After each entry, he would add a notation, like "P St hydrant," to indicate the physical location where he had picked up the readings.

When we got to the intersection with Grove, I turned right and called out the street name. Chris nodded and kept on copying and pasting. We dealt with Van Ness by zooming out to mid-block and parking. Chris took what readings he could and then gave me the green light to zoom up to McAllister. Then it was more of the same slow glide, except that Chris grunted about two-thirds of the way down.

"Something?" I asked.

"Could be. Let's finish up and then we'll take an accounting."

We coasted up to the place we began on Polk and I pushed the gearshift into Park. I watched as Chris massaged the information he had collected in the second window. A lot of it seemed to involve removing duplicate entries, but he was also sorting the data in a sequence that wasn't clear to me. When he was finished, he had three columns, one of which I concluded was the network name, the second clearly a location where the signal was strongest for that particular network, and the final was a Y or an N.

"What's the last column about?"

"It indicates whether the network is secured or not. Most of them are, but there are a few that aren't."

"Those would be the easiest to get into, right?"

"That's right, but unfortunately the unsecured ones don't seem to be particularly interesting. For instance, one of them is called traffic_court. We could probably fix a few parking tickets if we got in, but unless we can connect to the Elections Department network from there, it doesn't help us much."

"Don't lose that traffic court one. I've got beaucoup tickets to fix. But which ones look interesting now?"

He scrolled the window to the top and held the laptop up for me to look at the screen head on. "Which do you like?"

There were about fifteen networks in the final list, ranging from the prosaic mayors_office to the intriguing g_spot, but the one Chris had placed at the top was only three initials: CVT.

"I'll take door number one, Monty."

"I thought you might. That's the one I found on McAllister. There are only two problems. The first is it's secured. The second is the signal is pretty weak. If the encryption they are using is not the first and greatest, we may be able to break it or possibly we can guess the key. But first we've got to get a strong enough signal. Drive back to that spot on McAllister and let's see if we can fine tune the reception."

I wheeled the car around in a U-turn, drove past the spot where Chris had grunted and then did another U-turn to bring us up to the building side of the street. At Chris' direction I edged forward a few yards.

"That's as good as it gets," he said. "But it's still not good enough. We're dropping packets left, right and center."

"Dropping packets, eh? I hate when that happens. What are we going to do about it?"

Chris looked up from his screen with a deadpan expression that let me know I wasn't fooling anyone with my comment about packets. "Try holding the antenna out the window like I said before."

I punched the button to let my window down and took hold of the overgrown rabbit ears at the end where the cable connected. I pushed the whole thing into the night air, watching the rain glint on the polished aluminum.

Chris produced a neutral grunt and fiddled more with the computer mouse. "That's better, but it's still not good enough."

"What else we can do?"

"There's plenty of cable. The best thing would be to take the antenna right up next to the building. Preferably by a window."

"You mean take it *outside*?"

"That's right. I'll give you the thumbs up if you get to a place that works. Then, I'll either try to break the encryption or guess the key they are using. If we get past that hurdle, I'll try to get into the server where the election management system runs and see if I can access the database where the votes are tallied."

"How long is all that going to take?"

"Fifteen or twenty minutes if I'm lucky. Hours or never if I'm not."

I popped the latch on my door. "Okay, but if this is all a ruse to get me to stand outside in a rainstorm with a lightening rod in my hand, you are going to pay big time."

He grinned. "Wouldn't that be a knee-slapper?"

"Yeah, wouldn't it?" I stepped out into the rain, passing the antennae through the open window, and then threaded it and the cable around the front wheels, across the sidewalk and over to the building. I got a good soaking on the way, but there was an eave at the second-floor level that shielded me from the worst of it once I got up next to the building. I moved crabwise along the gray granite wall until I got close to a window and held the antenna near it.

Chris had turned on the dome light in the VW so I could see him clearly. He nodded, then pointed upwards. I held the antenna higher, and then higher again when he emphasized the gesture. When I had the antenna at full arm's length, he gave me a big thumbs up, flicked off the dome light and bent over the laptop.

Being a human radio tower is not the easiest of jobs. I took small comfort from the fact I was hidden in a dead zone between floodlights, and occupied my time shifting my weight from one foot to the other, and the antenna from one arm to the other, all while staring at Chris, looking for the slightest indication that things were progressing well. When I realized indications were not soon forthcoming, I switched my attention to a pair of earthworms that were squirming out of the waterlogged ground toward the relative shelter of the eave. Maybe they were covering an inch an hour, and maybe they had covered two-thirds of that when I heard Chris sing out.

He had the dome light on again and he seemed excited—but not excited in a good way. He gestured emphatically, urging me back to the car. I tucked the antenna under my arm and sprinted up to the passenger window. "Did you get in?" I demanded.

"Yes—all the way. Database, too. I'd bet anything the election was hacked this way. But forget that. There's a call for you."

"Who?"

By way of answer, he thrust out his cell phone. I ducked my head through the window and brought the receiver to my ear. "Hello. Who's this?"

"Mr. Ovaltine, it's—it's me—Casia. They say you have to come. They say you have to come now or they'll hurt me real bad. Please—" There was a shriek, and the phone at the other end clattered to the ground.

BETTER RED THAN DEAD

IT WAS DIEGO OF COURSE. HE DESIGNATED one of Wood's construction sites in the Mission as the meeting place and told me
I had fifteen minutes to get there. Every minute I was late would
mean one less finger or toe for Casia. If they ran out of digits, they
would find other things to cut. I was to come by myself and lose
the Glock. Cops would mean Casia's body would never be found
because she wasn't going to be on site.

"Then how do I know you'll let her go?" I asked.

"You don't," said Diego, and hung up.

It was a lose lose situation, but Chris agreed that doing what
they wanted was the lesser of two evils. At least we would be keeping
the ball in play and maybe Casia would not be hurt. With all the
crummy cards she'd been dealt in life, I couldn't bring myself to
simply walk away.

The corner of 14th and Mission was the address Diego gave.
I remembered it as the location of an abandoned federal armory.
Apparently Wood had obtained the property and was busy putting
up another of his low-income developments.

We made good time to the neighborhood, but I stopped about
three blocks away to let Chris out. I passed him the Glock and told
him to use his judgment.

"What does that mean?" he said, pinching the barrel of the gun between his thumb and forefinger like he was gripping a dead mouse. He knew how to shoot because I'd taught him, but he'd never been comfortable with the idea.

"It means what it means," I said. "I'm trusting you to do what you think is best. But if you do follow me to the site, please be careful and don't get yourself caught. You're the only one besides me that knows what the hell is going on."

He started to say something about picking a fine time to trust him, but I shooed him out of the car and sped up Mission to the edge of the property. It was 1:26. By my watch, I'd made it with three minutes to spare. In a desperate, message-in-a-bottle sort of gesture, I used those minutes to take out my cell phone and send my first text message. Then I powered the phone down and pulled the car up to the corner.

The hanger-sized brick building I remembered was gone. The only thing left was a gaping hole. Ten species of construction equipment ringed the pit with buckets, shovels and loaders dug into the earth like dinosaurs feeding. A chain-link fence enclosed the property, but the gate to it yawned wide open. A ramp of packed earth led from street level to the bottom of the graded excavation, where a sedan with tinted windows was parked with its headlights on.

I couldn't think of anything else to do but drive down the ramp and park by the sedan, which turned out to be a 70s vintage Mercedes. With the tinting on the Mercedes' windows and the only light coming from the cars' headlamps, I couldn't see in. I cut the motor on the VW and stepped outside. Mercifully, the rain had stopped, but my hands trembled as I closed the driver's door.

I stood frozen in the space between the cars. If Chris had decided to follow me, he could have crept onto the lot and hidden himself by the time I moved. I forced a deep breath into my lungs and tapped on the glass of the Mercedes. There was no response. I gripped the handle to the rear door, eased it open.

Roadrunner sat propped up in the back seat like a ventriloquist's dummy His eyes were half-closed and only the dullest reflection of the dome light came back from them. His fur hat had tumbled to his lap and there was a red blossom of blood on the headrest behind him. He'd been shot through the forehead, the entry wound like a vacant nail hole where a picture used to hang.

Diego was sprawled over the front seat. He'd gotten his from behind. Thick ropes of bloody saliva flowed from his mouth to cascade from the seat to his arm, and down his sleeve to the floor.

I still had my head in the Mercedes when I heard the other car. I pulled it out and whirled in time to see a stretch Hummer hurtling down the ramp. I clawed open the door to the Volkswagen and jumped into the driver's seat. I just managed to get the motor started, but it was wasted motion. The Hummer rammed me at a forty-five-degree angle, bulldozing me into the Mercedes and rattling me around the Bug.

Before I could collect my wits, two Asian guys in black pajamas came in through the passenger door and pulled me across the seat, out onto the muddy ground. One of them kicked me in the ribs for good measure.

I heard the passenger door of the Hummer open. I looked up to see the car shiver on its suspension and two stubbly feet and legs thudded into the earth like concrete piers.

"I believe the last time we spoke, the topic was death," said a voice above me.

The guys in the black pajamas yanked me to my feet, patted my torso down and shoved a gun into my ribs. Wu stood across from me in the same t-shirt and bloomer pants. The squid tattoo below his ear sagged in the fleshy folds of his neck, but his smile was vigorous—jolly even.

The fury from Gretchen's shooting rose within me. "You picked this fight, Wu. You nearly killed someone very close to me."

"And you killed my chef. And threatened me and my family. Neither of which will I forgive." He turned back to the Hummer and pulled out a pair of enormous cleavers with black handles. There were no characters written on the side—I gathered these were not the sort to be used as calling cards.

He looked at the cleavers almost wistfully, like they were an old baseball and glove from his youth. "I haven't used these for quite a while. The last time was to discipline one of my employees. He was a little shrimp of a guy and he'd always been kind of a fuck-up, so we had given him the affectionate nickname of Little Shit."

"Does this story have a point?"

"It has a punch line. Before I started in with the cleavers, Little Shit shit his pants." He grinned at me. "I told him he'd experienced an eponymous release. Because his name—"

"Yeah, I get it."

He nodded at his men, who backed me up against the dirt wall of the excavation. They stepped away, keeping their guns trained on me and blocking my escape route to the ramp. If there ever was a time for the cavalry, it was now. My eyes darted around the property, searching for some sign of Chris. I saw nothing.

Wu advanced, weaving the cleavers through the air in front of him. "If you're looking for your little fag friend, we've got him tied up in the back of the Humvee. I shouldn't think I'd let him play with guns in the future. Not that either of you have one."

My shoulders slumped and my breathing went to nothing. My hands and face felt tingly and numb. I thought of walking into the blades to get it over with.

Wu saved me by laughing. I vowed then I was going to hurt him somehow before it was over. "What is this really about, Squid

Boy?" I asked. "Why the rampage against me, the Lees and everyone else?"

"Playing dumb may suit your personality, but it's not a winning strategy." He touched the blades of the cleavers together like a praying mantis rubbing its foreclaws. "Now, they tell me you keep a knife on your ankle. You may take it out if you think it could be of any value."

It was disheartening to know he'd already factored the knife into the equation, but I leaned down to pull it off my ankle—then realized it was nothing but a trick. Wu bulled forward with surprising speed, slinging blades at my head and shoulders like a kind of grotesque Cuisinart.

I dove onto the ground, rolled past him and scrambled to my feet. He pivoted to face me and I backpedaled quickly, drawing him out between me and his men. That left me so many steps further from the exit, but at least I wouldn't be backed up to the wall or sandwiched between them.

Wu was already breathing hard and his face glistened with a greasy sweat. "Stand and fight, Riordan," he wheezed. "Or we'll shoot you."

He was right: both of his men had come up behind him and were busy drawing a bead on me with their pistols. I closed on Wu and feinted with the knife. One of the cleavers came whistling past my hand, shaving skin—and more—from my knuckles. I leaped back and pulled the hand to my midsection.

He threw a cleaver at my chest. I managed to lift both arms—one hand gripping the other—and the cleaver caught me square on the left forearm, just below the elbow. It bit into bone, hung there for the briefest of instants and then pulled out and plunked to the ground. I'd never felt so much pain.

Wu came charging in for the kill. I backpedaled like crazy, but caught my foot on a piece of rebar and launched in a near perfect back flop. It seemed like it took forever for me to hit the ground. While I sailed towards the black earth, I thought how puny my efforts had been. I worried about what would happen to Chris, but most of all, I wondered if I had hallucinated what I'd seen behind Wu and his men before I tripped—a backhoe blitzkrieging down the ramp.

I crash landed on my back and shoulders, but managed to avoid banging my head. I rolled to my right, fearing the bite of the other cleaver at any moment. It never came. What came instead were shouts, pistol fire and the soft thud of bodies hitting metal.

I rolled to a stop and pried myself off the ground. Wu was about ten yards to the left, watching as his pajamaed henchmen were scooped up in the loader of a real, steel-and-hydraulics backhoe. I'd lost my knife in the fall, but the cleaver he'd thrown at me lay partway between us. I sprinted towards it, flinging blood from the wound in my forearm as I came. I had my fingers around the handle by the time he turned. As I closed the distance between us, he brought the remaining cleaver up to swing at me, but I was on him before he could bring it forward. I chopped him in the neck just below his tattoo with everything I had. "Death," I shouted into his fat face and cackled like a madman—or maybe there was no "like" about it.

Wu was too stunned to even react. Blood spurted from the wound, spraying me and the front of his massive chest. He stood stock still for a moment, his cleaver still raised above his head, and then the blade slipped from his hand and he toppled backwards. He hit the ground with a sickening thud, his head wrenching over to reveal the deep V cut into his neck. He twitched and lay still.

My face, chest and arms were coated in blood—both Wu's and my own. I was laughing, mumbling to myself and trying to wipe blood from my cheek with a jacket sleeve that was already saturated when Red, the ATM thief, came up beside me. He looked at me, then at Wu and then back at me.

"Sweet Jesus," he said wonderingly. "And I thought you were taunting me about an ATM machine." He didn't wait for a response or explanation, but turned and ran out of the pit. "You owe me, man," he shouted over his shoulder.

He had trapped Wu's men in the loader against the wall of the excavation. I left them where they were and released Chris from the back of the Hummer. He was blubbering before I even got the gag out of his mouth and wrapped me in a hug in spite of the gore. "Don't ever tell me to use my judgment again," he said into my ear.

I extricated myself from his embrace as the wail of the approaching siren came to us. But there was also a muffled pounding emanating from the back of Diego's car. I reached under the dash of the car to pop the trunk and we found Casia hog-tied, but very much alive, in the back.

We had her propped up on the edge of the trunk by the time McQuaid and his partner Jerry skidded to a stop at the top of the ramp. There wasn't any friendly chit-chat about backhoes this time. They tumbled out of the cruiser to crouch behind its doors with guns drawn. McQuaid barked at us through the car's megaphone:

"Everybody down on the ground with your hands behind your head."

RETURN OF THE DRAGON

THE POLLS NEVER OPENED FOR THE RUNOFF election the next morning. After Chris and I got done talking, city officials finally accepted that the one in November had been rigged. They invalidated the results and scheduled it to be held again using the old paper ballot system in January.

"14th + mission. I dare u." was the text message I had sent Red from the car in front of the construction site. He got away clean and no one thought to ask me how I happened to be there at just the right time. Maybe text messaging wasn't quite the Valley Girl game I'd taken it to be.

Chris and I got thrown in the slammer. Chris got out the next day, but I ended up with a bail amount I had no hope of scratching together. It took three weeks of Mark Richie's time—and $24,000 in fees—to get me out. The murder charges against me were dropped when Chris located an adult toy store on Valencia Street where Diego bought the strap-on found at August Alley. The female clerk remembered Diego because his response to the question about whether the item was for personal use or should be gift-wrapped was, "Just put it in a bag, dyke." Likewise, the evidence clerk at the South San Francisco Police Station admitted that he had been bribed by Diego to release my gun and forge my signature (badly) on the locker release form.

The remaining charges of resisting arrest and criminal flight were dropped when Richie pointed out how much worse I could make things look for the city by talking to the newspapers. That was no empty threat, either. There wasn't a day that I spent in jail that the media didn't try to interview me. The threat of going public also carried the day for Chris and the charges against him of accessory to murder.

The Dragon Lady and Lisa came back to town soon after Wu's death hit the papers, and Lisa and Chris were frequent visitors while I was incarcerated. Lisa filled me in on how she and her mother avoided capture by Wu and regaled me with details of their subsequent adventures in Paris, which mainly seemed to involve shopping. Chris kept me apprised of the forensic audit the city was performing on the November election and all the processes, systems and software involved. It seemed his friend from the engineering staff of the now bankrupt Columbia Voting Technologies had been hired as part of the audit team.

"Exactly what sort of friend is he?" I asked.

"Oh, let's put it this way: I get most of the scoop horizontal."

I covered the speaker dingus in the Plexiglas wall that separated us. "Too much information."

The day I got out, Lisa met me at the Intake and Release Facility on 7th Street with Mylar balloons and champagne.

"Ready for your next session on the yoga mat, big boy?" Lisa whispered in my ear after planting a wet one on my lips. She was wearing a pencil skirt and black satin top with a keyhole cutaway. The view was breathtaking.

"That's almost all I've been thinking of."

She made a face. "Only almost?"

"Well, there were a few other little things, like not spending the rest of my life in jail and figuring out how to pay my shyster lawyer."

"Don't worry about that. My mother's already got it covered. She wants you to come by her office so she can thank you—and pay you your bonus, which she says you've more than earned."

"She has a point there. Tell her I'll be there later this afternoon—after I get my shoes polished."

She laughed. "Excellent. I've got a big evening planned for us after that."

But it turned out that I didn't have time for my shoes. I went instead to visit Gretchen at her apartment in Cow Hollow. She had been released from the hospital the week before, and while still a little wobbly, was up and about and making good progress in physical therapy. We sat at her kitchen table and talked about old times, not straying into her shooting or the case until the very end.

"After I passed out at my desk," she said, "Chris told me you threatened to kill this Wu character and all of his family."

"I did."

"I won't thank you for that—or for killing Wu. But thank you for caring enough to want to do it."

"Are you coming back to the office?"

"I don't know, August." Moisture welled at the corners of her eyes. "It has nothing to do with my being afraid—or what Dennis says. It has to do with you."

"If you mean all the violence—"

"I don't mean that, although I can't help but be shocked by it. I mean that you don't seem to realize you're being used."

"I don't understand."

"I've said more than I have any right to say. And I'm tired." She reached her hands across the table to take mine. "Come back and see me again in a few days, will you?"

I had taken a cab to Gretchen's apartment and now I walked up Union over the hill to North Beach and then down Columbus and across to Grant and Chinatown. It was two miles at least and it gave me a lot of time to think. Once onto Grant, I pointed myself towards the Dragon Lady's office, but stopped along the way at Chow's back scratcher emporium. We talked for a while and I left with one of his new bumper stickers. It read, "Change and Chow: They Go Together."

The violin player was not at his usual place outside the Dragon Lady's building—I assumed the incident with the cleavers had put him off his feed—but the red phone had been repaired and Lisa was quick to answer and open the private elevator for the short ride to the penthouse. She beamed at me from behind the reception desk when I stepped out. The furniture had all been resettled, the mangled carpet and smashed vases replaced and a spray of white orchids sat at her elbow. The sun was working hard to break free from a bank of puffy clouds, and filtered light came through the floor-to-ceiling windows, filling the room with a soft, diffuse glow. It seemed about as far as you could get from the fluorescent-lit, concrete and stainless steel bunker I'd been living in for the past few weeks.

"Go on in," said Lisa. "She's waiting for you. But don't be too long. We're having drinks at The Redwood Room and then dinner at Fleur de Lys."

"I assumed we were going straight to the yoga mat."

She giggled. "First things first."

I winked at her and then went up to the Dragon Lady's office door and knocked. I heard something I hoped was "enter" and opened the door. She was sitting ramrod straight behind her Napoleon's tomb-of-a-desk, wearing a tailored suit and enough jade to choke a real dragon, just like the first time I visited. The bookshelf had been righted, the other office furniture had been replaced and the divots in the desk had been filled without any telltale marks.

She gave me one of her fang-baring smiles. "Congratulations, Mr. Riordan," she said. "You have accomplished everything I asked—and more. That envelope is for you."

I pulled up a chair across from her and reached for the envelope at the edge of the desk. It wasn't fat like the one Calder had proffered, but it packed a heftier punch. Inside was a cashier's check for $35,000.

I set it on my lap. "I understand you picked up my legal expenses as well. All of this is much more than we agreed."

"As I said, you also did more than we agreed. But I would like to hear your explanation of exactly what happened. The city hasn't released any information and the media has been useless, my paper included. There's been nothing but a jumble of confusing, contradictory speculations. Some people, like Ralph Wood and Arthur Calder, seem to be running scared, but I don't understand why."

"So you're asking what I know."

She frowned at me. "Yes, isn't that what I just said? Does that surprise you?"

"Not at all. If I were you, I'd want the same thing. And it *is* a complicated business. I learned that electronic voting machines, or more accurately, electronic voting systems and processes, are vulnerable at many points—when the software is being developed and installed, at the precinct when the votes are cast, when the USB drives are collected from the machines, at election headquarters where the votes are tallied. All of those places."

"Yes, yes, I know all that."

"Well, the mistake I made was to assume that only one vulnerability was exploited. And that only one person—or several people working together with the same goal—were involved. It turns out there were a lot of fingers in the pie—and they all were groping for the plum from different directions. For instance, the chief engineer at CVT, Geiberger, built a sort of trap door into the touch-screen software allowing him to control the candidate who received the most votes on any particular machine. Calder bribed him to ensure that Lowdon won the election hands down, without requiring a runoff with Padilla or Chow."

"But that didn't happen."

"No, it didn't. And I'm sure Calder didn't pay Geiberger what he promised, which, coupled with the nasty divorce he had just been through, probably led to him going postal at CVT after they failed to settle his stock grievance. He didn't get the stock and he didn't get the money from Calder."

The Dragon Lady reached up to finger one of her clip earrings. Irritated, she pulled it off. "Yes, but why didn't it happen? Did the change Geiberger made fail to work the way he planned?"

"No, it worked perfectly. The problem, for Geiberger at least, was that the vulnerability he selected was upstream in the election process. He picked the first place you could tamper with the system—at the voting machine. But it turned out that the Green Party had somebody who picked the last place you could tamper with the process—at the Elections Department on the election management system. That was Raymond Fitch, aka Roadrunner, the kid who died in the car at the construction site with Diego Barrueta. They were both working for Wood to fix the election for Padilla. Well, maybe working isn't quite the way to phrase it in Roadrunner's case—I think he alone of all the would-be conspirators did it for his beliefs, rather than money.

"Anyway, during the November election, he hacked into a wireless network at city hall and accessed the voting database. Then he simply typed in the vote counts he wanted for each of the precincts, overriding whatever was already recorded. He intended to do the same thing for the runoff election, giving the victory to Padilla."

"There was a mention in the paper that this Roadrunner person had a paper audit trail from one of the voting machines. What was he doing with that?"

"Nothing, as it turned out. He had made up a set of dummy audit trails that matched the results he entered in the election management system. I think he hoped to replace the originals to make his hack more difficult to detect, but he couldn't get access, even though he worked in an adjacent office in city hall. While the electronic security for the election was bad, the physical security was not. All the materials from the precincts are kept in a locked room."

The Dragon Lady rolled her earring around in her palm, seemingly deep in thought.

"Other questions?" I asked.

"No, I ..."

I held up the envelope and sighted down the edge of it. "I can think of one question you might have. Who killed Elections Director Bowman?"

"Well, yes, you haven't explained—"

"Another might be where does Wu come into all of this, although maybe you already have a handle on that—seeing how you left the country to avoid him."

The Dragon Lady clenched the earring in her hand and sat up even straighter in her chair, if that was possible. She said nothing.

"I myself never found any evidence of his involvement in the election," I continued in a breezy tone, "but my associate has a pipeline into the forensic audit they're doing at city hall. They found that the votes recorded on the USB drives collected from the individual machines at the precincts often did not match the precinct totals in the election management database. That's hardly a news flash. Given what I told you about Geiberger and Roadrunner, you'd expect that the drives would show more votes for Lowdon and the database would show more for Padilla. The interesting bit was that there were more votes for Chow on the USB drives. In fact, when they reloaded the database with the drives from all the precincts, they found that Chow and Lowdon were neck and neck, which would have forced a runoff election between them, not between Lowdon and Padilla."

I gave her what I imagined was sort of an aw-shucks smile. "It's pretty confusing, isn't it? What that means is somewhere between the time the USB drives were collected at the precincts and the data from them was loaded into the election management system, the drives were either replaced or the numbers on them were changed. The only way that could happen was if there was a third group working to fix the election in Chow's favor, but since Roadrunner got in last taps with his changes, Padilla still got into the runoff, not Chow."

"And you're suggesting this was Wu's doing?"

"Undoubtedly. But to affect things that late in the process—and on such a scale—he would need to suborn someone high up in the Elections Department—and that was almost certainly Elections Director Bowman. The auditors got access to Bowman's bank records and found a deposit of $150,000 several months before the election. That was probably the down payment. But you can imagine Wu's chagrin when the election results were announced. After making that investment of $150,000, his candidate loses. Based on what I know about Wu, he probably didn't take that lying down. He probably thought he'd been double-crossed by Bowman and had him killed.

"Poor Bowman. He knew someone else had finagled the results, but he couldn't afford to launch an investigation or he'd risk exposing his own scam."

I fanned myself with the envelope and looked across the desk expectantly.

The Dragon Lady sighed. "Your veiled references to my relationship to Wu and the affected manner you've assumed since you walked in here hasn't escaped my attention, Mr. Riordan. Just where are you going with this?"

"I've been groping to figure out what the conflict between you and Wu was since the beginning. Chow suggested that maybe you had some business disagreement, and your daughter seemed to confirm that when she told me you were in a real estate transaction with him where he felt he was still owed money. Wu himself hinted at something along those lines, although the first time I talked with him, he suggested things between you had been smoothed over.

"What I can't help but wonder now is if the business transaction under dispute was fixing the election for Chow. Wu didn't deliver as promised, so you didn't pay. Wu tried to kidnap Lisa as leverage to get the money, so you mollified him with a partial payment—or at least the promise of one. Then you were friends again. But either you didn't come through with the promised money or you crossed or threatened him in some other way, and it was all-out war again—"

"Stop it!" she shouted and slapped the desk. "Stop it right now."

"Sorry, I'm such a motor mouth. But I'm curious—how much does it cost to fix an election? I imagine if you made a deal with someone like Wu it must run into the millions, especially when you've got to pay off election directors with hundreds of thousands of dollars. I spoke with Chow today and he told me an interesting thing. With all the shenanigans in the November election, he decided to get smarter about special interests and he did a little research into the companies that filed to develop Hunter's Point. He found one called Basis Construction he didn't recognize, but chasing a paper trail that led to Hong Kong and back, he linked it to you. I guess a few million to have your candidate elected mayor to approve your company's bid for a billion dollar opportunity is chump change. I don't think Chow is going to be quite as loyal to you as he was in the past, though. You know, now that Wu isn't around to threaten him with letter bombs and cleavers and things like that."

The Dragon Lady's face had petrified into a dark, flinty mask. "Are you quite finished?"

"No, but I'm working up to it. I'm still wondering about the final break with Wu. Why did he come on so hard against both you and *me*—even before I promised to kill him. It wouldn't be that you signaled to him in some way that I was coming after him before you skedaddled to Paris? Worst case, I would delay him, and possibly the investigation of my murder would bring some unwanted attention from the San Francisco police. In the best case—and I won't flatter myself into thinking you believed it was anything more than a long shot—I would come out on top, saving you millions of dollars and eliminating the one person who had evidence against you."

"None of it's true. You can't prove any of it."

"Those are two different things." I crossed a leg over my knee and looked down at my scuffed wingtip. "I'm not going to even try to prove it. But you better hope that the men from Wu's gang the San Francisco police have in custody don't talk or don't know anything to tell."

We stared at each other across the desk. Then she smiled. It was a queer, stiff smile like a crack in an ice cube. "Leave my office, Mr. Riordan. And don't come back."

I stood without saying anything and opened the door. I heard her pick up the phone and spit rapid-fire Chinese into it.

I went into the reception area. Lisa stared at her desk as she held her own phone to her ear. She hung up without saying anything.

"We still on for dinner, then?" I asked.

She looked up at me, and the eyes that met mine were as cold and opaque as obsidian. "*Sei gweilo.*"

The ugly words seemed to linger, to hover around us like blood in the water. I said, "I guess that yoga mat has sailed."

I turned and walked to the elevator. The few moments I spent waiting for it were long and uncomfortable, but I felt fine by the time I got off on the ground floor.

Chow broke all ties with the Dragon Lady, moved to the center politically and won the January election. His first act was to throw out all existing bids to develop Hunter's Point and establish a new commission to solicit and evaluate proposals. The bid from the Dragon Lady's firm, Basis Construction, was not resubmitted.

Ralph Wood and Arthur Calder both went to jail, Wood drawing a life sentence for his conviction on conspiracy to commit first-degree murder in the death of the Willmotts.

Maurice Salaiz won approval from the Planning Commission to develop senior housing on the property where his mother's bakery had stood for thirty years. She now resides in one of the units.

Casia's mom got a divorce from her stepdad. She caught a Greyhound back to Reno, where she enrolled in a local junior college. She sent a postcard to tell me she was majoring in philosophy with a specialization in nineteenth century Russian nihilists.

Gretchen made a full recovery and returned to work as my secretary. The first day back, she announced her engagement to Dennis Drent.

Chris and his engineer friend went on an all-gay cruise to Spain, Italy and the Greek Isles. He defrayed expenses by performing (as Cassandra) in the ship's popular show tune review. "On a Slow Boat to China" was his opening number.

I sent one more text message to Red asking him to meet me on a particular evening at the How Now? bar in South City. When he showed up, I bought him a beer, beat him two out of three games on the Junior Pac Man and gave him $20,000 in cash of the Dragon Lady's money. I told him my largesse did not extend to giving him a free pass for future ATM thefts, but there haven't been any more in San Francisco and I never collected the Bay Area Bankers Association reward.

AUTHOR'S NOTE

RESIDENTS OF SAN FRANCISCO WILL KNOW—AND PER-
HAPS now appreciate—that the city does not use touch-
screen voting machines. They should also be aware that San
Francisco is one of the few American cities to adopt ranked-
choice voting, which eliminates the need for runoffs. This was
done after the 2003 mayoral election, but in my fictional version of the city, runoffs are still possible, and, as it happens,
very useful to the plot.

The characters in the novel are also fictional, and while most of
the places are real, they have been used in ways that are complete
figments of my imagination. Likewise, the majority of the photo-
graphs at the beginning of each chapter are true portrayals of the
San Francisco Bay Area locales where the action takes place, but
some have been included not because they are literal illustrations
of a particular place, but because they suggest an atmosphere or a
mood that is *en rapport* with the text.

I would like to thank my fellow writers Harriotte Aaron, Sheila
Scobba Banning, John Billheimer, Bob Brownstein, Anne Cheilek,
Ann Hillesland and Donna Levin for helping me to make Runoff
the best I can make it. Thanks are also due to Bill Arney, Larry and
Ed Berger, David Dill, Ron "Eggplant Ole" Olson and Kurt Ribak
for their important contributions to the book.

Finally, I would like to thank my editor, Alison Janssen, who always knew what happened to the cleaver—and is smart enough not to take a thousand dollar bill in change—and my wife Linda, who put up with much more than usual from me this time around.